ISBN 978-0-9924455-0-8


https://www.behance.net/lholton
First published in 2011 lulu.com
Published by Adratea Publishing.

Alternate Book I : Alraune

Set in times.

# ALRAUNE

One fateful day, the worst thing that could ever possibly happen in the dungeon occurred. They lost a team member.

It wasn't like Cyrus, who ultimately met his fate deep down beneath the earth some months earlier; a loss that some parts of the town were still struggling to take. It was an abandonment. Magi's team had fled, and he was all alone.

His adventuring party had been formulated specifically to tackle one select region of the dungeon; a labyrinthine forest that existed under the ground, surviving somehow without the need for light. Mina, the librarian in Adratea had gone through all the botany books she had to find precedent for that sort of thing, but like so many other mysteries in the dungeon the forest remained one of its kind – sinister and dangerous.

Several expeditions into the forest, dubbed 'Underwood' by Siro who had been the first to explore revealed not much fauna in the way of malicious creatures, but there were several strains of deadly plants growing in that area; carnivorous vegetation, acid-spitting flowers, and a deep infestation of plant-like humanoids known as the Alraune. *Those* at least they had prior record of; a semi-intelligent species of monster that ensnares humans to increase their own numbers. Male alraune hunt for females, and vice versa. Siro had come out relatively unharmed from the Underwood because all of the alraune he had seen were male, and therefore left him alone.

This did bring him a lot of worry over the female adventurers of the town who also explored the dungeon, but wisely they left that region for the men to explore and set out in a different area for their treasure. Magi had joined the Underwood exploration team because it seemed like the best idea at the time, along with Ravendor and Darren from the Adratea inn and Warren the doctor from the town's clinic. He knew them all well (though not so much Warren but he seemed friendly enough) and felt that he could trust them with his back, so one dark night he set off in the party of four to reach the heart of the Underwood and survey what was there.

And that was when the ordeal began.

"Monster!" Darren shrieked as he pelted out of the cavern entrance like the hounds of hell were after him. "Monster, monster!"

The rest of his team was congregated at the entrance of the cave waiting for his return. Darren was agile, sneaky and light-footed, capable of all manner of stealth acts so whenever they explored a new, uncharted area of the dungeon it was often that they sent Darren in as a scout, as a yellow canary to make sure they weren't walking into a trap. Darren was good at his job, mostly, but he also had jittery nerves which caused him to be predisposed to running out of cave entrances yelling about monsters at the top of his lungs. It was a known weakness that his team was still trying to wean him out of him.

The other three waiting for him to return looked up from their respective distractions as Darren reached them, leaning over and placing his hands on his knees as he tried to catch his breath. Warren was helping to gauze Ravendor's arm where a violent flower had spat acid on him, and Magi had simply been waiting patiently for their scout to return. "So what did you see?" He asked Darren now, as if he hadn't just heard the shouts earlier.

Darren glanced at the other two first, but then fixed on Magi. He wasn't the leader, but he was as good as any to report to. "I-Inside...

near the exit… a huge monster. She was sleeping…" He breathed between pauses, being as non specific as usual.

"It probably will not be sleeping for much longer now that you have informed the world." Ravendor scolded as Warren finished bandaging him and he fit his burned arm back into his coat sleeve. He was the team's unofficial leader, simply for the fact that he was the oldest and the bossiest in the group. He stood up from where he had been sitting against a mossy boulder. "Did it seem dangerous? Describe it to us." He added.

"Well, it was one of those plant people things we've been seeing all around the wood, but bigger. *Much* bigger. I… uh, also think it was a girl." Darren explained, wringing his hands nervously.

"What makes you say that?" Magi asked, curious.

"It had… er… boobs."

Magi glanced at Ravendor. "That could be dangerous. Do you think it might be true?"

"They were actually kinda nice boobs now that I think about it…" Their scout continued on obliviously.

Ravendor shrugged. "I suppose it is logical to believe that there must at least be one female alraune in this dank, dirty forest, or else the population would collapse."

"Just like a termite colony, or a grove of faeries." Warren contributed helpfully as he packed up his first aid kit behind them.

"What?"

"Nothing." He answered demurely.

It was indeed rather risky. A female alraune would have no problems attacking and devouring all four of them, but then again, Magi had sort of been expecting this deep down in the Underwood. "If the monster has made her lair at the very exit of this forest where we must go, then there's really only one thing we can do, right?" He reasoned, awaiting their response. He was a young, strong and particularly handsome hunter-wanderer who had temporarily made Adratea his home. Both stoic and polite, but also rather friendly, he had made a lot more friends in town than probably he himself was aware.

Darren stepped back a little as the gentle swaying frond of a fern or some other bit of greenery brushed against his ankle. He was wary of bugs and other strange things in this subterranean forest, but all there ever was were plants, plants, and even more plants. He wondered how the other teams were doing elsewhere in the dungeon. Maybe they were *wishing* for plants right about now…

Warren made another interjection as he stood, brushing the dirt from his blue jeans. Usually he was the lab-coated, glasses-wearing nerdy-looking physician from town, but down there in the dungeon the glasses came off and the lab coat stayed neatly tied about his waist. It made him look like an entirely different person, a tall, strapping fighter whose physical prowess was exceeded only by Zagtakh and possibly Siro; the mayor. Warren folded his arms. "Yeah, but we've got to be careful. Alraune are called 'the man trap' for a reason, you know."

The fern brushed against Darren's ankle again. He ignored it. "I heard that once an alraune king or queen catches you… they suck out your very soul." He said in a small haunted voice, the wisdom coming from none other than his sagely grandfather who had been a master storyteller and derived a perverse pleasure from frightening the daylights out of his grandkids. Outside the cavern though, where it seemed to be safe it wasn't so scary.

"So it's like a succubus?" Magi asked. Unlike the others he wasn't so quick to dismiss old tales as mere fancy. The tales had to come from *somewhere* after all, and mankind wasn't as creative as it liked to think it was.

"What a load of rubbish." Ravendor scoffed as he loaded five fresh bullets into his gun.

"Maybe. It *did* have boobs." Darren said with a nervous laugh, trying to calm himself before everything went to hell.

The plant that had been irritating him brushed against his leg again but higher this time, coaxed by the breeze.

Only…

There *was* no breeze so far down beneath the earth.

Warren noticed it first. He tensed. "Darren! Your leg-"

Something lithe but firm wrapped itself around his upper leg. Darren whirled around. At first what he thought he saw was some kind of weird snake crawling out of the cavern, dark, forest green, but it was *way* too long for it to be some kind of reptile and if it were true wouldn't he have been bitten by now? Instead, the second thing that came to mind was an octopus… like a tentacle.

# · ALRAUNE ·

Darren screamed.

The green thing pulled hard against him like a lassoist roping in a captive calf. Darren was thrown onto his stomach and he hit the grassy, mossy ground with a soft slapping sound, bracing against the fall with his hands. By this time the others had seen it as well and were at attention now, Magi darting forward with his quick reflexes and trying to grab for one of Darren's hands, but as soon as his fingertips brushed against the other man's the green thing pulled again, not like a lassoist but more like a fisherman; reeling in his catch.

The dark-haired youth immediately slipped away from them, dragged on his belly back the way he had came into the cavern. Magi stumbled momentarily as his fingers grabbed only air, then he righted himself as Ravendor and Warren ran past him and joined the chase.

Painful bumps of jagged stones and knobs of reaching roots poked and prodded Darren as he was mercilessly dragged against them. He cried out in pain and fear as he was roughly manhandled backwards toward a point unknown, but he had a pretty good idea where it lay and that idea made him want to scream even more.

A length of tree root partially sticking out of the ground like an elongated letter 'n' or a right triangle caught his attention as he skidded by. Thinking quickly he threw his weight and arms out to grab at it, catching it with only one hand but for now that was enough. He stopped moving.

But that didn't mean the tentacle was going to give up. The scrapes and soon-to-be bruises all down his front welcomed a new painful sensation – a low, raw pulling sensation as his leg was slowly and persistently being dragged out of its socket. Though it appeared thin and flimsy the green thing was *strong*.

Tears began to form in the corner of Darren's eyes as his fingers began to slip, a weak, keening groan of exertion slipping from his throat as he tried to hang on. *Please don't let it get me*, he prayed to any gods who would listen, *I don't want to die like this! I don't want to die* ***ever****! Noooooo...*

He could hear the footsteps of his friends catching up with him and hoped desperately that he could hold on in time. Even as he thought that, two of his fingers slipped away from the root; just as Magi rounded the corner with a gleaming knife drawn to separate him from the tentacle.

"Darren!" He called curtly as he noticed how the young rogue had snagged himself. "Don't let go!"

That was easier said than done. Darren had the distinct feeling that if he survived this one of his legs was going to be permanently longer than the other, but if he survived he would take it. That'd be fine. It'd be all peachy keen!

He whimpered as he lost another finger and looked up at Magi and the quickly approaching Warren and Ravendor with fear bright in his eyes. "Help me…" He sobbed as Magi reached out for his wrist.

But when he grabbed for him again Darren was already gone, now being dragged and sometimes thrown at a speed in which the other three would be unable to match. Magi swore harshly as he rose again, but turned to Ravendor when he felt the other man put a hand on his shoulder. "There is no need to be hasty. We already know what has ensnared him." He said.

Magi was incredulous at how Ravendor could stand there so calmly and tell him to take it easy when they could both hear Darren's shrieks echoing further and further down the underground corridor. "Yes, I know, but it'll eat him if we don't do something quickly!" He snapped as Warren finally caught up to them, confused about the hold-up.

Ravendor took the curt response in stride but briefly touched his index and middle finger against the bridge of his nose as if he had a headache. "I know you are not a fan of the sport, Magi, but have you ever observed Zagtakh fishing off the wharf in South Adratea? He baits his hook with chunks of crab meat to entice his prey to swallow the lure; hook and all. This is what the alraune is trying to do with us."

"You think the monster is using Darren as bait?" Magi ventured, raising an eyebrow.

"But what if you're wrong?" Warren asked, doubting the monster in question had enough intelligence for such a scheme.

"Then I suppose Darren is merely the entrée." Ravendor answered with a wry smile which was met with a look of horror from Warren and a why-the-hell-are-we-just-standing-around-here look from Magi. He sighed. "Look, I am not saying we should come back later to pick up the bones, only that we should exercise some caution before running willy-nilly into the monster's lair. An old acquaintance of mine used to say that looking for a shortcut would lead you astray, and I find that as true now as it ever was."

Magi regarded him neutrally for a second, and then tore off down the tunnel again in pursuit of his friend. "And sometimes you just talk too damn much!" He called back, drawing his other knife from the small pocket at his belt. It glimmered coolly in the growing darkness.

Warren also thought that Magi had the better idea. Whether it was a trap or not Darren's life was at stake, and that was the most important thing of all. (Even if Darren getting eaten would finally stop the confusion new migrants into Adratea had about them being related, or brothers or something. Warren had been called 'Darren' enough times now for it to have gotten more than a little annoying.)

He unsheathed his two-handed sword from the scabbard at his back. It was almost too heavy for a normal man to use, but he'd gotten the hang of it after quite a bit of practice with Siro. "Magi's right." Warren said. "Er… about going on ahead. Sometimes you just *have* to rush in, you know? We'll be all right." And then he rushed off after his cloaked teammate.

Ravendor was left alone in the tunnel. He sighed again, his gut feeling telling him that they wouldn't be all right at all, and then followed the rest of his party with his gun at the ready.

"Wait! Wait for me!"

Maybe one of the main reasons why they weren't so prepared for the fight ahead may have lain with Darren not being very good at describing what he saw earlier, underwhelming his friends and placing them off-guard. Darren would have said in his defense that he had run out of the cavern *screaming*, and if that wasn't a good enough descriptor then nothing was. Who knows? Maybe in the end they should have listened to Ravendor.

As they ran into the main chamber of the cavern the air seemed to change all around them, almost as if it had grown fresher; purer. The cave was the size of a small church and almost shaped like one too, the walls and ceiling held up by a massive, intricate series of tree roots buttressing the stones like ancient, fossilized veins. Some of the main roots were significantly wider than a man and must have been decades, if not centuries old. Ravendor opened the shutter on the lantern he was carrying to illuminate the area and he and his party held in a collective breath at the sight.

This place must have been the very heart of the Underwood. Vine plants grew in hectic sprawls here and there and at the far back of the cavern he could almost hear a faint trickling sound that might be running water. All of a sudden he felt thirsty, but there was no time to worry about that now. Darren had been dragged into the center of the cavern by multiple green tentacles; they rose into the air like dancing cobras and lifted their terrified bait up with them, before a rise that almost seemed like an altar. Behind that, after the rise there was… no back wall. Nothing.

Instead there lay a tangled bramble of hundreds of vines, so thick and numerous that they resembled a ball of yarn that a curious housecat might have played with for a little too long. It was no less than a jungle back there.

Darren hung captured from three or four of those vines right now, like the hanged man from that deck of cards BW liked to play with so often in order to predict the future, as she called it. He had been lifted several feet into the air and was swinging from his ankle, while his arms and coattails swung down towards the floor. He had finally lost his hat as well and it was now lying on the ground beneath him, forgotten.

The three men had all been ready to burst into the lair of the alraune and take on whatever challenges that lay for them inside, but in taking in this new area and their comrade before them they paused. That was probably one of the first mistakes they made. Darren's breathing was shallow and harsh, full of the soft gasps and spluttering of the truly afraid. "Guys please…" He begged weakly. "Get me down from here…"

"Oh wow…" Warren said. There were so many vines here that there was no doubt as to what this could be – an alraune *nest* of some sort. After a moment of wonder he settled back to the task at hand and became determined, focusing on Darren as he raised his sword. "Don't worry; I'll have you down in a second." He promised.

He started out towards the middle of the chamber, leaving Magi and Ravendor behind them briefly until they realized they were being left behind and hurried to catch up with him. From his upside-down vantage point Darren was relieved to see his friends approaching him, until…

A vine darted up towards him, close to Darren's face like a charmed snake. It seemed to regard him silently for a second, and then slid itself up around his throat, noosing itself and pulling *tight*.

The rogue choked.

His arms that had been hanging limply over his head came back to life. One shot up to his throat to grapple and grasp at the vine cutting off most of his oxygen supply, while the other was thrown out straight ahead of his approaching allies, gesturing frantically for them to stop, stop before he choked to death. There was no telling how Darren had managed to link the strangulation with the approach of his friends so quickly, but at least in that he was correct. When Warren and the others stopped dead in their tracks the vine loosened and he could breathe again.

This was a nasty stalemate. They couldn't reach him to cut him free and if they tried the vines would simply wring his neck. Warren looked back at the other two as if searching for help. "So, uh, what now?" He asked.

Darren let out a weaker, softer cry like a frightened animal as the spare vines restraining his body seemed to grow bored with merely holding him and began to move, lazily at first, but then almost with interest as the little tendrils brushed themselves over all the scrapes and scratches he had accumulated while being dragged through the tunnel. His shirt was already slipping down enough due to gravity to reveal his skinny stomach and a bit of his chest, bleeding slightly in places from where the skin had torn. The movement of the vines stung and felt weird; he didn't like it at all. "T-The alraune…" He stammered in a raw voice, but found he could not continue.

So focused they had been on Darren that they had almost forgotten they were not alone in this monster's lair. Magi grabbed the kerosene lantern from Ravendor and tried to scan the back of the chamber with it, through that messy chaotic bramble of tangled-up vines. If Darren was right there would be an anomaly in those thin, creeping shapes, something that was not so much a mass of vines than a vaguely human form…

Magi felt Warren step back against him and brush the side of his arm against Magi's shoulder as he searched. It might have been, it might be… there!

The alraune. She could have been kneeling on the altar of the cathedral-cavern in some kind of monstrous prayer had she any legs to kneel on. The top half of her body was mostly human in shape, *mostly*, but from the join in her legs and downwards everything fell apart into the wriggling, writhing mass of vines that made up the back wall and reinforced the cavern. It was like she was part octopus – part plant-octopus, anyway. *I don't believe it,* Magi remarked silently to himself, *the monster isn't just living in this part of the cavern; she **is** the cavern!*

Thinner, more dexterous vines seemed to sprout backwards from her green forearms, and if Magi had the time to trace them all the way to their end he would have found the source of what was restraining and tormenting Darren. She was well endowed just like Darren had said, reminding Magi a little bit of Mieus; the barmaid who ran the Adratea Guildhouse. Ravendor and Warren were actually thinking the very same thing, but like Magi they also kept it to themselves. Were she a human being like the rest of them she would have been beautiful. Instead, like this, there was no question that she was merely a monster; no different from an animal.

When Darren spoke the alraune opened her eyes and stood, or more accurately raised herself upward on her tentacles. Magi sheathed his daggers and went for his bow, setting the blazing lantern down on the slightly uneven floor. The young hunter spoke to Darren slowly, so as not to agitate the creature behind him. "Just stay calm, Darren. We'll get you down." Magi paused for a moment then added; "Somehow."

"Oh for goodness sake." Ravendor griped at everybody in the chamber and half turned to the right, raising his gun. If the other two were useless or clueless then he'd just have to free Darren on his own. He fired four times, nearly depleting the six gun, the individual booming echoes sounding so close together that they almost became one loud, dull thunderclap in the low light. He'd double-tapped twice, almost bafflingly fast, and all four of the vines holding Darren up snapped in two.

The first two shots took out the vines holding his throat and midsection, and the final two destroyed the bindings around his ankle and the one spiraled up around the rogue's leg. Darren was fortunate. If Ravendor had aimed in a different sequence he would have fallen with the ropes still around his neck – already drawn tightly the alraune would have hanged him.

Instead he face-planted painfully onto the ground with the dead, bleeding vine-like ropes still attached to him. Darren shrieked and sat up quickly, ripping the now loose bonds away. They were cold and oozing thick green fluid, like a plant, like a…

Ravendor lowered the gun after hearing Darren shriek. "Blast, did I wing him? I can barely see in this darkness. Is he okay?"

"Hey, are you okay?" Warren called.

Darren looked up at his teammates as he pulled the organic noose from his neck. Suddenly he realized that if Ravendor had done a worse job at aiming he might not be there right now. Had the older man hit him? Was he still alive? The rogue took half a second for himself to check for injuries. Well, his head and front hurt like hell from the fall and being dragged and his throat stung terribly from the vines, but that was all. "I-I'm fuh-fine…" He rasped back to Warren in a dry, harsh voice, rising unsteadily to his feet.

Then he remembered the monster behind him. Darren whirled around quickly, almost *too* quickly as he nearly lost his balance and fell to the floor again.

Magi had been watching it while Ravendor and Warren were preoccupied with Darren. He was fascinated by it, really. When the shots had severed the vines from Darren's body the alraune had recoiled as if she had been shot herself, the monster collapsing against her own vines; mossy hair fanning out behind her as if somebody had just sliced her fingers off – and that wasn't very far from the truth. Her mouth was frozen in a little 'o' of agony, but it looked like she could not scream. Maybe she didn't have any vocal chords to scream with.

The cut, bleeding lengths of vine still attached to the creature whipped about violently, momentarily, until the alraune seemed to gather her bearings and withdrew them backward into relative safety. Magi fit a bone-tipped arrow against the drawstring of his bow. Suddenly he had a feeling that something horrible was about to happen, regardless of the apparent innocence or vulnerability of the creature before them. He didn't particularly *want* to put an arrow into the alraune, but he might not have a choice in the matter.

Maybe he was just a sucker for a pretty face.

That pretty face's expression darkened considerably in anger as she recovered from the injury. She stood as Darren whirled around and then vines from all directions, from behind her, from the ceiling and the walls ripped out of their places and lunged for the hunting party in rage. They came from seemingly all directions so it was impossible to run away; impossible to retreat. They attacked by catching and ensnaring, by pulling, by beating, and by lifting one high into the air and by bashing them hard against any available surface. It was a crude method of attack, but effective. There were simply too many tentacles for them to resist.

Magi's first and only shot in reaction to half a dozen vines lunging for him was a hit, but his arrows lacked the explosive power of Ravendor's bullets and the arrow simply twanged halfway through one of the reaching tendrils, piercing it easily but not slowing it down. Magi's eyes widened when he realized that his main method of attack was almost useless on this foe, and he dropped his bow more out of necessity than surprise as the vines reached out and grabbed him by the arms, the legs; everything.

One vine gripped his right hand - a major annoyance as Magi favored it over the other. He pulled his dagger out quickly on his left side and slashed blindly at the enemy all around him. The knife was unbearably sharp, with an edge that Trina the weapon-smith had forged to absolute perfection and that Magi had maintained with the whetstone. When it sliced it glided through flesh like silk without discrimination. Chlorophyllic blood flew and the young archer's legs were free once more.

Darren had been captured and throttled once by the dangerous beauty and he wasn't that willing to have it happen to him a second time. All that mattered to him now was the location of the exit, and getting there dwarfed everything else in comparison. He ran. In doing so he accidentally kicked over the lantern Magi had placed so carefully on the ground, spilling its contents. Without its fuel supply the little flame didn't quite go out immediately, but it would go out soon enough.

As for Warren, he was already having the time of his life. His heavy two-handed blade flashed unceasingly in the gradually increasing darkness, cutting down tentacles as soon as they got close like wheat before the scythe; clean, complete and thorough. The vines could barely touch him; the range of his vengeful blade was just too wide. One tentacle seemed to worm its way up from beneath him and grabbed him by the leg, pulling him off balance and attempting to trip him up so he would be prone and vulnerable, like Darren had been.

Warren would have fallen had Ravendor not been nearby and braced his friend's shoulder, then used his last bullet to take out the offending vine. The end of his gun barrel was smoking by this point and the swordsman steadied himself, kicking the dead length of plant away. "Thanks." He said quickly as he got back into a defensive position.

"Are you capable of covering me for a few seconds?" The dark-haired man asked him as he sidestepped to stand behind Warren. He half cocked the hammer of the revolver in his hands as he spoke.

"What? Why?" Warren asked.

"It takes time to reload." He replied with exasperation, as if this were common knowledge to anyone regardless of if they understood firearms or not. He fished in the pocket of his coat momentarily for fresh bullets, not waiting for Warren's answer before getting back to business. If his weapon didn't work he was toast anyway, regardless if Warren chose to defend him or not.

But the swordsman was happy to help. If it meant that he'd be able to blow a few more of those vines away then he was all for it. One of those vines came at them now and he cut it down to size; the pruned piece of flora collapsing bleeding into the ground alongside the tinkling of empty casings. Another came from behind him and this time Warren grabbed it with his bare hands, or at least one of them, winding it around his wrist of his own volition and then yanking savagely, the limb tearing with a deceptively meaty sound.

Blood fell, but he tried to avoid it. There was no telling what monster blood could do to you if it made contact with the skin. "Are you nearly done?" Warren shouted as he intercepted another tentacle, cleaving it with growing skill but also diminishing energy. This was tiring him out.

"Almost… there!" Ravendor responded as he loaded the last few new shells and snapped his weapon closed again. He was happy that he had managed to get through that unmolested, though that didn't last very long. A thick, strong vine seemingly came out of nowhere and whipped him harshly across the back and shoulder, forcing the man to utter a breathless "*Augh!*" before staggering to his knees.

Through that haze of sudden pain he could hear Magi shouting at all of them to retreat, to run the hell out of the cavern because this fight was going nowhere fast and they were being overwhelmed. Darren had already fled, and Warren helped Ravendor up while thinking that maybe running away might not be such a bad idea after all. If the alraune was part of this cavern then she wouldn't follow them.

… Hopefully.

"Everybody run! Get out of here!" Magi called again as his hands slick with the monster's blood strived to maintain a competent hold on his knife. His arm felt sore all the way to the socket and their one last light, the bleeding lantern, was going out. He wasn't their leader, and rarely did Magi attempt to make decisions on behalf of the entire team, but on this he was certain he had to act. He was familiar with people; if one dissenting voice cried an order in the absence of leadership it was always obeyed.

Tentacles bound Magi's body again. The alraune seemed to be making the hunter its main target now that Darren had run out of her reach. He didn't know why. Maybe it was because he seemed the most vulnerable, and Magi gasped as the grasping tentacles squeezed nearly all of the air out of his lungs, pinning his arms against his sides. So much for fighting back now.

"Magi!" That voice sounded like Warren.

The young hunter felt himself being lifted; felt his boots no longer touching the earth. He didn't think to look at the alraune again. One of his last thoughts before the creature raised him up and bashed his head savagely against the edge of the altar wasn't something selfless, or something heroic. Rarely is that so. Instead, it was;

*If she **does** try to eat me… I hope to the gods she kills me first.*

The sharp, painful impact removed him from the waking world.

"*Magi!*" This time it was Ravendor's turn to call his name. He started forth from Warren's side, as if to run at the many tentacles binding his friend, but he only managed a step or two before he realized that the swordsman had grabbed him firmly by the elbow. He tried to shake free from Warren's grip. "Let me go, damn you!"

Warren seemed grim. “Didn’t you hear him? He has a point. We have to get out of here before we run out of light or we’ll lose our bearings!”

Ravendor tugged again, harder this time. He was furious. “Bugger your bearings! I’ll not hand Magi over to that beast!” He roared.

But Warren had a pretty good grip on him and Ravendor would never have been able to get free even on a good day and in perfect sunlight. The doctor was conflicted, of course he wanted to run with him and save Magi too, but when it came to the dungeon he was strictly a pragmatist. Pragmatists tended to survive longer. They’d be no good to Magi if they got captured as well, and in the darkness they would be more than easy prey. They’d be dinner served up on a silver plate.

He started to drag the older man back to the entrance, trying his best to keep an eye out for any stray vines that might try to stop them. Now that she actually had a prize; a trophy to call her own the alraune seemed to lose most of her interest in them. Warren could see her faintly dark outline lift up the outline of Magi triumphantly, and with his imagination he could picture his unconscious face, the blood from the head wound pouring down his temple; everything.

He would regret this. He knew it.

“It’s fine! It’s fine! We’ll come back for him! I promise!” He shouted.

“No! Damn it, let go of me! *Magi*!”

And then the lights went out.

…

… …

…

Cold. Dark. A sense of weightlessness.

Magi finally came to in a world full of horrors.

The side of his head throbbed painfully from the blow the stones had granted him and he opened his eyes, though he could see only darkness. *The lantern must have gone out*, he reasoned blearily before remembering the last few moments preceding unconsciousness, the lashing tentacles, Warren shouting something amidst the confusion and then his team fleeing, distant, out of his reach.

All of them, they had run away. They were gone. But then…

What was he still doing here?

His stomach dropped down several inches when he tried to move his arms and legs and found them forcibly restrained. There was some slight give, but not really enough to allow him a proper range of motion. Something slithered between his legs and he flinched, recoiling.

"H-Hello…?" He managed to whisper hoarsely, wishing that he could brush away the hair hanging limply down in front of his face. Slowly, gradually, his eyes began to adjust to the darkness, just enough for him to discern basic shapes and outlines. Something moved behind him, and Magi's eyes widened in realization.

He hadn't even left the lair of the queen alraune. Dozens upon dozens of tentacles were sprawled about the cavern, of various thicknesses and strengths. The plant-like vines bound his arms, his legs, and even his torso. He was caught helpless like a fly in a web. His friends had let the monster take him and had left him alone to die.

The shocking realization filled him with brief energy and he pulled hard with his right arm, trying to wrench himself free. "N-No!" He choked as the vines readjusted themselves around the limb and yanked him back with just as much force to keep him bound once more. The grasping roots felt like they were being somewhat gentle, and Magi all of a sudden realized that they could probably rip him to pieces if they so desired.

The situation was beyond serious. He could die down here in the dungeon, just like others had. Magi glanced around furtively for anything that could help him to escape; a dropped knife or a sharp stone or *anything*, but it was useless. The vines had him suspended at least ten feet off the ground and they did not allow enough give for him to grope for his belt. Nothing was within reach.

Then, unexpectedly, the bonds loosened themselves around his body. It wasn't enough to break free, but it *was* somewhat reassuring, although eerie. Before his eyes the entire cavern seemed to shift, to move around as if it were one singular organism. It crawled, and something vaguely human approached him.

Though it was dark Magi could clearly tell that it wasn't human, and now he had the grisly opportunity to study it up close. It- *she* was female, and despite all the tentacles and mossy hair she had a lovely face. The young archer tried to recoil away from her regardless, his heart beating faster in fear. "Let me go…" He implored weakly, but the alraune only continued to look at him in silence. Maybe it couldn't speak. Maybe all of Magi's words were gibberish to her.

"Please… let me down…" He continued, and tiredly tried to pull free with his arm once more. This time it *did* come loose, but with Magi throwing his weight forward like that he unbalanced himself and nearly fell. He reached out for anything to grab hold of and steady himself and he grabbed the alraune by the hand. Magi froze, looking up at her, suddenly afraid that she would take it as an act of aggression. His head was swimming and he feared that he had a concussion, but he was even more worried that it would all be over soon.

Instead of attacking the alraune smiled at him. It was a peaceful, serene smile the likes of which gave Magi hope that he might get out of the dungeon alive after all. He managed a shaky smile of his own, just to show that he was friendly.

This seemed to delight the monster queen. Another vine came down from above them and took Magi's free wrist, securing him safely once more. She released her grip on him and while the vines pulled him back she closed the distance between them by crawling forward on her hands. Magi couldn't struggle anymore even if he wanted; he was too exhausted. "Wait…" He began.

But she ignored him. The alraune leaned forward and sealed his lips with hers, filling Magi's mouth with an intensely bitter taste. He couldn't really describe it; it wasn't gagworthy, more like the taste of bitter herbal medicine. The alraune's lips were velvety soft but cold, like she generated no body heat whatsoever. Magi squeezed his eyes shut as if to distance himself from the kiss, and when she finally released him he coughed and spluttered like he had been breathing foul air, which wasn't too far from the truth.

While Magi struggled to get over the alraune's kiss her expression transformed from serene to sultry. She began to retreat back the way she had come, to the heart of her lair. Between coughs the archer noticed her withdrawal and he panicked. "No, wait! Let me go! Come back!" He cried, but to no avail.

Magi was left alone, once again in the dark.

"How could you be such a coward?" Ravendor shouted at Darren loud enough for the young rogue to cringe. It wasn't often that he raised his voice like that, so to Darren it was a little too much like being chewed out by an angry father.

"I-I'm sorry! I was scared!" He shouted back at him from the floor of the dungeon, his jacket laid over his knee and his shirt knotted between his fists. Warren had made him sit and take his shirt off once they had gotten far away enough from the alraune's lair to be safe, intent on treating everybody's wounds before they continued the trek back through the dungeon and into the upper world again. There was still quite a ways to go yet. Darren's cuts looked painful but they were mostly superficial; they'd heal up fine in a couple of days.

"Finding oneself frightened of an adversary is hardly a justifiable reason to abandon your teammates." The dark-haired gunman said hotly, lowering his voice before he lost it or accidentally alerted a curious monster to their presence. His back was killing him from where the alraune had struck him and he was rather certain it had bruised, but it was a tiny thing not even worth mentioning to Warren compared to what they had lost.

"Leave him alone, Ravendor." Warren said tiredly as he dressed some of Darren's nastier cuts. "There's no reason to make him feel worse than he already does."

Darren would have thanked the doctor were he not feeling just as shitty as Warren had already described. He had run from the monster, run out of the cavern and minutes later his friends had followed – minus Magi. They had lost Magi. He couldn't help but feel that if he had stood his ground and fought with the others maybe his friend would still be there with them. If that were true then maybe losing Magi really *was* all his fault. Darren bowed his head in shame. "I'm sorry…" He repeated, his voice cracking.

Ravendor sighed and made a hand gesture as if to wave that sorry away. There was a lot of pent-up rage, and possibly desperation in that sigh. "No, you needn't apologize. I cannot allow myself to foist my regrets upon you. I am just… distraught. I should have done something when I had the chance." After all, Magi had been the closest thing he had ever had to a best friend in Adratea.

"We could go back." Darren said, disliking the idea even as it came out of his mouth. It wasn't that he didn't *want* to rescue Magi; it was just that he didn't want to have to share his fate. If Magi were there, maybe he would understand. Maybe.

To Darren's great relief Ravendor seemed to disagree with him, even though the older man would have liked nothing more than to go back and try it anyway. Warren had had to *drag* him down half of the tunnel, but he needed to be practical here. "With less teammates we stand an even smaller chance of surviving. It would not be wise. We must accept the fact that Magi has followed the path of Cyrus." At least he would leave no grieving widow behind, though he was certain the news would break Mara's heart back in town.

Warren finished working on Darren and rose as the rogue carefully pulled his shirt back on again. He looked surprised. "What? Are you saying you're going to give up on Magi just like that? What if he's still alive?" He demanded.

"But alraune… they eat people. They'll eat Magi too." Darren said, recalling the very brief bit of information they had looked up in the library prior to their first exploration of the Underwood. He couldn't remember much, as he had spent most of his time staring at the librarian girl Mina from across the room.

The swordsman nodded. "Yeah, they do, but we don't know whether or not they eat people outright or hold them for a while first or what." He rubbed the back of his neck with his palm. "The thing is, I think I remember reading that they tie their victims up for a while before they get down to the eating; to wear them out first so they don't put up a fight."

"Like an arachnid?" Ravendor ventured. The huge series of plant vines had certainly been spiderlike enough. "How long do you think the creature would hold a man like Magi for?"

"I really have no idea. I'd have to look at that book again." Warren admitted sheepishly.

After all the anger and frustration he had shown earlier Ravendor seemed to brighten a bit. "You are right, we cannot lose hope. If we set out for Adratea immediately we can look into this more and arrange a rescue party. With more people we may yet stand a chance."

"I just hope Magi can hold on that long." Darren said.

With no way to tell the time, no real concept of time's passage, he had no way to tell when the alraune's kiss had begun to take effect.

The headache was gone. That at least was a blessing, but what replaced it was a dazed lightheadedness that sent all his senses reeling into a fog. Touch was intensified, as if he could feel every inch of his skin tingling from the cloth, from the vines against his wrists and legs and the gentle caress of the air.

He panted softly, hungry, dehydrated, and unbearably, agonizingly aroused. It would have been incredibly embarrassing in any other circumstance, but as it was nobody else was there and he didn't give a damn anymore.

*... There must... have been something... in that monster's kiss...*

*Some kind of... aphrodisiac...*

*... nngh... haah... ahh...*

The worst torture of all was that he wasn't able to do anything about it. The vines wouldn't even let him get to his belt; anything below that was completely out of the question no matter how much it ached and pressed against the fabric of his pants.

So, perhaps it was more of a relief than a surprise when the tentacle-like vines came to life again and began to move on their own accord. They moved like snakes, feeling, groping and sliding up and down the hunter's legs and skin. He groaned softly at the contact, but that was the limit of his capabilities. Part of him was horrified that he wasn't feeling revulsion for the vines anymore, but that part was smothered away by the daze and the fog.

A vine managed to slip itself under his shirt and slide up against the contours of his abdomen and chest, his ribs, gently trailing the collarbone and then doubling back to tease a nipple. His breath hitched at that, while two other slender vines worked their way up one of his trouser-legs and the other attempted to loosen his belt.

Magi tried to wrack his brain frantically for any information he'd ever heard before about humanoid plants as the vines gave up at trying to get his belt undone and went elsewhere for their fun, and he tried to recall if he'd ever seen a book on cryptobotany in Mina's library as the limbs of the alraune attempted to coil around the outline of his straining erection. After that he didn't think much of anything at all. It was just too difficult. He hung his head wretchedly and let the monster do whatever it wanted with his body, because he had been defeated and now he was just its prey.

The cavern in the heart of the underwood's dungeon was silent, save for the heavy, quick breathing of the captured hunter. There was a sharp, pained gasp as the alraune violated him, and filled nearly every orifice he had with her vines.

Magi panicked when a tentacle was forced down his throat. The thick tentacle working its way into his lower body was almost enough to make him come then and there, the amazing feeling heightened by the pain, but when he had opened his mouth to moan the other tentacle had surprised him.

That bitter scent penetrated his senses again and rebellion rose up in Magi for the very last time. If a simple kiss could send him into this state then he was terrified that anything more would be enough to drive him mad. He bit down hard on the intrusion, digging into the plant with his teeth.

Suddenly his mouth filled with thick liquid and the bitter taste became overpowering. He must have hurt the plant somehow because the vine pulled itself out of throat in a hurry, damaged and bleeding. He swallowed on reflex to get the caustic taste out of his mouth, and then he paused.

That probably hadn't been a good idea. Fear gripped him, all the way from each of his limbs to the very pit of his stomach. It could have been poison, it could have been *anything*. It could have-

The effect hit him like a swift kick in the gut. He cried out, doubled over, eyes glazing from the immediate, insurmountable rush of pleasure that struck him like a tidal wave during a storm. The vines pushing their way into his body no longer felt so weird, so wrong. A numbness came down about him that blocked out only pain, leaving the rest of his body free to endure the pleasurable torment that the alraune wished to impart upon him. This was what it had been waiting for, and it had come much sooner than expected. For the prey to *willingly* drink her blood, well…

It appeared he wanted to be more than just a meal to her, and the alraune was fine with that.

Blood mixed with the alraune's fluid dripped slowly down Magi's legs. Strands of his hair were pasted to his forehead by sweat, now unkempt, like the hanging strands of a willow tree. He was panting and gasping like a woman now, like a bitch in heat, twisting his body with the tiny bit of leverage that he had to grind the monster's vines deeper and deeper inside of him. It could reach places that no other man had been able to before, and every time it nudged against his prostate the young hunter could barely suppress the urge to scream out loud.

His moans echoed in the cavern and warmed the cold heart of his captor. Magi suddenly pulled forward sharply with his left arm, as if to escape, and this time instead of holding him back with equal force the vines loosened and slipped away, giving him back full use of one arm.

He could escape. He had a hunting knife on his belt that he couldn't reach before, and he could use it to slash and stab his way out of the alraune's grasp for good. It was a long shot, but a shot nonetheless. It was better than being eaten.

Magi's free hand dropped down to his belt, but it was useless. His logical mind had long since gone, lost to the aphrodisiac and the pleasure. Perhaps the alraune had been testing him to make sure of that fact. The female body of the creature returned, watching with interest some meters away. She smiled slightly as he clumsily tried to unbuckle his belt, as if he were doing it while half asleep. The vines were heaven but they weren't enough, not really, not quite.

Eventually he was able to loosen his belt enough for the monster to reward him for his efforts. Magi didn't notice the alraune gently bind his arm again, only the vines slipping quickly and softly into his pants to grip his rock-hard cock. They began to move and squeeze against him, an almost undulating, firm pressure; better than his hand. Better than anyone's hand. The simultaneous stroking and fucking was unbearable and Magi nearly blacked-out as his whole body thrummed like a live wire while he came.

His body slumped, hanging limply from the vines like meat in a butcher's storeroom. In the calmness that followed afterwards he felt the touch of salt on his lips, and dimly realized that he had been crying. Had it been from the pleasure? The despair? Or the knowledge that soon his life would be over?

*"He was panting and gasping like a woman now, like a bitch in heat, twisting his body with the tiny bit of leverage that he had to grind the monster's vines deeper and deeper inside of him."*

All he knew was that despite his earth-shattering orgasm his blood still burned faintly with the touch of the alraune's curse. It was an addiction. He needed *more*.

When the plant-like beauty approached him and cradled Magi's hung head in her green, long-fingered hands, he did not pull away or recoil as they kissed once again, renewing the shadow of the taint in his blood. There was no longer any reason to try and resist, he guessed.

His body had already been claimed as her property.

It was nearing late afternoon by the time the Underwood exploration party arrived back in town.

There was really no time to rest so they took whatever as they could of it at the Guildhouse; a building that was both the local tavern and the town hall. The path from the dungeon worked its way through east Adratea first and foremost before hitting the town proper, which meant that it was inevitable that the three hurt and tired men had to pass by the Guildhouse before anything else.

Nearly every person in town was a member of the Adventurer's Guild, and if the town were to ever have a meeting related to the dungeon it would be there. It was also a good place for the Underwood exploration team to sit down and allow Mieus the barmaid to provide them with some food and something to drink. None of them were particularly hungry anymore, but at least the drink helped.

Mieus hardly even had to ask the reason for all the long faces. She wasn't a particularly clever woman, but she *was* observant. She'd seen four men go into the dungeon that morning and only three return in the evening. She could do basic math. Maybe Mieus' own form of unspoken sympathy was that she didn't try to flirt with Warren at all that afternoon and kept her ferocious contempt of Ravendor in check. Darren she kept on forgetting was there, but that was nothing new.

"So what happened to your buddy? Long blond hair, cuter than most?" The red-haired beauty asked with a sympathetic smile as she washed up some glasses. Magi hadn't been an especially talkative guy but he'd come to the Guildhouse often for dinner, sometimes lunch, and he was *always* present whenever there was a party going on.

"A monster took him." Warren replied, feeling just as exhausted mentally as he did physically. He and Mieus had been dating not that long ago, and even though it hadn't worked out (she was into things that scared the hell out of him) they were still on rather good terms with one another.

They'd only been sitting down for about ten minutes but there really was no more time to waste. It didn't matter how tired they were, Ravendor didn't think that Magi had the time for them to relax. He looked at Mieus. "But we believe there is a small chance he may still be alive. We must call an assembly at once. The whole town must attend."

Normally assemblies only happened on Saturday nights, but she guessed that this was a big enough emergency. Mieus folded her arms beneath her more than ample breasts and seemed distraught. "You're gonna go back and get him, right? He's one of my best customers! He's polite and tidy and doesn't break stuff like Trina and Zagtakh do." She paused for a moment, and then added; "and I suppose it would be terrible if some monster just ate him. Who'd pay his tab?"

"This is all my fault." Darren whimpered, starting up again. "The only reason it went after him was because *I* ran away. I mean, I'm glad I didn't get eaten, but still…"

Warren patted Darren gently on the back. "Why don't you climb upstairs and ring the assembly bell? The sooner everybody gets here the sooner we can figure out what to do." The physician glanced at Mieus. "That's if you don't mind." The building technically belonged to everybody but she was its caretaker, after all.

"Yeah, sure, it's just 'round the stairs up the back." She explained, jerking a thumb at the back door. Darren got up to do what was asked of him but it was self-evident in the way that he carried himself that he still felt guilty and discouraged. Mieus pouted at his back as he left. "Well this is depressing. I had a plan all worked out how the blond cutie was gonna pay his tab." She sighed.

Ravendor looked like he was about to say something insulting to Mieus but Warren was already sick and tired of that old chestnut and managed to kick him under the bar in time. He was just not prepared to listen to another one of their arguments today. As he put his doctor's coat back on again Warren asked; "I don't suppose you know anything about alraune, Mieus?"

"Me? Not really. I know they're fuck-crazy, though. I haven't been in the Underwood much because of the warnings, you know, 'you must have a cock to enter' and all that. I'm sure that's got to be sexist or something, but I got curious once. This plant person must have caught my scent or whatever and he would have had his way with me if I hadn't turned him into lawn clippings, first."

"Ah… you mean, they, uh…"

"I even thought about letting it catch me, just to see what it was like." Mieus continued blithely. "But I didn't want to get eaten afterwards, you see."

There was a short, uncomfortable silence. Warren and Ravendor exchanged a glance. If Magi *were* still alive, what was that alraune queen doing to him right now? The silence was gratefully dispelled when the bell anchored on top of the Guildhouse began to ring out loudly and clearly to the rest of the town, orchestrated by Darren as he held the rope like a bungee cord and was almost repeatedly lifted into the air.

Mieus held her hands over her ears as she wrinkled her pert little nose at the sound. "I've been here for ages now and I'm *still* not used to that ringing." She complained.

As Warren took his glasses out of his pocket and rubbed the lenses lightly with his sleeve Siro walked into the tavern. He hadn't been called by the bell, not really, but he had been nearby and it hadn't taken long to get to Mieus' humble little abode. Like Magi Siro was also blond, but his hair was shorter and a shade slightly darker, while he also stood significantly taller and broader than the lost archer. He possessed an attractiveness that nearly all the women in town noticed to some degree, drawn to the quintessential leader; the knight in shining armor. Siro was a swordsman of such skill that it made Warren's own talents pale in comparison.

He was also the founder and the mayor of the city of Adratea, and instead of armor today he was just wearing trousers and a shirt. Warren brightened immediately as he entered the room, putting on his glasses. "Siro!" He cried warmly. "Hello!"

Siro smiled back at him, but he seemed curious. "The bell is ringing." He observed. "Did something happen?"

"Well, it's a long story…"

But they didn't properly get into that story until most of the townspeople living in Adratea arrived. They came from all over the village so it took some time to build the crowd, and by the time the Guildhouse was full enough for Siro to begin the assembly it was already twilight outside the tavern, the dim orange glow of the setting sun fading away into the night.

Warren, Darren, Ravendor and Mieus were there, obviously, with Siro at the head of the group. The blond swordsman scanned the crowd seated at the tavern tables quickly. He could see the Sylvas sisters, Cassie and Trina, along with Mina, Mara and Sera seated at the back. It wasn't that great of a turnout. Over the murmuring din of the people chatting amongst each other he asked; "Has anybody seen Zagtakh or Reiyu? Where's BW?"

A couple of the women in the crowd looked around or behind themselves for a sign of the missing townspeople. Trina cleared her throat. "Zagtakh's one town over last I heard from him. Something to do with a trade route."

Mina piped up. "Don't you remember, Siro? You asked Zagtakh to negotiate trade between Adratea and Mistral. He won't be back for another three days."

Siro blinked at Mina. He'd forgotten. Well, he always had trouble keeping up with the dozens upon dozens of duties a mayor had regarding their town, but it was a forgivable lapse in memory. He chuckled at himself. "Oh. Right. Of course. What about Reiyu or BW then? They should be here."

The assembly shifted through itself but there was no sign of either person. It wasn't that surprising. Reiyu, the wanderer from the east would often spend unbroken days inside the dungeon, camping out and exploring the secret ways of the underground with patient meticulousness. When he had arrived in town not long ago a rumor had spread that he had come from a place far beyond any plane that the townsfolk knew about.

BW had told Darren one evening while cleaning her store that she suspected Reiyu might be from the distant future. She had laughed right after saying it, which could mean that she was just making a joke, but with her he could never be certain. BW herself could be practically anywhere, Darren thought, or something just as simple as the magician girl taking a nap and then sleeping through the ringing of the bell.

With or without them Siro had to start the meeting now. He clapped his hands once to get the attention of everybody again and spoke. "Okay, first I want to thank everybody for showing up at such short notice. I know the evening is supposed to be reserved for ourselves and not the dungeon, but we'll have to make an exception this time. An incident had occurred." He turned to Warren who was sitting far off to the right of him with the rest of his party. "Warren? Could you come up here and explain to everyone what's happened? I'm curious too."

Warren went slightly red and raised his hands in a warding gesture. "I, um, I'm not exactly good at public speaking." He stammered sheepishly. Secretly he had been hoping that Darren or Ravendor would be asked to do it instead, but he supposed he shouldn't have been surprised. Siro knew him a whole lot better than he knew the other two.

Luckily for him Siro could identify the embarrassed blush that had appeared on the physician's face and smiled reassuringly. He stepped down from the centre of the crowd. "That's fine. Ravendor, could you take the floor instead?"

The older man rose from his seat. Unlike Warren, public speaking was practically in his blood. "It would be my pleasure." He said, taking Siro's place.

For the next twenty minutes he recounted the tale of how his team of four had reached the deep dark Underwood, how they had encountered the queen alraune in the very heart of the forest and how, despite their greatest efforts, she had stolen Magi away from them. Ravendor had a particular knack for storytelling, so his recount was just as much enthralling as it was horrifying; as if this had not just happened this afternoon but between the pages of a fantasy novel available for lending in Mina's library. Darren was relieved to hear that Ravendor downplayed his involvement in Magi's capture to the others, but that did not absolve him of his guilt.

"… so, to put it succinctly, if there is any hope of rescuing Magi from the creature it must be due to a joint effort from the town. No one party is enough."

Barring a few slight exaggerations of the alraune's aggression Ravendor's retelling of what happened in the Underwood was more or less accurate. By the time he finished speaking Siro had his arms loosely folded across his front with a hand on his chin. He appeared to be thinking quite deeply.

Mara immediately raised her hand as soon as there was silence. She wasn't in a classroom and there wasn't really anybody there to take her question, so she stood up and took the floor. She was a beautiful, though rather plain looking woman with chestnut brown hair and determination reflected in her eyes. "If what you're saying is true then we have to go find him at once. There's no telling when he might get eaten! I'm going with all of you to save him." She announced.

Instead of welcoming the pledge of aid Ravendor shook his head. "No, Mara. It is appreciated, but I refuse to take a woman down into the Underwood." He said.

The woman looked astonished. "What? Why? You just said that you three need help! Is this because of that silly rule? The 'protect the maidens of our town at all costs rule'? We have just as much a right to place ourselves in danger as you do!"

Somebody shouted 'sexist pig!' at him from the back of the tavern. It had sounded a lot like Mieus. He'd never really had anything against female adventurers as teammates before, but it was just the situation that bothered him as the leader. Ravendor frowned. "I think I can live with the notion of somebody like Darren dragged off by carnivorous creatures and molested, but should I find myself with the responsibility of that happening to a woman I… I would not be able to live with myself. You may call me old-fashioned if you wish, and things being as they are that may be so, but that is simply what I believe. I am sure my comrades agree with me as well."

Warren looked uncomfortable when a handful of female eyes focused on him. "I'd hate to see something awful happen to you, Mara." He admitted, smiling nervously.

"Hey…" Darren began, objecting to being used in such a terrible example.

Rather than be defeated Mara threw an arm out to indicate the crowd, all feminine and alert. "But with Zagtakh and Reiyu absent who are you planning to take with you? We're all here. We can help you if you ask us, for Magi's sake." She said.

Warren stood now, and merely in the act of standing he commandeered the floor. "She makes a good point." He agreed. Mara brightened at the praise, and then he glanced at Mina studiously writing something down in the notebook that she always carried under her arms. She looked up when Warren mentioned her name. "Mina, can you do a reference search on 'alraune' at the library? We'll need as much information as we can get, no matter how small or insignificant it might be. Personal accounts, biology, history, behavioral mannerisms…"

"Weaknesses." Darren threw in.

Warren nodded at the rogue. "Yeah, and weaknesses. *Especially* weaknesses." He said.

The bespectacled woman seemed a little surprised at having such a reference question thrown at her so suddenly, but soon she smiled. She was quite confident that Adratea's library had all the information they needed; all she had to do was dig it up. "Of course. I'll try my best. It's a rather obscure subject - cryptobotany, so it might take most of the night to research."

Darren rose suddenly to announce; 'Don't worry, I'll help you!' to the librarian girl, but before he could get the words out he felt Warren's hand pressing against his chest to keep him from making a fool of himself. Everybody knew about Darren's obsession with Mina save for Mina herself. It was best not to indulge him.

"Don't worry, *I'll* help you." Warren said instead, grinning warmly at Mina. "I'm not an expert at botany but I'll try my best."

Trina raised her hand. "Cassie and I can make machetes for the rescue party to use. Nothing can hack apart tough vines like a well-sharpened machete, and from the sounds of your story you guys just aren't equipped well enough without them."

"It might mean the difference between life and death." Cassie added.

"But you know, we can't really work for *free*…" Trina began to drawl, but then her younger sister elbowed her sharply in the ribs and she grimaced. "Ow! Alright, well, I guess we'll discuss it some other time. How many do you think you'll need?"

"Three." Ravendor said automatically, even though the number wasn't really that impressive and not any better than it had been after running from the alraune in the first place. He had been hoping for more.

Heck, he had been hoping for Zagtakh to still be in town or something like that.

"Make that four." Siro corrected from where he was standing, off to the side.

Everybody turned to look at the mayor of Adratea and Warren made kind of a strange face. It was kind of a cross between worry and pain. "Siro?" He asked.

"You said that you need all the help you can get. I'm able-bodied and not busy right now, so I'll go with you. I'll replace Magi on your team until you can get him back." Siro offered kindly. There was a chance that Magi might not be coming back at all, but he was optimistic about the chances.

"Your offer is deeply appreciated, my friend." Ravendor said formally, and the two men shook on it in front of the crowd.

Mina wanted to remind the swordsman that he had a veritable *mountain* of paperwork back at his office (kitchen table) to plough through, but this was something more important than just a merry romp through the dungeon. Somebody's life was at stake. Because Magi was a citizen of the town this came into the mayor's jurisdiction as both a lawman *and* the representative of Adratea, but Mina also knew that if Siro was nobody at all he would still want to help. That was just the kind of man he was.

Warren came up behind Siro and grasped the blond man by the shoulders. He shook him gently and as he spoke his voice sounded slightly uneven. "Uh… can I talk to you for a minute, please?" He asked.

"Sure, what is it?"

"*In private*, if that's okay with you." He stressed.

The doctor led the mayor out the back door of the tavern and left the assembly to free to talk amongst themselves. The evening air touched their faces softly with coldness, and far off in the grass and the trees cicadas and crickets chirped their own faint little tune. Warren finally let go of Siro's wrist once they were alone.

"What the hell are you thinking? You can't get involved in this!" He snapped.

"It seems like your team needs my help." The swordsman answered, seemingly unfazed by Warren's sudden irritability.

"You don't understand." Warren continued, this time sadly. "The alraune *abduct* humans. They took Magi, they tried to take Darren; you're attractive enough so they'll try to take you too! Adratea needs you, Siro!" He implored, looking away.

Siro wanted to smile reassuringly at him, but didn't. The doctor looked a little too anxious for airy, baseless reassurances. "It's fine. If anything happens to me the town will elect a new mayor. They'll probably even be a lot better at it than I am now." He said.

Warren let out a deep sigh, then added after a few empty moments; "*I* need you, Siro."

Ah, so that was what this was all about. Siro's expression softened. "So what are you saying?" He asked.

Warren stared mutely at the ground for a moment and then adjusted his glasses that had begun to slip a little down his nose. "It might be selfish of me to say this, but it doesn't matter as much if Ravendor or Darren go back into the monster's lair and get eaten. It would suck, I guess, but at least it wouldn't have been you. Don't you get what I'm saying? I'm terrified of losing you." He admitted, turning back to look at Siro with pleading grey eyes.

When Siro smiled at him it was an illustration of warmth, of endearment. "It's not like I'm utterly helpless in combat, you know. You worry far too much. I'm certainly not going to stay in town just because something *might* happen to me, just as it might happen to the three of you. Besides, worry is a two-way street. I have to come with you to protect you from the alraune as well."

The doctor still looked a little miffed at him, but his resolve was slipping. "Don't try and turn the argument back on me." He grumped.

"Come on, I want to help Magi. You and I will protect each other; I trust you with my back. That way if anything happens at least it will happen to us together." Siro reasoned, taking one of Warren's hands. The other man didn't resist him. "I love you, Warren." He said.

Warren sighed, giving up, but he was grateful that Siro understood how he felt even during times when he himself wasn't all that certain. "Yeah, I know. I love you too." He smiled bashfully. He still wasn't that used to saying it out loud just yet.

Siro placed his hand on Warren's shoulder and pulled him close. The two men kissed.

"You do realize I've been standing here the entire time, right?" BW said from where she was standing at the window.

Warren and Siro broke their kiss quickly in surprise. The mage girl was standing on a wooden crate Mieus had left under the windowsill, containing god knows what and merely labeled in black paint; 'spares'. They hadn't noticed her because she had been exceptionally quiet, and truth to tell in the darkness and from the corner of the eye BW looked like a gargoyle set in stone, all hunched over and brooding.

"BW!" Warren stammered, still mostly in Siro's arms. "What are you-"

"Oh can it. You two aren't doing anything I don't already know about and honestly it doesn't matter anything to me." She interrupted, hopping off the large crate and returning to her normal, rather diminutive size. Suddenly she flashed them a dazzling grin. "So you guys didn't see me at all? Ha ha! Darren was right! Hiding in plain sight really *does* work!" She laughed.

After he pulled away from Siro for propriety's sake Warren folded his arms and looked steadily at BW. She was a magician who had just appeared in Adratea one day and then set up a bazaar in the middle of town. Nobody was really certain where she had come from, and, like Zagtakh, she seemed to be a demi-human capable of socializing with other humans. Her shape was human save for two big wings on her back colored a deep midnight blue, something so weird and completely out of place that it caused people to wonder where in the world she had come from; if she had come from this world at all.

When asked about it BW's story was anything but consistent. Sometimes she'd say that her wings had come from an alchemy experiment gone horribly wrong, while at other times she'd allude that she came from a village of demi-humans that all looked just like her. Once or twice she'd even admitted to being an angel from heaven come to punish the wicked. Everything was uncertain with her, and that's what made BW strange, mysterious and possibly even dangerous.

"We were, er, waiting for you to show up." Warren murmured. "You were out here the whole time? Why didn't you come in when Siro called for you?"

The young girl shrugged. "When I got here Ravendor was already blathering on about the dungeon or whatever and I didn't feel like interrupting anything. You guys are going on an adventure? To that underground forest?" She asked.

Before Warren or Siro could answer her the back door opened again and Darren stuck his head outside. He looked anxious. "S-Siro? Mieus is picking a fight with Ravendor again and I think you ought to-"

"Darren!" BW cried eagerly, interrupting the rogue's plea. It wasn't a cry of annoyance, but of joy. She rushed to the youth and embraced him, crushing Darren's head against her small bosom. "I'm so glad you're okay! I heard terrible things happened to you in the dungeon!"

He struggled briefly for a few moments but then realized it was useless and gave in. "Yeah, but I'm fine now. Nothing really that bad happened to me." He tried to reassure her.

The girl opened her mouth to reply to him, but then realized they weren't alone and glared at the other two men. "Do you mind? We're about to have a moment here." She said.

Warren and Siro exchanged a glance. It expressed mutual, silent amazement at how BW could just bust in one their special moment and then demand time for her own. Still, it wasn't worth arguing about and apparently the mayor was needed indoors anyway, so the two left BW and Darren to themselves. As they were leaving the dark-haired rogue noticed that Warren and Siro were holding hands, but didn't think much of it once the winged mage girl hugged him again; much more tenderly this time.

"Warren is mean. It might not matter so much to him if you get eaten in the dungeon but I'll sure as hell be sad. You'd be really hard to replace." She sighed, glad that he had come back at all, then pulled back to look at him from an arm's length away. "You've got to stop letting everyone else in your team walk all over you."

That was easier said than done when he was the smallest and weakest of the group. "So you heard about what happened in the dungeon? With the alraune?" He asked.

"Most of it, yeah. It doesn't sound too good for you guys, especially if it's an alraune queen hiding out down there." BW smiled knowingly. "Did you know the alraune species was created by a sorcerer?"

Darren blinked at her. "You know about them?"

"It's part of my job to know about these kinds of things. Alraune nectar is actually a really potent ingredient in a lot of potions and tinctures, but incredibly hard to secure short of capturing one and putting it in a cage in your lab. There's a story told by alchemists and mages alike that alraune came into the world when a sorcerer cursed a dying man as he was hanging from the gallows, and the seed that was spilt when he died grew the mandragora root; the distant ancestor of the alraune."

That was a lot more than Darren would have expected to hear from BW. She acted rather immature most of the time but every so often she'd pop up and say something or quote a source that by all rights should be beyond her ability to grasp. The effect was slightly unbalancing, leaving many people unsure whether she was going to say something sagely or stupid or what. Darren looked a little uncomfortable. "Seed? You, um, mean…"

"It could be literal or symbolic or whatever; I don't know. I guess it doesn't matter. The most important thing right now is that there are alraune in the dungeon, and it has Reiyu!" She announced.

"Magi. It has Magi." Darren corrected.

"Oh, well, I knew it was someone from the inn." BW chuckled. "I'm glad to hear that, 'cause Reiyu still owes me thirty silver pieces from last month's poker night."

Darren walked over to the large crate BW had been standing on earlier and sat down, planting his elbows on his knees; both hands cupping his chin. He felt tired, sore, and utterly worn out. Somewhere inside the Guildhouse the fighting seemed to have ceased, no doubt due to Siro's intervention. "I have to do something." Darren said raggedly, his words riddled with guilt. "It should be me still down there in the dungeon, but I was so much of a coward that Magi took my place. I know I should be happy that I'm not plant food… but still…"

BW looked at him sitting there wretchedly for a few moments then shuffled over and sat down beside him, wrapping an arm around the rogue's thin shoulders. He leaned into the half-hug; into her warmth that was so precious in the rapidly cooling evening. "So you're going to go back with the others?" She asked softly.

He thought about the question. Going back would be risking his life again, but not going would be risking everybody else's lives and embracing himself as a coward for good. He didn't want that, even if it felt like he kind of deserved it. Darren nodded, grinding his chin into his palms. "Yeah. Yeah, I think so. If I don't I'll probably regret it forever." He said.

The mage girl smiled at him again and this time it was sincere. She brought her hand up and ran her fingers through his semi-long black hair. It seemed he had lost his hat somewhere. It was probably still down there in the monster's lair. "That's really brave of you, Darren. See, I *knew* you were a good guy beneath all the obsessions. Let me help you out, okay?"

"Help? How? I wish you could come with us but you can't, there's no way Ravendor would allow it." Darren protested, but he had a feeling that if she came with them then maybe things would turn out alright.

"Yeah, it'd be easier to just turn myself into a boy rather than argue with that wet blanket." She joked, holding her chest as if to flatten out her breasts with her hands. Knowing her, though, instead of it just being a jest it was equally possible that she was being serious, too.

Darren laughed a bit with her but as he trailed off he added; "Oh god you can't actually do that, can you?"

"I can do a lot of things with alchemy, and a lot more things with magic. I could probably make it work." She mused out loud, grinning evilly at him.

"Please don't get any ideas." He reassured her, liking her just the way she was. It might make their budding relationship a little more awkward than it needed to be.

"Why, with the right materials I could probably transform you into a beautiful, bouncy-"

"BW, stop!" Darren half laughed, half cried and grabbed her suddenly in a kiss. Back when they'd started seeing one another he never would have dared seizing a potentially volatile mage girl like that, but over time he had realized that while she did indeed have a short fuse love and kisses never set it off. He was grateful for that, and also grateful for the comfort provided when she slipped her hands around his sides for a close, gentle hug.

When she pulled away from him at last her grin has gone from evil to silly. "But you know being a girl is a lot of fun too." She giggled, blushing severely.

He kissed her again, and then a third time. Like this things didn't seem so daunting; didn't seem so bad. BW's hot breath washed over him briefly and it smelled like fresh ginger for an ephemeral second, as if she had been chewing on some just prior to coming down to the Guildhouse. "Their weakness is fire, in case you're curious." She said in a low voice.

"Huh?" He honestly had no idea what she was talking about.

"The alraune, dummy! Don't you remember? They're human-shaped, but when you get right down to it they're just plants. If they were ever human in the past they're not any more. Like all plants they go up in smoke when you torch them." She explained, then a thought came to her suddenly and she seemed worried. "Do you think Siro, Warren or Ravendor are quick enough to learn my fire spell overnight?" She asked.

Darren considered the possibility. All three of them were particularly intelligent people, but even so he didn't think it'd be possible. None of them were gifted in that area, and neither was he. The rogue shook his head. "Do you have a backup plan?" He asked instead.

"Maybe… but I'm not sure. It might not work. I've never tried it before." BW replied faintly, thinking hard but not giving away what her plan was in the slightest. From out of the blue she shot another question at Darren. "Hey, how good are you at throwing?"

"Throwing?" He echoed.

"You know; rocks, darts, horseshoes, whatever!" She pressed. It didn't matter what he could throw, just as long as he could wing a target easy enough to mark it.

And now, finally, they could talk about something Darren was actually *good* at. Bows and guns and what have you were a little too complicated for him, but nobody in town had been able to beat him in a game of darts yet. From his belt the youth took out a small throwing knife. The cold steel was muted by the darkness, but there was no misunderstanding what it was. "Oh, well, point out a target to me and let's see if I can hit it." Darren said, testing the balance of the blade in his hand by holding it at the very tip.

BW glanced around obediently for something for Darren to kill. At first she thought of that bad-tempered white cat that Mieus kept around and loosely called her 'pet', but it was nowhere to be seen at the moment. Instead, she looked at another crate some distance away, also made of wood and listed simply as; 'misc'. It seemed like it hadn't been touched for a very long time.

"Do you think you could hit the centre of the letter 'c' on that crate over there?" She asked. It was such a small area that she didn't think it was possible, but you never know; he might surprise her.

Darren squinted into the night. He stood. "I'm not sure. Let me try…" He murmured.

He threw the small dagger at the target. It spun tightly in the air and hit the side of the box with a wooden sound, blade first, so at least it stuck. BW ran over to the target and crouched, checking out his handiwork. She reached down and pulled the knife out of the wood, inspecting the thin hole it had made.

"It's not exactly in the centre, but it's good enough to pass." She commented casually, walking back to Darren and pressing the knife handle-first back into his hand. He sheathed it in his belt and she seemed satisfied. "It should work. It'll take all night, but I think I can give you the fire spell tomorrow morning."

"How?"

BW stuck her tongue out at him. "You'll find out tomorrow morning when I'm done, so be patient until then. I love handing out surprises." Before she turned to leave she took Darren by the hands again. "Be sure to get enough sleep tonight. You look tired." She said, and the youth felt a little touched that she'd notice something like that.

But something bothered him. It was just a tiny little detail BW had said as if she had given it no mind, but it was odd and out of place, and, frankly; strange. "You said; 'if the alraune were ever human in the past they're not anymore.' What did you mean by that?" He asked.

BW looked at him when he said that, and it finally felt like he was looking at the cunning, intelligent side of BW and that it was looking right back at him, just beneath those deep, dark red eyes. It was like looking into the eyes of someone capable of reading his mind. For Darren it felt like the glance must have taken a whole lot longer than it needed to, but in reality it was only a second or three before she turned away.

"Well… I'm sure Mina and Warren will dig that information up out of the library before daybreak, or at least eventually. I could just come out and say it, but I hate to be the bearer of bad news." She sighed airily, offhandedly; shrugging. She looked back at Darren again as she started away from the tavern. "I'll be back here at dawn, so tell everybody just to sit tight until then. You'd better not stand me up, Darren!"

He waved meekly at her. "Bye, BW."

Soon she was gone, wandering back into the darkness towards her store. When Darren went back inside again to convey her message to the others the assembly was well on its way to wrapping itself up anyway, and the rogue butting in with the message that BW was going to help them in some way, maybe, but he didn't know what, was the vague full-stop the townsfolk needed to collectively throw up their hands and continue discussing it in the morning.

Of course, some people weren't that happy with this arrangement. Ravendor in particular wanted to gather up his party and leave for the dungeon almost immediately, convinced that the longer Magi spent down there in the darkness the smaller his chances of survival. This was impractical while their team was still confused and exhausted, and it was one of the only reasons he relented when Warren and Siro told him how reckless his plan sounded. They needed time for everyone to sleep, for Mina to research, the Sylvas sisters to forge, and for BW to work whatever magic she had under cover of secrecy. Magi just had to hold on a little longer, that was all.

In the end everybody decided to go home. The meeting was adjourned by the mayor and under the starry, partially cloudy sky people paired off into small groups and walked back towards the centre of town. Some of them lived closely to one another and it was better than walking alone. Darren had a room at the inn over on the far west of town and while he usually walked home with BW after these meetings, at least until they hit her little cottage in the middle of the business district, that wasn't possible tonight. He walked home with Ravendor instead and the entire journey was mostly silent, except for the rogue's stunted attempts at conversation and the gunman's noncommittal, one word answers.

Darren was relieved when they finally got back to the inn. The windows were dark and the place seemed empty, almost lonesome as they headed up the dirt path to the building, which only reinforced the knowledge that Magi was gone and Reiyu was gods knew where. If Reiyu were home at least his lights would be on; he usually didn't go to sleep until midnight or later.

All the tenants of Adratea inn had their rooms upstairs, while Ravendor lived in the inn master's room on the first floor. Darren glanced at the other man in the glow of a freshly-lit candle, examining a ledger he kept at his desk in the middle off the lobby, probably checking to see if anybody had left him a note while he had been busy in the dungeon. "Hey… are you alright?" He asked awkwardly.

The older man didn't turn to look at him. "I am fine, Darren. Just get out of here. We need to be ready by dawn tomorrow." He said, but he did not seem to be that fine at all. He looked a little shaken up by all that had happened that day.

"I have some leftovers from last night in my room if you're too tired to cook and…"

Ravendor cut him off. "Actually I think I am just going to go straight to bed. Thank you for the offer, however."

The youth sighed. "Well, alright. 'Night then."

"Goodnight."

He climbed up the stairs silently, the light-footedness of his profession promising that not even a single step creaked or groaned as he made his way to the top. It was dark up there too, but he knew where the candles were and fumbled in his pockets for a match to light.

A floorboard creaked as something up there with him moved. Darren froze, going still in mid-fumble, like a rabbit that had just caught sight of an approaching predator. Magi was gone, Ravendor was downstairs, and Reiyu was still absent. What was…

Something started scratching furiously at the walls.

Darren lit the candle as quickly as he could, nearly burning the tips of his fingers in the process. He scoured the second floor lobby and then breathed a deep sigh of relief. It was only Fortinbras the inn hound, a black afghan that had started out as a stray hanging around western Adratea but had gradually wormed his way into the comforts and lives of the people living at the inn. When Darren had entered the animal had been curled up outside of Magi's room, but even the rogue's stealthy footsteps were no match for his sharp, attuned hearing.

When Fortinbras realized the humans had returned he had began to scratch frantically at Magi's door. The hound liked to sleep on other people's beds and did it on some kind of rotation; tonight it had seemed to be Magi's night for the huge, hairy hot water bottle to appear. He looked at Darren imploringly to open the door.

The rogue smiled wanly and picked up the now burning candlestick. "Magi isn't coming home tonight, boy." He told the animal as he unlocked the door to his room. They were modest accommodations, but comfortable and more than enough for someone like him. "You can stay with me. Come on." He held the door open for Fortinbras to gallop through.

The dog immediately took up a third of his bed and became one great big, immovable shag carpet. He patted the creature for a few short moments before getting ready to settle in for the night.

Tomorrow was going to be a really long day.

The lights in the library did not go out that night, even as the other buildings grew dark all around.

Mina Walman climbed down the steps that led to her small apartment above the book repository, carefully balancing a cup of hot coffee in each hand. The coffee was black and strong, so with luck it would keep her awake until the very crack of dawn. She brought it over to the table in the work area of the library, littered with piles of books and ledger files.

Warren was somewhere behind those piles of books. After a bit of searching she found him and handed him something to drink. They had been going over reference materials for hours now and they needed a break. "Find anything new?" She asked, sitting on the edge of the table and looking at her friend.

"A few things." Warren replied as he accepted the cup of coffee, but didn't take a sip. The night was warm and balmy, even as late as it was, but the sea breezes from the south maintained a slight damper on the heat of summer. To be perfectly honest he would have preferred a glass of lemonade.

He raised a clipboard covered in messy scrawls and paused for a moment to adjust his glasses. "Well, not really much more than we knew already. I was right back in the tunnels though; many accounts profess that alraune don't devour their prey immediately after capture."

Mina had also found some brief evidence of this, though unspecified in a couple of exploration journals. Why only 'many' accounts, though? Why not all of them? She smiled. "Well that's good to know, at least. Let's hope the monster put him in a corner or something so he can get some sleep."

The physician returned her smile, although the quality of it had changed. Warren looked tired, with faint shadows under his eyes and less than tidy hair. He was always on everybody's cases about 'taking care of themselves', yet Mina had begun to realize that her friend was one of those kinds of hypocrites who never listened to their own advice. "I can't imagine what that would be like. No light, no sound, and with a monster that might be planning to rip you to shreds."

Rising from where she was sitting Mina softly put a hand on Warren's shoulder. "I can take it from here if you want. You have to be ready to leave at dawn and it's almost midnight already."

"What's wrong? Are you worried I might turn into a pumpkin?" He asked wryly, but then interrupted her with a gentle laugh when Mina held in a breath to puff herself up a little in indignation. "It's fine, Mina. Please. Just give me a little longer, okay? Let me help a little longer."

He picked up another book she had pulled off the shelves as a result of her reference search, but paused as he read the title. He read it again, just to be sure, his brow furrowing a little in confusion. "Uh, Mina? Why did you put this in the pile? Why is this even *in* the library in the first place?" He asked.

The librarian leaned forward and looked over his shoulder. "Oh that? I'm not sure, but it was in the catalogue with a 'cryptobotany' tag on it. I didn't catalogue this entire library by myself; some of the other girls in town helped out." She giggled as she continued. "Maybe there is something about alraune in there after all."

"*'Sexual explorations through cryptozoology; a gentleman's guide'*" Warren announced, reading the title out loud. He gave Mina a sidelong glance and smiled a bit. "You can, er, explore that way?"

"I don't see why not."

"Sounds kind of dangerous." He couldn't help but imagine some kind of stodgy explorer type trying to stick his willy into all manner of monsters and fought the urge to laugh just like Mina had. Despite the title it *looked* credible enough; bound in leather just like any other academic journal. Warren flipped the book open and started to search for clues again.

While Warren read Mina cast a quiet glance towards the window, darkened now in the late night but still partially illuminated by the house next door, the second storey bedroom window lit as if its owner BW were still awake. It wasn't that surprising; the mage girl certainly seemed like the 'stay up all night and then sleep until noon' type.

A brief shadow seemed to move behind the curtains and then was gone again, prompting Mina to think about the man who lived next door to BW, just as she lived next door to her.

Without taking her gaze away from the window Mina spoke. "Warren, what's your opinion of Siro?" She asked.

For his own merit Warren didn't actually startle, though his heart gave a slightly more vexing 'thump' than usual. Instead, he tore himself away from the page he was reading (something about an angry sorcerer and a corpse, he would have been creeped out had he not heard of worse) and gave Mina an inquisitive look. The look spoke of mild curiosity, and that was true, but behind it there was something else. Slight nervousness. "Hm, what do you mean?"

After all, he had never *told* anybody about his relationship with the mayor before. There was no reason for it, and besides that it was his private business. Back in the city, where civilization was a little tighter, mentioning that you were interested in anything other than the opposite gender was a free ticket to getting your face kicked in out the back of an alleyway somewhere. He *still* had no idea how BW had picked up on it. Her crystal ball, maybe.

Warren noticed the wistful expression on Mina's face as she looked out the window and he understood, his expression softening a little. Like attracted like, and she was a little crazy for the mayor as well.

"He's at the clinic fairly often because he stresses himself out so much with his headaches, and you two seem to be friends so I was just curious." Mina added, glancing back at Warren. He had closed the reference journal softly but still kept a finger between the pages – an impromptu bookmark made only to last for a few minutes. She continued. "I was just wondering if you knew anything about him, that's all."

"Gee Mina, you're supposed to be his secretary or something. I would have thought you'd know more about Siro than me." The doctor commented.

"Yes but I… always wanted to know if he talks about me… when I'm not around." The librarian sighed, stretching the sentence artificially. They were wasting time talking about something that didn't really matter, but Mina didn't care. They needed a break anyhow. "You're his physician, so…"

"So I could tell you about stuff like how he once trod on a nail and needed a tetanus injection or something like that?" Warren joked.

"You know what I mean!" Mina responded with a short burst of laughter, though not at the joke. Warren wasn't very good at playing dumb, and he was intentionally misunderstanding her. "You're a guy *and* his friend, so I just thought you might…" She trailed off, unsure how to continue without repeating herself.

In truth Warren could tell her a lot about Siro. He could tell her about how he looked standing glistening in the shower with streams of water running through his hair and down his skin, tracing the musculature just as he had with his hands the night before. He could tell her about how Siro had a weakness for lovers in glasses and preferred it when he kept them on, though that might only encourage her; he wasn't sure.

In the end telling her that Siro probably wouldn't be interested because he had already found somebody else and even *worse*, fallen in love with them would probably do Mina more harm than good. Warren said nothing. He was in the business of making people feel better, after all.

He went back to the book and awkwardly ended the conversation. His eyes swam momentarily at the small, blurred text, and he blinked a couple of times, adjusting his glasses. Maybe he really was more exhausted than he thought.

Mina felt a little put off at the evasion but if Warren didn't know he didn't know, and it was no use pressing him. They both decided to get back to work instead, but the librarian was certain that she would send him home at the turn of the hour. That was the limit.

According to the grandfather clock in the library they hit a breakthrough at five minutes prior to her self-imposed curfew. It wasn't a pleasant surprise; Warren nearly choked on his coffee as he turned the page.

"Mina!"

Mina was jolted out of the hefty task of drawing a sunflower on the outside of the margin of her notebook. It wasn't very professional but she was well into her fifth hour of study, so…

Warren looked grim. He was still reading the subsequent page of the monster sex book. "Magi might be in a lot more trouble than we thought. There's a section in this chapter about alraune regarding… transmutation." He said.

"Transmutation?" The word sounded vaguely familiar but she couldn't quite remember its meaning, though it didn't sound very friendly.

Rather than try and explain it Warren merely showed the open book to the girl. "This."

It was a word-heavy journal, strangely so considering its topic, but there *were* illustrations. Not photos, this book seemed to pre-date them, but the artist had been meticulous enough. It was almost as if they had drawn it directly from life.

The picture in question was of a dark-haired buxom woman entangled in the vines of an alraune king. Entangled in more ways than one, entangled intimately, bare-breasted and held up with far too many vines to count. It would have been great porn stash material were Warren into that sort of thing, but he was more concerned with the anomaly in the picture; the thing that just didn't make sense.

Mina's first impulse after realizing what the picture detailed was to look away. She scrutinized it instead, even though the whole illustration was kind of horrific to her. "That poor woman…" She said out loud, and then realized another thing. "Is that what's happening to Magi right now?"

"Probably. Sorry for showing you something like this, but take a closer look at the drawing. Look at her arms and legs." The physician instructed.

She did so. For several moments she wasn't able to see what he was talking about, there were just so many vines everywhere and the picture, while meticulously drawn, was small on the page. The woman's hair hung in long loose strands against her pale breasts, while the alraune's vines curled against them almost possessively. The set of the woman's jaw made it impossible for Mina to tell if she was in extreme pain or pleasure.

And then she saw it. Mina's eyes widened. "Oh my." She breathed.

Some of the vines in the picture didn't connect to the alraune at all. They were coming from the *woman* instead.

Of course. Transmutation; the changing of something's form into something else. Like lead into gold, or a caterpillar into a butterfly…

Or a human into another alraune.

Were Magi not a strong man, a hardy man, and one accustomed to such hardships he never would have been able to survive down there; entangled in the alraune's trap.

A weaker man might have broken under the physical onslaught alone; hanging from his arms until the muscles burned and screamed in pain and then finally went numb. He was hungry, thirsty and tired, and while he fell into unconsciousness often it was nothing like proper rest. The blood from his injury had dried but his head still pounded at rhythmic intervals, almost hard enough to make him want to vomit had he anything left to throw up.

The only time the pain and exhaustion receded was when the alraune raped him. There was enough time to rest, and to hurt, but these were merely quick breaks just so that Magi's mind and body didn't snap under the pressure, and by a hair's width – he held.

Instead of going insane to the pain, the pleasure, instead of breaking outright… he bent against the creature's ministrations. When she had first violated him there had been resistance, tenseness, and an awful amount of blood. The alraune's nectar – her blood – healed and soothed while it also set his senses aflame. When she was not there… when she wasn't…

"Al… rau… ne…" Magi sighed faintly, his voice a dry whisper. He was dying of thirst, absolutely drying up, and he would do *anything* for anyone, *anywhere* simply for a glass of water. His eyesight had improved significantly thanks to his time spent in the darkness and he could hear the sound of water nearby, of an underground stream perhaps that tempted him and nearly drove him mad. He wasn't sure how long it had been since he'd last had a drink, but all he knew was that the strange bitter substance the monster fed him frequently from both directions did not suffice. If he had to, and if the alraune understood what he needed, he would gladly let the creature fuck him again if it would only let him have some water.

Tears prickled behind his eyes for the umpteenth time that night, but crying would be a waste of moisture so he forced those tears away. "Alraune…" He said again, more coherently but softer this time. You know, maybe she was *waiting* for him to die of thirst so she could-

Magi flinched involuntarily. Along with the burning thirst his arms itched terribly and sometimes sharply enough to make his entire body twinge. It would have worried him if he didn't have more important things to worry about; though he was a little curious as to how he could itch so badly when both his arms were dead.

The vines around his wrists shifted slightly and a flood of pins and needles poured down his limbs. Magi groaned and fell back against more vines so he didn't drop down to a broken leg, and for a short while he just waited half consciously for the terrible burning and jabbing to stop. When it felt like he could move his arms again he looked at them, weakly.

Both his outer forearms from his wrists to his elbows were horribly bruised. They were splotched blue and purple and even the very faintest shade of green, as if he had been in a serious accident and had protected himself with both of his arms. He couldn't remember how or why it had happened. Had it been when the alraune had smacked him hard against the altar? Or when he had been fighting the vines with everybody else? Could it have been when it had forced his legs open and pulled his arms back to-

His memory was too muddled up. He couldn't think.

He scratched at the itching bruises absently and his fragile train of thought was cut short as a bolt of livid pain helped to resuscitate his limbs. Just touching it had hurt as much as if he had slammed them against a hard surface. So he couldn't scratch them, not unless he wanted that kind of pain again.

Thinking about not scratching reminded the young archer briefly of his mother and that hot summer so many years ago when he had caught the chicken pox from some other kid in his village. She had still been alive back then, and he could remember her auburn curls and faint rosewater perfume as vividly and as dimly as any other son could with such an ocean of time between them.

*'Don't scratch, Magi. You'll only make it worse.'* He could hear her saying. *'Keep doing that and you'll never get better.'*

After so long he felt a sharp pang of homesickness, but quickly pushed it away. There was no point in remembering, but at least it had managed to keep his hands still.

It occurred to him that if he managed to remain lucid long enough he might be able to climb down to the ground and get a drink of water from that invisible stream. *That* would be even better than scratching.

*And Magi, Magi you idiot,* he told himself tiredly, *if you can reach the ground you might be able to escape!*

That idea had barely even occurred to him. How long had he been down here? Time had ceased to hold meaning. He had to gather his thoughts…

"Alraune… I am… dy…ing…" Magi said slowly, in a flat tone. He tried to heave his body up and away from the safety of the vines, paying no mind to the advanced state of undress he was in. It didn't really seem important.

Unfortunately for the young archer, even a light-footed and dexterous man would have had trouble untangling himself from and descending down the alraune's snare. Whether it had been a misplaced step or the loss of grip, or just simple gravity; Magi fell.

It was not a killing distance to the ground, but it *was* a crippling one. He grabbed wearily at a loose vine and then gave up.

What he did not expect was for the vine to grab back. It felt him leaving and snatched at him before he could hit the floor, grabbing Magi by the wrist and causing the youth to cry out in pain as his shoulder was nearly dislocated from its socket. He gritted his teeth as he stared down at the bottom of the cavern. He was so close to freedom but now he hung there like a puppet, and the vine cutting into his bruises hurt so, *so* badly…

The alraune was quick to approach him again now that he had drawn her attention by falling. She pulled him up with her vines back to a more comfortable altitude and laid him against the tangled mess with ease.

Prey became lethargic and careless after being fed too much nectar; that was just how things were.

"Water…" Magi said to her, desperately, but there was no use. She did not understand his language, and even if she did she would not have obliged him. Water was not something the alraune had to worry about except through her roots. She pressed her green, too-long fingered hands up against Magi's upper arms to check him. He was pale and clammy and cold.

And simply seeing the alraune there again awoke something almost Pavlovian from deep within Magi, something which whispered to him that he was hurting terribly and the alraune with her promise of monstrous pleasure could banish it away. It was simple. In these circumstances she was his lifeline; the only hope that he might yet live another day. She was everything. She was…

… his queen.

And he didn't even have to taste her to feel those bitter pheromones in the air.

Magi made the first move. He leaned forward and kissed her on her deceptively human lips; soft and moist yet neither warm nor cold. The alraune hesitated for a moment, a split second almost indistinguishable from how a human girl would have reacted, with brief surprise and even a little uncertainty. That did not last long however as the plant creature was already fairly certain as to what she wanted.

She kissed back, pressed up against him as the vines at Magi's back pressed him gently into the alraune's embrace. Two firm, yet soft globes of pseudoflesh were pushed against the young archer's naked chest as the contact slowly warmed her, the creature obtaining her own body heat vicariously through him. Magi was taken aback by the kiss, by how even the most gentle of contacts was already beginning to lessen the headache, the thirst, the pain in his shoulder.

He felt the alraune's grip on his arms increase slightly as he deepened the kiss, exploring tentatively with his tongue a place that might even be as deadly as the very cave he was trapped in. Vines thinner and more sensitive to the alraune's wishes tightened themselves about Magi's body, clinging but not painful, like a lover to the object of one's affections. As strange as it felt it was something of an embrace.

The taste of blood filled their mouths as Magi accidentally ran his tongue against a few of her teeth and realized that they were razor sharp, curved and pointed like those of a shark, or some kind of piranha type creature. She had a sweet mouth specifically designed for both kissing and tearing through bloody flesh and Magi was already far too distracted to realize the irony that this turned him on even more somehow, despite all logic and reason.

In response to the bloodletting the monster girl rose into action, excited by the taste of Magi's blood just as he had been cursed by hers. She shoved him roughly against her tentacles and pressed even harder against him, sucking at the cut with her generously moist mouth.

Magi's hands came up and cupped the alraune's huge and heavy breasts. He had sort of expected them to be firm and unyielding like some kind of statue – she was a plant after all – but he was delighted to find that they were soft and full; if a little bit rubbery. Their perkiness more than made up for that and he happily caressed and handled the ample cleavage, rolling his thumbs over her hard nipples as their kiss became even more fervent and needy.

He did not resist her as the alraune pulled away and parted some of the vines at Magi's back, allowing the youth a little more room to recline. Her deep green eyes were half-lidded and her mouth was a sultry smile. Magi smiled back too, a small trickle of blood oozing down his lip from where she had nicked him outwardly, and there were more within. He was lucky he hadn't lost his tongue to her.

She trailed one of her long fingers up along Magi's standing member, from the base to the tip, and glanced at him as if to gauge his reaction. The archer shuddered at the touch but it was only a tease, and Magi looked so dazed it was almost like he wasn't even there at all, his higher faculties banished by the alraune's bittersweet nectar and kisses.

She opened her mouth in a little 'o' shape and revealed her tongue, so long and snakelike that there was no way she could have ever mimicked human speech. It was built for finer things than that. She dipped her head downward towards his cock.

"*Nyaaaah...!*" Magi cried out loud as she engulfed him completely. This was strange. When the alraune had wanted to fuck him before this she would have done it with her vines and filled him until he would pass out from the painful pleasure, but this was different. This was... this was...

It was far too good to waste trying to think about unimportant things. He'd done this before in the past, once or twice at least, but he'd always been the one providing them; not receiving. Was *this* was it was like? With the alraune's skill this was just too good. He didn't even worry about her teeth anymore.

Unconsciously Magi gently placed a hand on the hungry monster's bobbing head as if to guide her movements. Her hair was just as soft and mossy as it looked, and he feared that he could probably break it easily if he pulled hard enough. He stroked it instead while his breathing deepened, trying to control himself so he wouldn't come right away.

In the midst of all this the youth hadn't even noticed that the bruises on his outstretched arm were deepening, becoming less purple-black and more... green.

When his cries became more insistent and the alraune could feel him throbbing all the way down her throat she wisely withdrew (mindful of her teeth at the end. Her prey would be useless if it's most important bit was cut off). He had a bitter taste of his own, and it was almost as intoxicating as the coppery tang of his blood. The monster licked her lips thoughtfully.

Without any regard for his own safety Magi moved suddenly. He grabbed the alraune by her hips, just above the mantle where her body fell apart into those tangling vines and lifted her on top of him into his lap. His arms were shaky from hanging trapped for so long but the alraune acquiesced to his silent demand without hesitation.

He slid his hand beneath the vines coming out of her body and felt around for what he logically suspected was there if the alraune was human enough. He found a softness and a wetness down there that clung enticingly to his fingertips and caused his partner to press against him suggestively, grinding against his fingers and the hardness in his lap. Magi withdrew the digits and guided his cock towards her instead, pressing into her with one eager, satisfying thrust.

She melted around him and clung against his body for support, her arms around his back, his upon her hips, cheek against breast. The alraune couldn't move against him all that well but then again she didn't have to, Magi pumped in and out of her smoothly, desperately, relying entirely on adrenaline and blind lust. He tried to shrug off the vines that writhed around him in response to the alraune's pleasure, as far as he was concerned he was in his own little world, where pain and tiredness and thirst could not reach him.

When he shifted his angle just slightly the alraune responded with trembles, clenching her hands against Magi's back and digging thin bloody trails across his skin with her razor-tipped claws, tightening the vines around his waist until it must have hurt. She couldn't moan or scream in pleasure and she couldn't pant or gasp either, but her constant trembles and shudders against her human partner was enough to show that she wasn't feeling nothing; that she as a living creature was enjoying it just as he was.

The vines all around the cavern slackened and loosened as the alraune stopped paying attention to them. The human creature was making itself useful already. With its seed…

Magi thrust against the alraune one last time and then held her firmly against him with an iron grip as he came. He let out a loud moan, releasing all the frustration and fear he had felt since waking up in this cavern and realizing that he would have to die here. It didn't seem so important anymore.

He was coming so much, he'd never had an orgasm this long before. It felt like he was pouring everything he had left into the alraune's beautiful body, feeding her like the captured prey he was supposed to be. Maybe she would eat him after all of this was over.

After what felt like an eternity Magi finally came down from his staggering high. He was panting and sweat stood out on his skin, and when he withdrew himself from his captor the alraune lifted herself off him almost effortlessly with her vines and looked at him in an odd way, in his almost-nakedness and spent cock covered in her nectar and countless bloody scratches.

She smiled and crept away.

Magi could hardly remember what had happened to him after that. Perhaps he had blacked out or something due to exhaustion or sexual torpor but what he *did* know was that when he came to again he was lying horizontally on his side, stretched out, as if he were in a kind of weird hammock made out of vines. It was infinitely more comfortable than hanging there like a piece of meat.

Not long after that Magi slept. Not unconsciousness, but true, honest sleep.

And his thirst was forgotten.

It was dark, but he could see. Still, he felt about on the ground for a little while to figure out who he was, where he was, and how he was-

But he already knew all that, and stood. It was just one of those kinds of dreams. *'Hello?'* He called out tentatively into the still air and walked- no, kind of stumbled his way to the back of the queen alraune's lair. His knees wouldn't work properly, they kept locking up at the most inappropriate times, and there was a tangible bitterness to the air…

*'Hurry up Darren, we don't have all day!'* Mina admonished him at the altar impatiently. She was wearing a wedding dress.

It wasn't the normal kind either; it was the *other* kind, the kind you would find in dirty magazines and the minds of perverted young men. It pushed her cleavage up to an almost impossibly bountiful state and the fabric was dirty, the flowers upon it wilted, and showed leg all the way up to her garter belt. He swallowed hard as he memorized every inch of her perfect body.

When she lifted her veil of cobwebs she…

*'You've been procrastinating for far too long, you even ran back into town to hide, you snivelling little rat!'* BW scolded, her voice piercing and accusatory in the overbearing silence. She was where Mina was; she was the same woman. It suddenly occurred to Darren that this person didn't even look like *either* of them; it was only his dreaming mind that insisted on calling her 'Mina' or 'BW' despite all evidence to the contrary.

*'But I…'* He began to say, but then realized no sound was coming out. The thought carried itself anyway regardless.

It was enough for Mina to interrupt him mid-thought. *'No excuses! I want you to get up there and take Magi's place right now, do you understand?'*

*'Yeah, quit being a 'fraidy cat and face him, you coward!'* BW added, placing her hands on her nonsensically voluptuous hips.

*'Not a whit like his father,'* his aunt muttered sadly beside Mina or BW, forcing an exasperated sigh, *'a hero, he was. Went out and saved*

*our town, he did! And look at this! Too afraid to even trade places with a friend!'*

*'A-Aunt Selina...'* Darren began to say.

She hit him with a table leg. *'Off you go, then! Off you go!'* She ordered as Darren recovered from the assault and cradled his head in pain.

*'Magi?'* Mina asked calmly from the ground.

*'Yes?'*

Darren whirled to his side and looked up. The hideous, tangled mass of plant vines continued to make up the far wall, but they were calm. Not unfriendly at all.

Perched somewhere about twenty feet above them was Magi. He was sitting down amidst the stationary vines like a child in a swing – unmolested and unharmed. He even seemed curious as to the conversation going on below him, as if his post wasn't a confinement but a choice.

BW waved up at him with a smile. *'We've brought Darren! You can come down now!'* She called.

Magi brightened a little at the good news. *'Really?'* He asked, but then he seemed to remember something. *'Oh, but you had better ask the alraune first. I am her property now.'*

Cold hands touched Darren on his shoulders. He felt it as though it were touching his bare skin despite wearing a shirt and a coat at the time. The fingers were too long and thin; way too long to be human.

*'One human is as good as another to me. I don't care.'* The alraune said. Her not-words sounded like ice; sounded serpentine.

Darren's heart kicked it up several notches and tried to escape through his mouth. He choked it back reflexively, his eyes wide. *'But I... but I...'* He stammered and tried to back away, but only succeeded in backing up against the alraune's breast.

Mina smiled in a rather disturbing fashion and his aunt Selina laughed. *'That's good to hear. Magi, you are free now!'* The librarian announced.

The hunter suspended in the vines above them chucked softly and began to climb down. He did it with a surprising amount of grace, despite the seemingly random placement of the vines and the sheer drop down. When he almost reached the bottom Mina or BW reached out for him and helped him with the last few feet. He offered a gentle *'thanks'* in response.

And then the three of them (or four if you counted the Mina and BW woman as separate entities) turned to Darren. They did this simultaneously, robotically, as if they were all on the same circuit. Their eyes were dead.

The alraune wrapped her cold arms about him firmly.

Darren shrieked.

He tried to rip himself out of her grasp and run towards his friends, but that dead-eyed stare shocked him to his roots and when he broke free, somehow, ripping himself away, he only managed a step or two before he realized there was no place for him to go. There was the darkness, the alraune, and his friends who wished to give him to the alraune. Nowhere at all.

Just like it had happened before during the day the monster's vines found his ankles and wrapped and pulled before Darren could even register he had been grabbed. They got both his legs this time and within a second Darren was hurled onto his stomach and dragged backwards a few steps, the vines coiling up his legs in symmetric, perfect little spirals. He gasped and reached out with his hands to claw at the dirt and stones of the altar, pulling forward as the alraune pulled back, but Mina came forward as well, the folds of her delicate wedding dress rustling as she stepped on one of his hands.

The heel of the dainty, off-white slipper felt like a needle going into the back of his hand. The young rogue cried out and pulled his hands away in a hurry, protecting the injured one with the hale one. More vines took him now, these ones grabbing him by the arms and rolling him onto his back. From there he could look up and see the alraune before him, at his feet, looking at him with apparent disinterest.

*'He looks tender.'* The alraune commented, whether to herself or to the others Darren didn't care to know. *'But not quite tender enough...'*

*'I don't know what that means!'* He cried as more vines swarmed over him, batting them away to no avail, rooting him to the ground; trapped, caged, defenseless...

He heard Mina giggle out of the range of his vision. *'You could always try tenderizing him.'* She suggested.

*'Mina, no-'*

*'We'll just be on our way then.'* Magi said.

*'You can't-'*

*'Bye, Darren!'* BW called as he heard them walk away.

*'No! Youcan'tbeserious-'* A gentle tentacle slid up his trouser leg all the way to his inner thigh. *'Gah! Come back! Come back, please!'*

More vines tore through his shirt and squeezed his wrists and chest. *'I need...'* Darren began to cry as tentacles got past his suddenly loosened belt and slid into his pants. He shook his head wildly, trying to get away, trying to clear his vision as it was blurred by tears.

Vines suddenly gripped his cock that had, completely without his knowing during the process of his binding, turned rock-hard. The squeezing was a pleasant sensation, but it made him want to throw up. *'Somebody,'* he croaked, tears rolling down his face, *'please, please help me...'*

He looked back at his assailant and his eyes widened in shock. The alraune was gone. The vines were still there, but the alraune was gone.

In her place was the dream woman in her wedding dress. The vines seemed to be growing out from under her gown. Darren went stock still, arms bound, his clothing torn and cock pressing so very obviously against the fabric of his trousers…

*'I just realized...'* BW or Mina said with satisfaction as they lifted a slipper up and toed thoughtfully at his erection, stiletto heel poised mere centimeters from his scrotum.

Darren felt like his heart was going to explode in fear.

*'... you really* ***are*** *a little pervert, aren't you, Darren? Hahaha.'*

The slipper pressed…

And Darren passed out.

The young rogue sat bolt upright in his bed. He didn't scream, but he emitted sort of a hoarse croak that didn't quite make it into sound.

Fortinbras raised his head from where he had been resting it against the youth's knee and gave him a bemused look. The rogue didn't notice him; he was too busy trying to get his heart to stop pounding like a jackhammer in his chest, the sheets and covers of his bed knotted tightly between his fists. A dream… it had been a dream.

It had seemed so vivid, so real, and after some moments of putting himself back together again Darren felt under his covers and his clothes and realized with embarrassment and slight shame that he had come in his sleep. Ugh, well, better than wetting the bed he supposed. He groaned softly and slipped out of bed, heading to the only window in his small room at the inn. For a moment his knees felt like they were going to buckle and his heart skipped a beat in dread, but it was just stiffness and nothing more. He peeled back the curtain slightly.

It was still dark outside, but there was some very slight lightening of the horizon that spoke of dawn just around the corner. The rogue heard the dog slide out of bed as well and pad towards the door, and rather than risk a wet rug he opened the door and let the afghan outside into the hall.

Was a dream like that merely a reflection of his guilt? It seemed so, with the switch and the two girls and his aunt mocking him, but what about the tentacle vines? What the heck did *they* signify? He had no idea about dream interpretation; that was more in the way of BW's line of work.

Not that he'd ever tell anyone about it, ever.

*Especially* about how it had felt, even with the pain and terror… kind of good.

Darren cleaned himself up, ate a small breakfast and got dressed; black coat, black pants and grey shirt. They were the proper clothes for blending into a cave-like environment. He belted his dagger scabbards and checked the blades briefly for sharpness and signs of rust. They looked good, though he would have preferred to sharpen them beforehand, but he didn't have time. Lastly, he went for his hat and…

No hat. He had lost it in the dungeon. It completely threw Darren off his morning. It had been his favorite hat (it had been his only one too) and it had brought him luck. Well, hopefully he could search for it after they rescued Magi today, provided they weren't all murdered and eaten by monsters.

By the time he was ready to go it was still night outside, but the darkness was fading. The rogue locked up his room and climbed down the stairs to the lobby of the inn, remembering to change his inn tag to 'out' as he passed by the board. He noticed that Ravendor's tag was also on the 'out' position too, and the candles were freshly lit in the lobby. It seemed like he wasn't the only person awake at this hour.

But the innkeeper hadn't strayed far. The Adratea inn had a small porch out the front and a long bench for tenants to sit on, and when Darren went out onto the ground floor balcony Ravendor was on the bench, his boots on one armrest and his head against the other, with a lantern hanging above him on a hook providing light for the book he was reading.

He didn't get up or offer Darren any kind of greeting as the rogue stepped outside. It was cooler out here, and that was refreshing. A soft breeze from the south touched his face and brought with it the faint scent of the waves. Hard to believe that such a huge dungeon beneath their town could be so close to the ocean.

"What time is it?" Darren asked, more to himself than anyone else.

Nevertheless, Ravendor checked his watch and showed that he was at least aware of Darren being there and not just immersed in his book. "Four forty-five in the morning." His arm cast a brief shadow over his face as he looked and then he went back to his reading.

"You're up early."

"I was under the impression that was the plan." The older man replied dryly.

"Well yeah, but… couldn't sleep?" He pressed, trying to make conversation. Maybe he hadn't been the only one having bad dreams, too. That would be reassuring.

"There are only so many hours in the night." Ravendor said vaguely.

Suddenly Darren was reminded of his dream again, of the person who might have been Mina or might have been BW, or could have even been both calling Magi down from the vines, calling him down and Magi casually climbing down, as if he were up there for fun. And then the vines were reaching him, pulling him away, coaxing him to take Magi's place.

Darren swallowed hard and tried to focus on anything else except for his thoughts. His eyes fell upon the cover of the book Ravendor was reading. It was an old book, not in the distinguished sense, but in more of the beat-up-paperback-fallen-to-the-back-of-the-bookshelf sense. He recognized the author, barely. "Asimov? That's the one with the robots, isn't it?"

"Mm. Warren lent it to me." He said as he turned a page, distracted, as if it were all the explanation required.

"Is it good?"

"It's readable."

"I didn't think you'd be interested in science fiction novels." The rogue admitted, leaning against the doorframe of the inn.

"You shouldn't presume too much about people." The innkeeper advised as he dog-eared the page he was on and got up from the bench. He stretched a little, rolling his shoulders, and then winced as he remembered the bruise.

"I had a nightmare." Darren said awkwardly, regretting it the very second the words passed his lips.

"Oh, poor boy. Did you dream the librarian installed heavy curtains in her bedroom?" Ravendor asked with syrupy sarcasm as he bent over and picked up the supply bag he had prepared earlier by the straps. He tossed it to Darren who caught it easily.

"N-No, of course not." Darren argued, frowning. He was always the pack mule. "Never mind."

"If we wish to make it to the Guildhouse on time we had best leave now. Are you ready?"

"Yeah. As ready as I'll ever be, I guess." He replied, trying to push the nightmare to the very back of his mind and trapping it there, so he would never have to think about it again.

He wasn't very successful.

Things grew better over time. He wasn't sure how or why it happened, but the pain and the desperation faded over the course of the night and then, when the sun came up miles above the surface Magi had been freed from both his hunger and his thirst

It must have been around eighteen hours since he had separated from his friends or had access to a water canteen. Didn't humans die after a few short days of being deprived of water? Why wasn't he the least bit thirsty now? At least the sound of the trickling stream behind him didn't bother him anymore.

The Underwood had become surprisingly comfortable and he could now see perfectly well in the dark. His breathing was slow yet shallow and he hung from fragile vines that did not discomfort the muscles in his arms. Magi smiled in an unfocused, wistful manner.

*'I wonder if the others will come back for me?'* He thought.

The alraune at his side informed him that she thought it was highly likely.

*'I don't know about Darren, but I guess Ravendor and Warren will come back. They're just that kind of people.'* Warren because heroics seemed right up his alley, and Ravendor because… well, he didn't know. Maybe because he liked to think that his friend cared enough about him to risk his life for him in the dark. Magi would probably do the same.

The alraune asked him if they were coming back with the intention to hurt her again.

Magi turned his head to look at the green-skinned woman made of vines close to his side. She looked back at him with surprisingly soft, concerned eyes. It was almost a human expression. He opened his mouth to say something to her out loud, but all that came out was a dry wheeze. His voice was going, no, it was more than going; it was gone. He had spoken his last.

As he looked at her the young archer felt that he had to do more than just hang there and wait for his party to show up and kill her. She could have granted him a painful death but instead she had chosen life. His life. A new life.

Magi did not fear her anymore.

He reached a bruised hand out to her and she looked at it quizzically, before making the obvious connection and placing her long-fingered hand in his. At last, surprisingly, the alraune asked him if he wanted to go back to the upper world where all of the other humans lived.

*'No.'*

The monster girl asked him why.

*'Because I'm not needed there. I never was. I am just a stranger passing by to them. I will stay here.'*

Adratea had only been a brief stop on his journey anyway. Staying there for half a year and moving on to the next country had been his plan. Who was to say that perhaps the alraune's lair hadn't been his destination all along? He had wandered to find himself. Instead he had found… her. And that was good.

Magi shifted his vines slightly against hers so he could lean over and get a better grip against the wall. His pale green hair slightly obscured his jade eyes. He moved in to kiss his lover sweetly on the lips.

*'I will not let anything happen to you.'* He told her.

*'I promise.'*

As the sun was rising over the town Warren and Siro found themselves the first of the party waiting outside of the Guildhouse, ready to go. They hadn't really expected to be the first ones there despite Warren living mere minutes away, but the night before the doctor had been so worn out from the dungeon and from study that he hadn't made it all the way home and had crashed at Siro's place instead. Not even Mieus was up yet; the Guildhouse remained locked and quiet.

Warren stretched and yawned again for what Siro felt must have been the tenth time since they had arrived. "That's what you get for staying up most of the night." He scolded as he sipped from his tartan thermos. It felt like it was too warm already for hot coffee, but he needed the caffeine buzz to properly wake up.

"Oh, don't give me that." The younger man grumped, definitely not a morning person. "If I hadn't been helping Mina we might not have even had any leads to go on when we rescue Magi." He knew it probably hadn't been smart, but it *had* been necessary.

Siro proffered his thermos to Warren who accepted it gratefully. He then leaned back against the wall of the Guildhouse, loitering in such a way that he as the mayor should have had issues with. "So what exactly did you and Mina discover in the library last night?"

The brown-haired man blinked at him. "Didn't I tell you already?" He asked.

"Not really. The only thing I could get out of you last night after you collapsed into bed was 'whhhhgnnhbllllhhh…'" Siro responded with a laugh as Warren stared at him.

He looked moderately embarrassed. "It was kind of late, I guess…" He began, but then an idea came to him and he passed Siro his thermos back before kneeling and searching for something in his dungeoneering backpack. He pulled out the library book he and Mina had been studying the night before. Crinkled sheets of paper torn from notebooks and crumpled notes peeked out between the pages like curious mushrooms.

"What's that?" Siro asked.

"It's the book about alraune Mina and I found. I thought it wouldn't hurt if we took it with us." Warren explained. He had to be careful with it though, as he had neglected to officially borrow it from the library. If he lost the tome it would be gone forever, and he was pretty sure that Mina wouldn't stand for that.

"Well, er, where do I begin…?"

The mayor didn't really know much about the situation save for what had been discussed during the meeting the night before. "I hate to ask such a morbid question, but at least I can do it while no one else is around. Is it likely that Magi will still be alive by the time we get down there, or…" He hesitated for a moment, trying to think of a better way to phrase himself. "Or are we going to have to kill the alraune out of revenge?"

Warren regarded Siro with a worrisome smile. He hadn't actually come out and said 'dead', but the doctor knew what he meant. He sidled closed to his partner a little bit and opened the book on the section he had marked the night before. "Actually, there's a pretty good chance that Magi is dead by now. I didn't want to mention it to the others in case they lose hope but I also don't want to sugar-coat the facts to you, Siro. There are three states we might find Magi in. The first is we'll find him either dead or eaten. The second is we will find him captured and exhausted, but still alive. The third…"

He trailed off. Warren sighed. "The third is the most unlikely but the trickiest situation. I hope it doesn't come to that, but if it does…"

Siro tried to fight back his impatience. Warren had a habit of just going on and on about something without explaining what it was, first. It was annoying, but he could also see that the good doctor was trying to postpone the bad news. "What is it? Tell me." He insisted.

Warren flipped through the pages of his book until he found the picture of that trapped woman he had shown Mina earlier. Siro leaned over to study it. "It's possible that the alraune might have tried to transmute him. They are a magical species in nature and produce offspring by breeding with themselves, just like certain kinds of plants do, but these offspring contain no genetic variance from its parent; they are almost carbon copies of a lesser form."

He was talking about the smaller alraune they had seen here and there in the Underwood, but those had all been male. "What do you mean by 'transmute' him?" Siro pressed.

"Without genetic diversity an entire colony of creatures could succumb easily to a single threat. There is also no chance for evolution in a creature that cannot improve itself. So… alraune kings and queens, that's what you call the large colony parents, take genetic material from *outside* of their species. They do it forcefully by hunting for-"

"Humans?" Siro cut in, unable to help himself. "Is that what you're saying? The alraune took Magi so she could breed with him?" Folklore spoke of alraune as creatures that fed on life energy, like incubi and succubae. Warren's explanation seemed to support this… in a more scientific way.

"Yes, but humans and alraune aren't genetically compatible. Not only are we a different species, but the divide between the animal and vegetable kingdom is so great that even if Magi were, er, 'forced to donate' the alraune would not be able to produce any variant offspring. It just doesn't work that way. It would be like trying to breed a cat with a stalk of celery." Through the wall Warren could hear someone moving around in the Guildhouse. It was probably Mieus.

It was getting a little harder for Siro to follow. He was a bright man, but he hadn't been subjected to the same kind of schooling Warren had. The extent of his knowledge in the sciences had been watching his best friend's father work the alchemic magic that he had been renowned for, but that was neither here nor there. He needed to listen. Siro sipped his coffee thoughtfully as Warren continued.

"So, to combat this problem the alraune species managed to make one single evolutionary jump on its own. Their kings and queens are so rare that it's unlikely a pair will find one another and reproduce successfully in a lifetime, so when an alraune catches a human of good genetic stock it… transmutes them. Into another alraune." Warren concluded solemnly.

The mayor of Adratea was silent for a moment as he let the entirety of that information sink in. It was a lot to try and comprehend and if it were true it would make their rescue significantly harder. He got up from where he had been leaning against the wall. "So what are the chances of that?" He asked his friend.

"Low, but possible. I don't really know for sure." The other man admitted sheepishly.

"If we get down there and Magi has been turned into a monster what should we do? Should we try to rescue him anyway, or leave him there, or… put him out of his misery?" Siro asked out loud. Warren might have felt that he was addressing him, but in truth he was asking himself or nobody in particular. It was his turn to sigh now. "This isn't exactly great news. Are you going to tell the others as well?"

"I'd rather not." Warren replied, surprising Siro.

"Oh, how come?" He found himself asking.

And Warren's reasoning was not a scientific one, but a personal one. "It's just that everybody in this town likes Magi. He's a likeable guy, even if he is a wee bit introverted. If I told everyone what I've just told you right now I believe everyone would lose morale, which will be a useless downer or a bringer of false hope if we go down there and find him still human or murdered. I don't want to do that to people if I can help it." The doctor said softly.

Ah, so Warren was thinking about everybody else first. That was actually quite like him. "But what if we find Magi and he *is* a monster? What are you planning to do then?"

"I don't know. I guess I'd just like to cross that bridge if we ever reach it. There's no use worrying about it until then. I'll take Mina's book with us; hopefully it'll provide us with some advice if we end up needing it."

Warren snapped the book closed, running his fingertips briefly over the leather binding. He stowed the tome back in his bag and with it, his glasses. He smiled at Siro and the change was immediate; he'd gone from cute and nerdy to handsome and capable in just a few short seconds. "The thing is, one of the main reasons I don't want to share this information with the others yet is because of Ravendor." He said unexpectedly.

"Ravendor?" Siro echoed, nonplussed. "I would think that he would want to know about this just as much as the rest of us."

"I know, but I've been friends with Ravendor for a long time, way before I came to live here in Adratea. I know him well enough to say that this whole thing with Magi has him pretty upset, even if he doesn't openly show it. Magi *is* his best friend, after all, and I think he feels responsible over what happened to him. I don't want him to assume that this mission is hopeless until we're absolutely certain that it is." Warren explained.

The blond swordsman thought about this and nodded. "Well, if you're sure. I'll keep it to myself then, I suppose."

"Thanks, Siro."

The front door of the Guildhouse creaked open and Mieus stepped outside, stretching. She was wearing short denim pants and a white blouse that was knotted suggestively at the front. It did not leave much to the imagination without it being outright provocative, even if it *did* seem a little unusually hickish for her to wear. She spied the two men loitering on her property and approached them.

"Morning boys. It's going to be a hot one today." She smiled, a hand on her hip.

Siro and Warren echoed a 'morning' back to her in turn, the both of them trying to avoid the natural gravitation of their eyes to her obvious assets. Warren knew that Mieus always got a sick kick out of it when she noticed people looking.

As Siro spied Trina and Cassie approaching on the road from the west, the former carrying a large sack effortlessly over one shoulder, Mieus continued. "Have you two eaten? I could whip you up some breakfast before everyone else gets here if you'd like." She was a pretty good cook, at least compared to some of the other women in the town (there was a reason why Magi frequently ate dinner at Mieus' place, besides not wanting to cook for himself), but the two swordsmen respectfully declined. Warren had already made breakfast for the both of them earlier, zombie-like, and had in effect nearly burned Siro's house down.

"We're good, Mieus, thanks." Warren yawned diplomatically.

But the least she could do was invite them inside so they wouldn't have to feel like a pair of idlers. Inside the Guildhouse the chairs were still stacked on the tables and the small stage was bare, the curtains closed to the light of morning. Mieus methodically went from window to window and briskly let in the sunshine.

Soon enough Trina and Cassie arrived, and not long after that came Mina, Sera and Mara. Mieus ended up having to open the bar early and started serving tea, coffee, orange and apple juice instead of her usual repertoire of alcoholic beverages. Eventually Darren and Ravendor showed up as well and the party was for the most part complete.

Cassie idly played a few keys on the Guildhouse grand piano as her big sister pulled a wooden case out of the sack she had been carrying and opened it proudly. From it she drew four sharp blades. They were machetes, tempered in steel. She swung one experimentally to test its balance and the sound it made as it passed through the air was quick and tight; pleasing to the ears.

"You know, I should be getting at least a hundred per blade." She said conversationally as she lowered the weapon and proffered it to the nearest rescue party member, namely Ravendor. He took it from her like he had no idea what to do with it, which was probably the truth. The others also received machetes of their own, handed out one at a time with great care.

"I made these last night so they won't need to be sharpened for a while. The blades are honed, but they're made for cutting through undergrowth, not monsters, so don't you dare try to use them in battle! It's not a big deal if you lose them, but I'd like to get them back from you guys after you return with Magi, okay?" Trina instructed; one hand elevated in lecture while the other was hooked on the waistband of her jeans.

Siro and Warren looked at their brand new machetes and then at each other. They smiled, and then there was a clashing of steel on steel as they crossed blades together with a triumphant shout.

"Hey!" Trina cried. "What did I just say?"

Across the other side of the table Sera and Mara were sitting together quietly, somewhat removed from the rest of the group. Sera was young and elfin with auburn hair and green eyes but she seemed forlorn, cradling her hands around the noticeable bump in her abdomen that was her baby to be.

Mara touched her on the shoulder softly. "Are you alright, Sera?"

The touch seemed to bring Sera out of her reverie and she smiled sadly at Mara. "I'm sorry; this just reminds me of the night I lost Cyrus." She explained, and then looked to the rescue party poorly trying to organize itself while Trina hovered over them. "It began almost exactly like this. Different people, a different challenge, but…" She sighed. "It brings back bad memories."

That was understandable. It had only been a few months ago and Cyrus had been her husband, the love of her life; the father of her child. A wound that deep was not going to heal quickly. Mara was mindful of her choice of words. "I hope this time we'll have a different conclusion."

Sera nodded and then glanced at Mara. "You really care about Magi too, right?"

She knew that Sera wasn't just talking about friendship. She blushed and stared down at her glass of apple juice. So far it had been one-sided, though she had had high hopes for the future. "Magi is… he doesn't deserve to die. I wish I could go with them."

"If I didn't have this little one with me," Sera patted the curve where her pregnancy expanded her belly, "I'd go with them whether they liked it or not, and Ravendor can just suck a lemon." She announced, which prompted Mara to chuckle.

"Pardon? You ladies wish me to do *what*?" Ravendor inquired politely from over both Sera and Mara's shoulders.

Mara's giggle condensed into a cute snort when she realized they had been caught. She exchanged a glance with Sera before turning to study him. "We were, um, talking about Magi. We want you to bring Magi back." She explained.

The older man raised an eyebrow. "That goes without saying."

Mara stood, becoming utterly serious, almost pleading. "I really mean it, Ravendor. I want to come with you, I really do, but I know that I can't. There isn't much that someone like me could do anyway. But still… you have to bring Magi back to me. I haven't-"

She suddenly realized that she was being a little too sincere over her feelings and floundered, eyes widening. "I haven't, uh, I haven't finished with his laundry yet. He needs to be alive so he can come and get it back." She managed after a while.

This time it was Ravendor and Sera's turn to share a look, his of confusion and hers of knowing amusement. He patted Mara reassuringly on the shoulders and gently pushed her back down into her seat. It was the same kind of gesture one would make to calm a child, and Sera haphazardly wondered if Mara would have taken offense to it were she not busy being worried about Magi.

"We will do all that we can; I can assure you of that. Don't worry, Mara. We'll try our best." He told her.

Before she could reply the front doors of the Guildhouse swung open and BW stumbled inside. She rarely came into the building voluntarily and she found the weekly town meetings boring, so seeing her show up was a bit of a surprise. She looked tired, and she was carrying a small bag of something in her hand.

"So this is what the dawn looks like, huh? Hi everybody." She mumbled to the room, moving over and sitting down heavily next to Darren.

"You didn't sleep?" He asked, but he wasn't that surprised. BW sometimes didn't even see noon, so this was probably a new experience for her.

The girl paused in the middle of rubbing her eyes and looked sidelong at him for a bit, then smiled and shoved the bag of whatever she was carrying into his ribs. He flinched and something that sounded an awful lot like marbles jangled inside the bag. "Well I didn't have the time to sleep. You're leaving so quickly that I didn't have a choice. There's no way you'll win against the alraune without *these*."

Before Darren could ask what was in the bag Mina leaned over him curiously, touching him gently on the back in the process. The youth went beet red, and not just from the embarrassing dream he had had the night before. Having Mina touch him even idly was almost too much for him to take. "What do you have there?" She asked innocently.

Darren made an almost inaudible squeak as he observed BW's face. For a split second her expression darkened into something frightening, but then it faded quickly like a passing storm. It wasn't that BW hated Mina, but she hated Darren's idolization of Mina. The other woman wasn't even vaguely aware of it. The winged girl smirked at her. "Want to see?" She asked. "We'll have to go outside."

"Why's that?"

"'Don't think Mieus would be too happy if her home burst into flames."

Darren took the bag very carefully away from BW. "Let's, uh, let's do that then." He advised.

After a few minutes of informing the rest of the town the citizens of Adratea gathered outside of the Guildhouse once more. All they had been told was that BW had developed a weapon overnight, which was making a lot of people feel kind of nervous.

The mage girl addressed the small crowd of people, folding her arms. She frowned. "Well, we all know that girls aren't allowed to come on your stupid mission to save Magi or whatever. I don't like it. You can't fight a mythical creature like the alraune without a little magical power to back you up, but I know that apart from Warren who can work white magic your rescue team is as magical as a clump of dirt. It's not your fault," she added, glancing at Siro, Darren and Ravendor, "some people are just born with it. Others aren't."

Siro sighed in nostalgia. "Ah, I remember when they tested me for magical talent. My parents were so disappointed." He smiled.

"So," BW continued after the mayor's brief reminiscence, "I made these marbles here to replace me, kind of, while you guys are in the dungeon. You can open that bag I gave you now, Darren." She advised.

The rogue did as directed. He reached his hand into the small satchel and pulled out half a dozen tiny orbs the size of small marbles but black, with a fiery red streak through the centre that made him think of a cut and polished cat's eye. What he noticed most of all, however, was that each small stone was slightly warm to the touch. The heat was almost pleasant in his hand.

"What are these?" He asked warily, as if they might explode at any moment.

BW grinned broadly. "They're what my fire spell looks like when crystallized. If you throw it hard enough and it hits something it'll ignite, just as if I were there. I made two dozen of 'em, I hope that'll be enough."

Darren experienced a cold shiver. "So they're little bombs? What if I drop them or bump them while they're still in the bag?" He asked in a small voice.

Sera reached over and plucked a fire marble from Darren's palm. She studied the small, perfectly round gem with fascination. She was something of a mage herself, but she had never seen anything like it before. "This is alchemy applied to magery, right? Did you add a safety to it?"

BW blinked at her. "Huh?"

The pregnant elf sighed, exasperated but also slightly endeared. BW seemed so tired that she could only offer an explanation, not anything as complicated as trying to answer questions. "You know; something that keeps a clumsy person from setting themselves on fire." She clarified.

Something very obvious clicked in BW's mind. "Oh! Yeah. Of course. Don't be silly, of course I'd do something like that." She exclaimed.

Sera smiled, indulging her. "Really?"

From the crowd BW heard Ravendor mumble to Mieus; "I find that hard to believe," followed by the barmaid chuckling softly.

Her colour rose. She didn't mind it when people didn't trust her, but BW hated it when people doubted her. Maybe she'd let the comment pass were she properly rested, but she was already a little overtired and cranky, so…

"Here, I'll show you." She pouted, slapping the palm full of marbles out of Darren's hand.

Half of the village recoiled. The ones that didn't either had poor reflexes or hadn't entirely been paying attention in the first place. Sera seemed to be the only one who knew better and didn't bother panicking as the marbles fell and bounced against the hard, barren ground.

"See? It's perfectly safe." BW assured them.

"B-B-Buh… BW?" Darren stammered.

"Yeah?"

"*Never* do that again."

When Mieus realized she hadn't been in any danger in the first place she scowled, roughly shoving Ravendor who had moved to stand in front of her out of the way and into Mara. "Move it, you! Gah! I don't care how safe those things are! *No* trying to detonate bombs outside of my bar!" She shouted angrily.

"Are you okay, Mina?" Siro asked.

Mina nodded, embarrassed. She had ducked behind him in surprise. "Y-Yes…"

Sera crouched down and scooped up the dropped marbles. Their heat had not dissipated and only increased when she curled her fingers around them, like hot pebbles. "You have to warm them in your hands for a while before they can be thrown?" She guessed.

BW beamed at Sera proudly. “That’s right. The only way you could blow yourself up is by warming them and then tossing them hard at your feet. I’m not talking about a casual throw here; you’d have to hit something hard enough to break glass to set one of these babies off.”

“That settles it,” Ravendor said after apologizing to Mara for nearly knocking her over, “we will divvy these trinkets evenly between the members of the party. Thank you for your contribution, BW.”

The magician shook her head in response, and from the way she stood and the sureness of her voice there was no way she was going to budge. “Now wait a sec! These things are perfectly safe but they’re still pretty dangerous. I didn’t make them to be shared like candy; I made them as a gift for Darren. Only Darren is allowed to use them.”

While Ravendor looked at her appraisingly Darren goggled at BW. “What? These are for me?” He asked, surprised.

BW sighed and rubbed her eyes tiredly. “Would I stay up ‘til dawn using up all my energy for anybody else? If you guys are so adamant about not letting women come with you then you can at least honor my wishes and let Darren keep his gift, okay?”

Ravendor nodded. “Very well. That does sound fair.”

Cassie nudged the dark-haired rogue softly in the side. “You ought to thank her.” She whispered.

And Darren in turn felt all the stares of the crowd alight upon him. He could feel his awkwardness increasing. “Ah… thanks, BW. I’ll try not to waste them.” He promised, transferring the marbles back to their small, safe bag. “Maybe when I get back we can go out or something…”

BW laughed and shook her head, walking past Darren and patting him fondly on the shoulder. “Nah. I’m gonna go crawl into bed and sleep for the next two days. See you guys later if you’re still alive! Bye!”

Sera also mumbled a goodbye to the meeting and they left it together, the two redheads heading for home.

“Cold…” Warren murmured.

“Really cold.” Siro agreed.

“Let’s… let’s just go.” Ravendor sighed, holding his head in his hand. “Mina, Trina, Mara. Cassie and Mieus. If fate deigns us never to return do not search for us. There is no point in putting more people in danger.”

"Just try your best," Mara told the four adventurers as they prepared to leave. "Really, that's all we ask."

Of course, the alraune was not blind to the encroachment of enemies on her lands.

She was too... permanent to venture very far beyond the border of her cavern, and beyond the Underwood she could only guess of the hostile world out to harm them, but she was not unaware. She had eyes and ears in the forest, servants and monsters alike, and through them she waited and watched for the humans to return.

They would come to rob her of her prize; that much she was certain. The human-suitor had said so himself. The tall one with the blade would return to them, and so too would the one with the instrument that created painful sparks and smoke in the darkness. If the little one came back, the one that smelt so strongly of fear... well. It had been a long time since she had been able to *feed*.

She had almost fed on the human-suitor instead, but he had shown traits to her that were too desirable to be digested. He was asleep now, hanging beside her, building up his strength for when the humans came back. His transition into her mate was taking up the lion's share of water and nutrients from the earth, but he would not be whole in time. It was a gradual process and he was just beginning to become beautiful to her. Beautiful but weak, helpless, like a child.

That didn't matter. The alraune was prepared to fight for him herself, and this time there would be no holding back.

Ravendor was the point this time, with Warren and Siro making up the body of the party and carrying between them most of the rescue supplies. Warren had been managing it by himself at the start but Siro had kindly offered to share. Darren trailed behind the three men in front of him, bringing up the rear. Their path was stony and uncertain, but pendulously it etched a road for them to follow, spiralling deeper down into the depths.

"So what is the one thing in the world you couldn't live without?" Warren asked his party, trying to make some conversation amidst the silence of their march.

"What on earth are you talking about?" Ravendor responded from up ahead, the very act of him being at the front meaning that everyone behind him was getting a free face full of cigarette smoke. It might have meant that he wasn't entirely aware of his surroundings, but it could also just mean that he didn't care.

"It's like you couldn't function without it. Not having it would mess up your entire day, or you couldn't see yourself being happy with it gone." He elaborated, laughing at the end. "Like with me. I don't know what I'd do if I didn't get to sleep in on Saturday mornings."

"Oh, like a creature comfort." Siro volunteered helpfully.

"Something like that, yeah." Warren agreed, halfway in the process of climbing over a tricky rock formation with the others. He could feel an uncertain dampness from the moisture in the air. They would be nearing the Underwood soon.

"I guess I couldn't live without legs." The blond swordsman speculated, smiling.

Warren stared at him. "What?"

"Well, you wouldn't be able to walk anywhere. You'd be stuck in one of those chairs with the wheels on them, and I don't think I'd be able to live with something like that. I like going for long walks."

"I don't think that really counts, Siro. Everyone needs legs." Warren commented in an amused manner.

"Unless you had a really nice cart." Darren chimed in from behind them.

"What about you, Darren?" Warren asked pleasantly, giving up on Siro for the moment.

"Oh gee, I don't know. I have no idea." He did, but he wasn't about to tell the others. It would be too embarrassing, especially when Mina barely even knew that he existed. She was his reason to get up in the morning; the reason he was even there in Adratea at all.

"I find it most important to practice proper nail-care." Ravendor interrupted, who could frequently be found at his desk in the inn giving himself a manicure on slow days. "Ragged cuticles would simply drive me mad. I don't know how others could stand it."

Siro smiled and Warren suppressed a laugh. "You're kidding, right?"

"No, it's very important."

"More important than those cigarettes you're always smoking? Look, just… can you go to the back of the line behind Darren? We're choking here." The doctor complained.

The older man regarded him for a moment, and rather than having to move to the back with Darren he put the cigarette out on a moss-encrusted wall. It hissed as it made contact with the dampness of the stones. "So sorry." He said at last.

There was silence for a few minutes while the party continued to walk. Darren couldn't help but drag his feet and tried to stay focused on the back of Siro's cloak, because at least he seemed to know where he was going.

"Actually," he murmured after some time had passed, "I don't think I'd be able to live with myself if Magi is dead. It was my- I mean, our fault that we left him there."

"Don't say such things." Ravendor snapped at him. "Magi is not dead."

Fortunately the memory of the safest path through the Underwood was still fresh in their minds. They wandered through low-lying grasses and seemingly prehistoric ferns, shaded by the trees that sprouted out of the cavern's floor and laced by entangling, numerous vines. Bioluminescent mosses and fungi gave the Underwood just enough unearthly light to see by, barely, but they lit lanterns when the darkness seemed to close in all around them and relied on their own light source.

The plants grew quickly. What had once been a thin path just over twenty four hours ago and dotted with acid-spitting flowers had grown over again, barring the way. At first they hesitated and wondered if they might have taken a wrong turn somewhere, but Ravendor managed to find evidence of their own footprints made the day before imprinted in the soft soil and knew they had to press on. The machetes Trina had forged for them finally came out.

She had made them well. They slashed through the reaching branches and vines like nobody's business and Siro and Warren seemed to be enjoying themselves at least a little as they cut their way through to the alraune's cavern.

Darren felt a deep sense of unease as he followed his comrades into the jungle. It felt a bit like somebody was watching him, even though he was the last one at the rear of the group. It was almost like he could imagine eyes peering at him from all the different, dark alcoves hidden in the forest just out of the range of the lantern he was carrying.

"We're being watched." He said quietly as he walked, trying not to be too loud.

Ravendor, who had ended up in the back anyway while Warren and Siro went hog wild with the machetes nodded slightly. "That doesn't surprise me."

"Why's that?"

"Haven't you noticed? The last time we were here we practically had to mow our way through hostile foliage." The older man explained, remembering all too well the acid burns hidden under his coat. It still stung quite badly from time to time.

"Maybe we scared them off." Darren said hopefully, but didn't quite feel it himself.

"Perhaps. That would be nice."

"Almost done!" Siro called from the head of the group. It was beginning to look like the plants blocking the pathway were thinning.

"I think the cavern is just up ahead." Warren commented, ripping out a network of vines with his bare hands. This was… yes, this was where they had stopped to gather their wits after the alraune had chased them out of the cavern yesterday. The entrance to the cave was right over there, open and yawning like a hungry mouth. Plant vines hung down over the entranceway now, a lot like the vines of the alraune and this worried Warren.

They made their approach but stopped just shy of going inside. It was an unspoken thing, like nobody wanted to be the first one to descend down into that deeper darkness. It hadn't been as unnerving before because they had been in a hurry to rescue Darren, but now, knowing what was at the end of that path…

"Well Darren, off you go." Ravendor said expectantly.

It took Darren a second to realize what was being asked of him. He gawked at his friends in disbelief. "W-what? No! I'm not going back in there alone, not like last time."

"You are our scout."

"I've already done it once, I'm not gonna do it again. Why don't you go, Ravendor? You've got a lantern too." Darren argued. Usually he didn't bother trying to protest when the others pushed him around, but this just wasn't fair.

Ravendor knelt slightly and looked down the mouth of the cave. He remembered it being long but not especially precarious. It was just dark, and he did indeed have one of the kerosene lamps in his hands. The older man sighed. "Very well, if I must."

He began the rocky climb into the mouth of the cave. It was hard going, trying not to slip while at the same time trying to keep the lantern safe from bumping or cracking against the stones. At about halfway down he heard Siro call out; "wait a sec," and he clambered down into the cave as well.

"Let me go on ahead. I just realized that I'm the only one here wearing body armor, so I should stay up front. Lend me your lamp." He explained, extending a gloved hand for the precious light source.

"Be my guest." Ravendor agreed a little too quickly for Siro's liking. The lantern was pressed earnestly into the swordsman's hands.

"Siro!" He heard Warren cry disapprovingly from the cave entrance and within a few seconds he was down there with the other two, leaving Darren all alone. The physician wiped the dampness off his hands using his doctor's coat then realized with a wince that it would probably cause a stain.

The mayor smiled at him. "Don't fret, Warren. I'll have everybody right behind me. We'll walk single file and-"

"And watch your ankles for the alraune's loose vines." Warren finished up for him, still not happy with the idea of his partner going first.

"Hey!" Darren cried, struggling into the cave. "Don't leave me up there by myself!"

Together they pressed forward, back into the unknown.

*It is time. They are here.*

*Do you know what you must do?*

*... yeah.*

*Kill them. Kill them all.*

"*Magi!*"

The shout echoed through the alraune's lair loudly and clearly, much to the horror of nearly everybody within.

The other three members of the rescue party jumped on Ravendor. Warren quickly attempted to slap a hand over his mouth to shut him up and the other man immediately and unsuccessfully tried to shove him off. Darren made an unpleasant keening noise in the back of his throat.

"What are you, crazy?" Warren snapped, shaking him firmly and by proxy Siro, who he had slammed Ravendor into. "Do you want to let the alraune know we're here or something?"

Ravendor shot him a reproachful look. "Mnn." He mumbled.

"Ugh, fine." Warren sulked and let him go.

The innkeeper stumbled away from Siro and Warren but backed into Darren who slunk back against the wall. He looked extremely put off at being grabbed so suddenly. "That does not matter now. The monster has known we are here since we entered this Underwood; there is no need for this pretense of secrecy. Magi, however, if he can answer us…"

He paused all of a sudden, listening to the hollow silence, then shouted yet again in an even louder voice; "*Magiiiii!*"

There was another hasty scuffle as his party piled on him again. Siro glanced over at Warren in worry. "Do you think she heard us?"

"Maybe. But if we-"

Before he could continue a low grinding noise filled the air. It wasn't that loud but it was persistent and strong; the soft sound of stone pressed hard against more stone. There was a leathery sinewiness to it as well, and when Darren nervously adjusted the shutters of his lantern to let out more light he and his party could now see why. He swallowed hard.

The walls of the alraune's lair were thickly laced with vines, like a delicate spider's web veining through the many layers of dirt and stone. Those vines were squeezing the cavern, *squeezing*, causing dust and dirt and lichen to spiral down from the ceiling and walls. It didn't seem like the tunnel was collapsing but it *did* feel like a warning. A threat.

"Guys…" Darren began to say.

Of the four of them Siro was the first to step forward and proceed into the centre of the cave, his own lantern warding against the darkness.

He seemed to walk without fear, only curiosity, moving ahead. "Magi?" He called at a more tolerable volume, yet still causing an echo. "Are you here?"

He didn't get a response from the darkness, but that could just mean their friend was unconscious, or possibly gagged. After some seconds the swordsman could hear his comrades following after him, so he placed his lantern carefully down on the ground and opened the lid, exposing the burning wick. Siro looked over to Warren carrying the supply backpack. "Did you bring torches?"

"A few."

"Can you light them? I can't see anything in here."

He unsheathed his sword as Warren knelt to search through his pack. They could be attacked at any moment, and if that happened Siro was ready to do some defending. He was used to slaying monsters but the magnitude of the alraune… he wasn't certain yet. As a wooden torch wrapped in kerosene-soaked rags burst into greater light Siro heard Ravendor taking the safety off his gun, and that at least was a reassuring sound.

Warren swept the torch this way and that as their eyes adjusted to the changing of the light. The altar they had seen before became visible, finally, and upon it…

The alraune. She was just sitting there, reclining on her dozens and dozens of vines, pieces of the cavern, watching them silently with perfect, alien night vision.

She did not look happy.

The men from Adratea came together in a line, forming a small group. Siro didn't feel so perturbed by the alraune's presence until he realized her many vines connected to the huge tangled mass at the back of the cavern, and that she was bigger and stronger than any single monster had a right to be.

As she lifted herself up and raised the writhing, deadly vines connected to her arms without any fanfare, indeed without even a sound apart from snakelike slithering, Ravendor suddenly shouted; "Darren!"

Darren was caught off-guard, unsure whether to go for his daggers or the bag of gems given to him by BW on his belt. "Y-yeah?" He quavered, frightened but certain he would not run away. Not again.

"Find Magi! We three will keep the alraune busy while you search!"

The youth hadn't been expecting that. "But-"

There wasn't time for arguing. "Do it! Nobody here can move like you can! Find him!"

When the vines came at them they were ready this time. They had not forgotten the brutal defeat they had experienced the day before and thanks to Trina they now had a way to fight back. She had explicitly told them not to use the machetes in combat and only use them for cutting back undergrowth, but what else was the alraune but a huge infestation of undergrowth with a personal agenda? Vines were vines. As a multitude of the strong, grasping coils leapt out at them Sylvas steel flashed for the first time in the darkness.

Darren backed away from the rest of his party as severed tentacles dropped dead around the three other men, spurting ichorous blood. Warren and Siro braced themselves against the ground and stood firmly in their place, daring more to come, a sword in one hand and a machete in the other. Warren had been splattered with the creature's blood. Siro turned to him slightly, but before he could say anything Warren replied; "Don't worry about it, it's alright."

He hastily wiped the blood from his face with the back of his wrist. As he did this Ravendor rushed past him and Siro and left their defensive protection, a move that frankly surprised Warren quite a bit. He was running directly towards the alraune and those vines, what was-

The first vine he managed to twist in the middle of a step and dodge, but the second got a firm grip around his gun-arm and tried to pull him forward, attempting to disarm him of both his weapon and his balance, but Ravendor hacked at the prehensile limb with the machete in his off-hand and severed it in two rough strikes, then closed the distance between himself and the alraune quickly. The monster seemed surprised by this, not expecting her prey to simply run up to her on the altar within striking distance. Her vines were made for long-range attacks, not close-quarters combat.

Ravendor tried to slice at her with the machete but she recoiled from him and the inaccurate, wildly flashing blade. He didn't have the same degree of control over it like Warren and Siro had and couldn't land a hit, for though the alraune was rooted to the spot there was a certain grace to her movements and she managed to evade each time, skulking back against her cavern's wall.

Realizing he was just wasting his time with the blade and only really needing to get close enough to powder-burn distance with her Ravendor suddenly let go of Trina's machete and allowed the weapon to go spinning into the dirt, freeing up his off-hand to rapidly work the hammer of his pistol. *That* was way too fast for the alraune to handle, and before she could weave out of the way of his aim he unloaded three rounds directly into her chest.

Smoke rose from the small bullet holes in her once beautiful, full breast. She didn't fall down or flinch very hard, even though were she a human Ravendor would have directly hit her in the heart multiple times. Of course, she was a monster; an abomination. It was entirely likely the alraune didn't have a heart at all.

Siro tried to intercept them as quickly as he could but he was just a few seconds too slow. A thick vine came up out of the ground at Ravendor's feet and punched up with such force that it hit him squarely in the jaw and he fell back, staggering into the dirt. The blond swordsman popped up at her left, sword raised high and prepared to cleave a trench through her side when she suddenly spun towards him, her long fingers outstretched as claws and raked him hard across the chest.

She was deceptively strong. Siro was knocked down by the attack and sparks flew as her claws dug deep trenches through his body armor, leaving permanent scratches behind. She might have eviscerated him had he been wearing anything lighter. The mayor of Adratea groaned as he got back up to his feet, unharmed but a little dazed.

Warren hacked away at another vine that went for him as he tried to follow his friends. He went to the alraune's right, attempting to box her in. "Keep on top of her! Get up, everyone! Darren! Have you found Magi?" He cried, trying to make sure at least *somebody* was giving orders, but he was just flailing. He had no idea what he was supposed to do, and that panicked him.

Rattled but still conscious Ravendor attempted to push himself up again, but stopped halfway as something restrained him. He could feel something wrapping around his leg and it was tightening *fast*. He holstered his gun so he could get both of his hands free; as he had a hunch he'd need them soon. "Oh dear..." He moaned, feeling the alraune's vines dragging him backwards, away from his friends.

The alraune herself retreated, not liking the idea of being outnumbered. She skittered up the wall tangle of her own vines like a spider, moving with speed and precision out of their reach.

But the humans, well, *they* were still within her grasp.

Vines burst out of the tangle like spears, two of them aimed for Warren and Siro. They were of impaling width and sharpness, but Warren reacted first. He threw himself into Siro, unbalancing the both of them and hurling them into the floor, but causing the vines to miss them.

Almost.

A vine grazed by Warren's side as he moved and blood flowed. The doctor roared in pain and when he hit the ground on top of Siro he did not get up again.

"Warren!" Siro called, trying to squirm out from under him. "You idiot! Are you okay?"

"Augh… my side… ribs…" He choked back in a weak voice, then let out a shuddering sigh. "I'm alright…"

It looked as bad as it sounded. The two swordsmen managed to get up without incident but Warren's right side was stained with blood and he was stuck hunched over, trying to hold his wound together with his hand. Blood was oozing out between his fingers at a steady rate. He had gone as white as a sheet, and Siro all at once felt sick to his stomach at the sight.

Warren crouched to pick up his sword again and nearly fell over, hissing in pain. He decided to leave it there instead; his balance was more important than a blade and he had actually trained for this eventuality instead. He tried to smile at Siro encouragingly but it didn't quite come out right. "I can heal it later, don't worry…"

"Can you heal it now?" Siro could hear himself saying.

Warren looked at him oddly. "It takes time…" He protested as Siro walked towards him.

"I will protect you." He said.

The other man laughed at his seriousness, but it became a groan of pain as he slowly sunk to his knees, acquiescing and putting his life directly into Siro's hands. He pressed his own hands deeper against the wound and the twisted grimace he made was almost painful to look at, but then Warren started to say something under his breath, some kind of chant, and the mayor knew that the healing process had already begun.

His partner was a doctor first and foremost, but that did not mean magic didn't exist. Warren was one of those rare kinds of people, one of the people blessed with the gifts of both worlds; of magic *and* science. He could have become legendary in either field, but Warren would probably be the first to admit that he preferred being a master of none; that he wanted things to work both ways. *He* worked because of this, and it was one of the reasons Siro loved him for it.

He rested his sword against the right pauldron of his cloak and stood beside Warren; waiting for the vines to return. He would be ready for them.

"I don't suppose I could get a hand here?" Ravendor complained in a strained voice, slowly losing the fight with the alraune's pulling vines. There wasn't much for him to hold onto in the first place and it didn't look like anybody was available to help. Siro and Warren were clearly busy and Darren had up and vanished. Goddamned Darren! He had most likely already fled.

Siro glanced at him apologetically. He just couldn't defend two people at once so far away from each other. "I'm sorry." He said.

The older man smirked sarcastically as his fingers began to give way in the soil. So much for his perfect manicure. "Well that's alright, I'm sure I'll be fine." He grumbled seconds before his arms gave out and he was forced to let go, sliding uncomfortably on his stomach to wherever the alraune had decided to take him. He thought fast and tried to roll onto his back, reaching for a small hunting knife he kept somewhere on his belt.

It wasn't really something designed for combat; it was more of a utility knife than anything else. The vine that was dragging him had wormed its way up his leg and was squeezing just a little too tightly for comfort and circulation. There wasn't enough time to properly brace for the pain so without a second thought Ravendor plunged the small knife deep into the vine and his own leg.

Only the tip of it pierced through his clothing and went into the flesh but it still hurt like hell. Ravendor growled in pain and ripped the knife out again so he wouldn't be pinned against the vine but it didn't seem to notice the stab wound at all. Bullets and blades couldn't harm her, not unless the vines were completely lopped off, and he didn't have time for-

All of a sudden the vine dragging him bucked wildly and he realized too late what the alraune was planning to do. The vine had been pulling him towards the edge of the cavern and when it moved, flinging him against the rocky surface it was like being smashed against a brick wall. Ravendor managed to get a scream out a mere second before he crumpled and was knocked unconscious, and only then the vine decided to let him go.

Siro heard that scream but he was too occupied to do anything about it. Vines kept coming at him at least one or two at a time, sometimes at Warren; sometimes at himself. He could cut through them easily with his sword but the tentacles were just unceasingly constant, one after the other, and sooner or later his arms were just going to give out. They were beginning to burn already and he could feel himself sweating, and even worse than that he could sense the semblance of control he held over himself beginning to slip.

He got headaches sometimes. They were usually stress related, or at least that was what his doctor told him. Other times he got the opposite, a perfect clarity, something that only happened when he felt he was totally synched with his sword. It was a good feeling yet he was always afraid that someday he might become addicted to it. Killing monsters helped to bring it out but cutting down endless tentacles that did not die and just bled more… it did something. It calmed him. It excited him. Endless…

He wasn't sure when it started, but when there was more blood on him than anything else Siro started to laugh. A vine grabbed his ankle. He jammed his sword into the ground and sliced it in half. A thin one grabbed him by the throat. He ripped it out with his bare hands. One grabbed Warren and interrupted him for a second in mid-concentration. It didn't stay whole for very long.

His gauntlets were getting slippery from all the alraune's blood. Was the blood dangerous? He couldn't remember.

"Siro." Warren said evenly, eyes still closed. He focused better that way.

"Y-yeah?" Siro grinned in more of a showing of teeth than anything else.

"Calm down. Think about your blood pressure." The brown-haired man instructed. He was no longer panting or gasping in pain. Warren rose from where he was kneeling. In truth that was the last thing he was worried about right now, but Siro sometimes had issues with bloodlust. The poor guy was barely even aware of it, but Warren knew.

The swordsman hesitated. He put down his blade. "Oh, damn, I..." He mumbled.

And then a vine came just for him, and this time he wasn't ready for it.

Warren came forward and caught it in time. His hand came down like lightning and without even a blade he tore the vine in two.

He grimaced afterwards. "Ouch. I don't think I did that right." He admitted bashfully.

While the rest of the rescue party was occupied with distracting or killing the alraune, one other member was having problems of a different sort. Contrary to popular opinion (or just Ravendor's opinion) Darren had not fled. He had picked up the burning torch Warren had dropped earlier when he had readied his sword and had crept into the shadows at the back of the cavern, intent on searching for Magi while he was temporarily invisible to danger.

It was reassuring to know that he wouldn't have to fight, or at least not yet, but Darren was also kind of afraid. He didn't want to find Magi as a pile of bones, or a half eaten corpse, but if that was what he was now that was what he was going to find, and that scared him. If that happened it would be entirely his fault – as Magi's fate had meant to be *his* fate instead.

If he was anywhere he would probably be somewhere in the back of the alraune's tangle of vines. He didn't want to go near them in case they noticed his presence but the vines *themselves* were not sentient; they were just a small part of the alraune's whole. If he told himself this it was a lot easier to press forward, to use the bright light of the torch to illuminate the bramble of vines.

"Magi?" Darren called quietly, walking parallel to the wall of vines but being mindful not to get too close to the altar where his friends were fighting. The ground around the vines were bare, kind of damp in places, but there didn't seem to be any place where a human could be hidden, even secretly. The rogue hoped that Magi wasn't actually *in* the bramble, as a child he had gotten caught in a blackberry field for an afternoon and didn't relish those memories very much.

He looked up and then realized there was also another dimension to consider in his search. If the alraune could climb walls, and it looked like she could quite easily, Magi could be up there, above him, hanging like a fly caught in a huge spider's web. Darren sighed. That was why he had been chosen to be the searcher; climbing was his specialty.

It would be hard to scale the vines while holding the torch with one hand, but it had to be done. He couldn't search without light. The youth anxiously placed a boot on a sturdy-looking vine, testing the footing.

He half expected it to move under his weight. It didn't. A little more confident now Darren began to scale the wall of vines, moving upwards foot by deliberate foot. The vines seemed to grow thinner the higher he went and he took extra care not to torch the vine. *That* would probably give him right away.

Far away at the altar Darren thought he heard somebody scream. He tensed, clinging to the vines a little tighter than usual, but he had to ignore that. His job was here. The others were on their own now.

"Magi, are you up here?" He called again, raising his voice to a more normal level. He got nothing in response for some time, until out of the corner of his eye the young adventurer could have sworn that he noticed movement to his left. Not a *lot* of movement, mind you, but movement all the same.

"Okay." He said to himself to reassure himself of progress and leaned over a bit, trying to find a footing path to progress horizontally without going up or down. This was certainly a lot more complicated than his usual training nights, which normally consisted of crawling about on other people's roofs or drainpipes; practicing his rogue-like skills.

He discovered a good looking path amongst the thinner vines but then realized he would definitely need two hands for the job. There was nothing else for it. He began to hear laughter coming from the ground as he clamped the torch between his teeth (it sounded like Siro and frankly as creepy as hell) and took the vines with both hands this time. Darren climbed and the light from the torch did the rest of the work for him.

He found Magi.

It wasn't a very encouraging sight.

He was hanging there limply from vines bound tightly around his arms, held up yet dangling there without much support. His arms must have been screaming in pain before they finally went dead, even then they looked like they had been deeply, horribly bruised. His clothes were in tatters, he was *covered* in a sticky kind of something along with mud, dust and dirt. Blood stained his thighs and what was left of his jeans. He looked white and clammy and anemic.

He looked dead.

Without thinking Darren reached out and touched him, just on his neck, needing to know if he was still alive or not. He was cold but not 'dead' cold, sick cold, not *rigor mortis* cold. He felt Magi take in a shallow breath and Darren in turn let out a deep sigh of relief. He was unconscious but still alive.

"Geez, what has it done to you?" He muttered very badly through the torch stuck in his teeth. Sick of the obstruction and needing more room to move Darren took the torch out of his mouth and wedged it between some vines, mindful to leave the flame a safe distance away from the bramble but deep enough to stick. He turned back to Magi again, drawing a dagger from his belt. Maybe he could cut him free…

It could have been the firelight casting weird hues in the enclosing darkness but Magi in his sickness seemed different. His normal blond hair looked a sickly shade of green and it seemed a bit longer than usual, a lot longer than it had been the day before, actually. Darren wasn't certain. Maybe he was just seeing things.

"Magi," Darren called, trying to rouse him by patting him gently on the cheek, "wake up!"

In response the other man didn't wake up immediately but he did furrow his brow and turn his head away, like a child unwilling to get up and go to school. He looked annoyed.

Darren didn't have time for this. He wanted to get Magi down from there, and quickly. He took the archer by the shoulder and shook him firmly. "Come on, we have to get out of here before the alraune notices us!" He pleaded.

It wasn't helping. Darren would just have to cut him down and carry him to the ground himself somehow. He wasn't sure how he was going to do it, Magi was already bigger and heavier than he was but he'd just have to try anyway.

"Hold still, this won't take long." The rogue reassured his friend, moving his dagger to the vines binding Magi's arms. They were on pretty tightly, for a few moments Darren couldn't find the join, though that might have had something to do with the weird angle he was at.

Strange... green alraune vine connected smoothly to green skin, bruised and hurting skin... Magi's skin...

Darren's blood suddenly ran as cold as ice. He turned to look back at the other man, slowly. Magi was awake. He had green eyes.

Magi didn't *have* green eyes.

And the sound he made when Darren's hand slipped, when the dagger cut into the vine *just* enough to draw blood, alraune's ichorous blood, well, that sound wasn't even in the least bit human either.

At first he couldn't see anything at all and worried that he might have gone blind, but after blinking once or twice he realized that his vision was just blurred, just red from all the blood dripping down into his eyes.

He touched his brow and when he did he pulled his hand away and found a bloody handprint. "Dear lord... my head..." He murmured weakly. How long had he been out for? It could have been seconds, it could have been minutes. He wasn't sure.

It felt like he had been run over by a carriage. Ravendor tried to stand. He didn't quite make it the first time and his back definitely felt like there was something wrong with it, but he pushed himself up against the wall he had been slammed against and he held.

He pulled his gun out again and thumbed back the hammer but this time he didn't feel confident enough to hit the broad side of a barn, let alone the alraune herself or her vines. He started to stagger forward to where Warren and Siro were defending themselves but paused once he heard the scream.

There were two screams, actually. The first sounded like somebody had awoken a giant snake, a cobra or something that hissed and snarled in what could have been either anger or pain, and the other sounded a *lot* more familiar. It was Darren's scream.

The young rogue had been utterly surprised by the attack. Magi had just lunged at him like a wild animal while he was in such a precarious position; hanging from the vines high up with just his hands and feet for support. When Magi went for his throat Darren recoiled instinctively from the attack, throwing up his arms in self-defense and therefore losing his hold on the wall. He cried out in panic and fear as he fell.

As fortune would have it Darren was not only talented in wall-climbing but also in taking a fall. A normal adventurer might have broken a bone hitting the hard stone floor but Darren tumbled instead, rolling and landing in a knee-bruising, skidding crouch. All of a sudden he feared for the fire bombs on his belt, knowing that impact set them off and he had almost certainly rolled over them at least once, but his pants hadn't burst into flames so he was good in that regard.

Darren's heart beat hard in his chest. He was on the ground now. He was safe. He looked up to where his burning torch remained stuck up there in the bramble and where Magi had been waiting for him.

A light, soft noise was all the warning Darren received. The archer dropped down nimbly to the ground in one controlled fall, landing in a crouch of his own. By all rights he should have broken an ankle doing that, but Magi clearly wasn't human anymore. His hands touched the soil lightly with his fingertips, as if grounding himself there, and he peered at the younger man through strands of hair made wild by his stay in the dungeon. He looked like an animal. A monster.

The vines weren't helping him one bit to look any more human. Now disentangled from the alraune's bramble Darren could see that Magi had two long vines of his own, only two, thin yet strong and extending outwards from his bruised forearms about six feet long; the length of a tall person. They moved fluidly, almost independently as Magi moved his arms. The sight made Darren feel a little sick inside, wondering, fearing what those bruises and vines must felt like bursting out of his skin.

Magi rose, pulling himself into almost a standing posture but he swayed a bit on his feet. It was possible his legs had weakened since the alraune had captured him or his transformation had begun, but he braced against the ground with both of his vines and got his support from there instead. Darren watched the roots caress the ground carefully, finding purchase, then took the time to stand up as well.

"Magi," Darren said unsteadily, now on his guard, "what happened to you? Come on, it's Darren. Your friend."

The words did not seem to affect him. It was as if he could no longer understand human speech. Instead of answering or making any noise at all Magi's hand flashed to his belt and grasped his one remaining dagger; the only weapon he had left from the human world. It was still sharp and gleamed in the lantern light; also made of Sylvas steel. He charged.

Magi may have been having trouble standing but he could still *run.* He sprinted towards the anxious Darren and slashed frantically with his knife, trying to tear a canal through the rogue's throat and chest.

Darren was faster. His hands moved down to his dagger-sheaths in only a fraction of a second and he brought his twin knives up into a blocking stance against Magi's own weapon, grinding steel against steel. The metallic crunch it made was strangely satisfying to the ears.

"Stop it!" Darren pleaded.

But he pulled away instead, sweeping his arm backwards, adjusting his grip on the single dagger and slashing forward again at Darren's right, attempting to cripple one of his arms. Darren parried automatically with his right dagger, the weapons striking with a '*ting*' noise and grateful that all those self-defense classes hadn't been in vain.

Magi reached out with a bare hand and attempted to grab the other man by the coat sleeve. He succeeded but not for very long as Darren pulled himself backwards and shrugged himself away. The archer slashed again. He wasn't very accurate but his fervor more than made up for it. With Darren not fighting back it would just be a matter of time until he landed a lucky hit.

And how could he fight back against Magi when rescuing him and bringing him back to the surface had been the entire *point* of their mission? He didn't understand. Why was this happening? It wasn't supposed to be this way!

"I'm sorry!" The rogue abruptly yelled, losing it. "I *know* it was supposed to be me instead of you but *come on*! This is ridiculous!" He shoved at Magi hard, as if to push him away, like a little brother trying to get away from a hated noogie.

Unfortunately that brought his arm close to Magi's face and Magi reacted with an alraune's instincts. He had yet to develop the razor-sharp incisors that the species possessed but the urge was still there, and blunted human teeth or not being bitten with all one's might still really hurt. He sunk his teeth into Darren's arm and he yelped in pain, twisting automatically in his grip and making it even worse.

Somehow he managed to struggle free, his arm throbbing in raw, unadulterated agony, but then Darren made his next mistake. He had forgotten about Magi's newfound ambidexterity in his extra limbs and by the time he felt the vine wrapping around his foot it was already too late. Magi pulled him off-balance and shot another vine out to coil around his neck, squeezing like a python and cutting off the supply of air to Darren's brain.

Darren was flipped over onto his back but he barely felt it as he let go of his daggers and grappled madly at his throat, ineffectually trying to pull the far-too-strong vines away. Sometimes he could almost dig his fingers under the vine and pull a little, but it would just snap into place again after his strength wore out. The youth gurgled weakly. Magi was too strong for him.

It was almost like adding insult to injury when Magi, not satisfied with the hold he had on him so far cracked the vines he possessed like a whip and lifted Darren into the air a little, then smashed him hard into the floor. The young adventurer didn't even have the breath left to cry out, but when he felt the impact his vision grayed around the edges and didn't come back.

Now Magi seemed to be patient. He adjusted his dagger one last time, blade downward, holding it firmly and ready to plunge it deep into the chest of his former friend. He smiled. There was no warmth to it.

A single report echoed through the dungeon. Magi felt it more than he heard it. It surprised him.

The dagger flew out of his hand and landed some distance away from him. His fingers stung a bit from the sudden disarming. Magi turned his head in the direction of the obstruction.

"Let him go."

Ravendor had his gun trained on him. He didn't feel like he could hit the broad side of a barn in the state he was in, but he *had* been able to shoot the knife out of Magi's fingers. It must have been his lucky day.

But now he only had one bullet left before he'd have to reload. He hoped one would be enough.

Magi appeared to hesitate when he saw Ravendor. Maybe he recognized him, or maybe his mind was still human enough to remember what the gun was and what it could do to him if he disobeyed. His alraune queen could take a bullet with ease, but he didn't look like he was quite ready for that just yet.

The vines binding Darren went slack. He rolled onto his side in a hurry and began to cough, taking in great lungfuls of sweet, sustaining air. Tears rolled down his cheeks as he tried to stabilize himself, pulling away at the vines that came free without a hassle. That had almost been the end, he was sure of it.

All at once Magi looked like he had no idea what he was going to do next, like he had been in a trance the entire time and it was only now that he had some doubts over what he was doing. He seemed confused… and perhaps just a little bit frightened.

Ravendor appeared to be rolling with the idea that the alraune had transformed Magi into a monster quite better than Darren had, despite Siro and Warren neglecting to mention a thing to him beforehand. He was older than all the others. It was possible he might have heard about something like this before. His tone was soft and steady, contrasting weirdly with his head injuries and the blood oozing down one side of his face. "It's alright. You do not have to do this. You can just sit down, if you like."

Magi looked at him mutely. He couldn't speak, didn't have the ability to form words anymore. The silence seemed to be enough, somehow.

The gunman was not daunted. "You have been through so much," he said gently, "if you sit down now and do not resist we can take care of the rest. Everything will be all right."

But he was *lying*. He knew what the humans wanted to do to his queen, even *if* a very small, lost part of him wanted to believe every word that Ravendor said. He had to protect her. Needed to protect her…

He would *die* to protect her.

Abruptly Magi switched targets. He didn't care about Darren anymore. In a burst of frankly baffling speed he dove towards Ravendor, making a sound in his throat that was truly horrifying to hear. Ravendor quickly took a step back and fired on reflex even though he had been entirely bluffing and hadn't ever intended on shooting Magi in the first place. The bullet missed anyway, winging its way past Magi's shoulder, and before he could do anything about it the older man was hurled onto the ground, his best friend on top of him.

Darren didn't climb to his feet so much as Warren appeared at his side and helped him up as carefully as he could. Dark red marks had already begun to form around the youth's throat from the strangulation. "Are you alright?" He asked.

"Y-yeah." Darren nodded and winced, hands on his skinned knees. A thought suddenly came to him as Siro approached; quickly heading to the scuffle that was taking place in front of them. "The alraune! Where is she?"

"She retreated once Magi stepped into the fray but I'll bet she'll be back any second now." Warren told him, frowning. "It's good to see Magi alive but he… he's been turned, hasn't he?"

"I don't know what you mean!" Darren said sharply. "But he's growing vines just like that monster with the breasts!"

Warren sighed and then flinched as he shifted weight to his injured side. He had healed it but it would still ache for some time longer, regardless. "I was afraid of that. Ravendor!"

"What?" He cried irritably, straddled by Magi and trying to fend him off with just his bare hands. It was a relief when Siro came up from behind them and grabbed Magi roughly by the arm and one of his vines, pulling him away.

"Don't hurt him! I think we might be able to save him!"

Magi struggled angrily in Siro's grasp but it seemed like he was tiring. He had been pushing himself from the very start for the sake of protecting his love but he was still in transition; not quite a human but not yet an alraune. His vines were too underdeveloped and with his legs he could barely stand anymore. He couldn't do this on his own.

Before Ravendor could answer Warren or move to get up, they heard another monster shriek in the darkness. It was the first time they had heard the queen make a noise and compared to her Magi had sounded like a kitten in distress. It hurt the ears, it wasn't speech, but it felt like the very embodiment of the '*put my mate down you bastards*' sentiment. The alraune climbed back down to the ground. She was bleeding. There was a lot less of her than there was before, but she had returned.

When Magi saw her he tried to wrench himself out of Siro's grip but he was too strong for him. He wanted to go to her. Without warning Siro felt uncomfortable, as if he were restraining Romeo from reaching his Juliet. He found himself wondering if maybe this was more than it seemed, and maybe coming back and dragging Magi up to the surface again might not be for the greatest of good.

He felt Magi begin to tremble in his arms. Initially he thought that the blond archer was about to fall over, unable to support himself on his weak legs, but when he didn't Siro then realized that Magi had started to cry.

The alraune didn't attack. She couldn't, not with Siro holding Magi like that. One wrong move and the human could snap his neck. As Ravendor picked himself up off the ground the plant creature and the almost-plant creature locked eyes for what could have been the very last time. One single, silent thought was exchanged.

*I love you.*

Nobody seemed to notice when Darren walked out into the midst of his party. He was carrying something in his hands – a bag. His face was full of pent-up anger. With his good arm, his dart-throwing arm; he pitched.

They didn't realize what it was Darren had thrown until it hit the alraune squarely between the breasts.

The cavern ignited. For a split second the alraune's home was lit up as bright as day and then there was fire, fire everywhere, catching on anything and everything close enough to burn. The monster queen became engulfed in the flames. She screamed again, this time not in anger but in pain. It jellified the organs, made one feel absolutely sick inside, because after all in the end it was just a woman screaming in agony and nobody liked to hear that.

For the first time in… ever, really, Darren was the only one who had any idea of what to do. Suddenly he was yelling his own style of expletives at the monster, babbling frantically as he lobbed a second fire gem at the enemy, and then a third. His hands were shaking; it threw off his aim a little bit, but still…

"*Damn you! I'm not going to die in here! I'm not just a scout! I just want to help damn it and I'm not* ***into*** *those kind of dreams damn it and it was a mistake and* ***you can't tell me what to doooo, Aunt Selina****! It's not my fault! It's not my fauuuult!*"

One of the gems struck the massive tangle of vines behind the alraune and caught. Immediately there was a brushfire and it spread fast. The alraune herself writhed in the flames and made hand and vine motions as if to beat herself out, but it wasn't enough to extinguish the spell and she turned instead, uprooting herself, putting her back to the party and attempting to flee.

Darren pulled his arm back to fling a fifth gem at the retreating figure but Ravendor got behind him and caught his wrist in time. "For goodness sake calm yourself." He hissed at him, disgusted.

When he felt somebody touch him it was like all his rage turned into lead and sunk downwards through his body, seeping out from the soles of his shoes and into the floor. It felt like the older man holding his arm was the only thing keeping him upright. "It's not my fault." He said again, weakly.

Before Darren had a chance to collapse somebody else did it for him. It was Magi. He had watched the whole thing in Siro's arms and the screaming, the burning, the listening to his mate's cries of pain – it had been too much for him. He didn't pass out, not really, but Siro felt Magi lose all the strength in his legs and his vines ceased their constant movements. The archer just sort of slid out of his grip; folding up in on himself in the dirt.

He was harmless now. He wasn't going to go anywhere.

Soon the alraune was gone, disappearing behind her burning bramble to the caverns behind. Of course there was more dungeon behind her; it was the only way to press forward, and besides that they had heard a stream trickling up ahead the first time they had come here, so maybe she was moving fast to try and put herself out.

Warren appeared to be the first one to get his wits back into proper working order. The alraune was important but so was Magi. He hastily swung his supply pack off from behind his broad shoulders. "Well don't just stand there, you three!" He commanded urgently. "You should follow her! Take the rest of these torches and ignite them on the vines. We have to make sure she doesn't come back!"

Siro accepted a torch as Warren passed him one. "What about you?"

"I'll stay here. I need to see if Magi is alright. Is that okay?"

There were enough torches left for Darren and Ravendor as well. They were both beat-up pretty badly but Warren couldn't see to them until their jobs were done. It reminded Darren a bit of a good old-fashioned bonfire night in his hometown as he held a new torch again in his hands. "Will he survive?" He asked hesitantly.

Their doctor didn't feel like it was the right time to be asking frivolous questions. "Don't worry about it right now; that's my job. Find the alraune quickly and burn her!" He instructed.

Ravendor didn't need to be told twice. He had seen what the creature had done to his friend and he was already on the hunt for blood. The gunman lit his torch on the burning bramble and was gone, following the alraune through the unknown paths of the dungeon ahead. Siro was seconds behind him and not long after that Darren followed.

Warren found himself alone. Well, not really, he still had Magi near him even if he was sprawled on the ground like a ragdoll in a near-catatonic state. He smiled sympathetically at his fallen comrade, unpacking his medical supplies and with it the book of crypto-botany he had stolen from the library. He didn't have much to work with but at least he could make Magi comfortable for a time.

He winced once again in pain as he knelt, putting on his glasses which had thankfully not cracked in the previous battle. He rolled Magi gently onto his back.

"Okay then, let's see what she's done to you..." He murmured.

It looked like the alraune had been blocking a stream or a tiny underground river when she had moved into her lair years, decades, or maybe centuries ago. It might have been how she had grown so strong, damming up all the water and sucking the silty nutrients out of the soil. The caverns beyond were more like eroded tunnels, muddy in places, branching outwards in many different directions like a maze.

The three men separated without discussion; it just seemed like the most logical thing to do. Ravendor heard Siro and Darren choose their own paths but he didn't care, he didn't need them anyway for what *he* was going to do. He was following freshly-made tracks, long thin tracks, like vines being dragged through the mud.

The torch illuminated well in the darkness. He just had to follow. Water splashed up around his ankles as he rounded a bend in the road and found the stream, killing the tracks, but that was alright. This was where he needed to go.

He stopped abruptly and swore under his breath when he remembered something important, taking precious seconds to reload his gun. Bullets didn't harm her but he felt unprotected without it and he had no idea when he would need to fight again.

He was panting slightly from running, exhausted, injured and absolutely *dying* for a cigarette. Ravendor waved the torch around the tunnel. He couldn't see anything suspicious so he pressed onward, trying to ignore the chilling cold of the water around his legs. Soon he heard movement up ahead, not from a person but of water being displaced, splashed around, like a person trying to take a bath.

For a human the tunnel was a dead end. It finished in a small cul-de-sac that fissured off into a huge crack in the wall, too thin and jagged for a regular person to squeeze on through. When Ravendor entered the chamber the alraune turned to him, horrifically burned and smelling like an autumn brushfire, but still alive. She had put herself out in the stream. The fire had disfigured her but she was still beautiful, somehow.

Her once long and numerous vines had all been torn, cut or burnt away. She was human-sized now, with thick stumpy vines where her legs should have been that resembled an octopus instead of the tangle of a forest. Her arm vines had fared no better. She glanced at Ravendor, whirling around like a maiden startled in the midst of bathing, and there was *real* fear in her deep green eyes. She was afraid.

Not of him but of the thing he was carrying. The torch. Until tonight she might not have even known what fire *was*, or how badly it could hurt her. Well, she knew now. She backed away from him, pressing herself up against the wall, her gaze not leaving the flickering firelight for even a second.

Realizing the importance of what he was holding Ravendor thrust the torch out at her menacingly. She recoiled further into the wall even though he was far away enough for the flames not to be a threat. Her long-fingered hands grasped at the stony fissure behind her, but she did not move.

It would be easy to ignite her and to keep her burning until she finally twisted and crumbled, even in the midst of all that water. He could hold her up against the wall. He might burn himself a bit, and he might end up with some nasty scratches, but it *was* doable.

But… even though she was a monster, even though she had hurt Magi… she was a woman. He had never raised a fist in anger against a woman in his life and felt uncomfortable about starting now, despite the circumstances. If he burned her she would scream, and he would stop. He wasn't certain that he had the nerve, not right now.

But she *deserved* to die for what she had done to Magi, right?

Right?

Ravendor lowered the torch a little. No. No, she didn't. She could have killed Magi, could have eaten him up as quickly as she had caught him and that would have been the end of it. If that had been the case Ravendor would not have felt the slightest remorse if he burned her. Instead she had kept him alive, mutated him, granted, but she hadn't taken his life. If he burned her now he would be worse than the alraune and her motivations.

In a way he was actually *grateful* to the alraune that she had chosen to spare Magi's life.

And in the end they both wanted the same thing; they both wanted Magi. Ravendor and his party had already taken him back. It was over.

"Listen to me," he said slowly, deliberately, so that even a dumb animal could get the message. "You can't have him. He belongs to *us*. Get out of here."

He stepped forward, waving the torch at her again. He raised his voice. "Get out! *Go!*"

Ravendor raked the torch at the monster-girl close enough for her to feel the heat. The alraune cried out at him, angrily, sadly, and then a curious thing happened. She managed to squeeze her body into the thin fissure behind her, bending in ways that no human could, retreating like a giant spider into darkness and the damp. She went to a place where not even Ravendor could follow her, but he was fine with that. Let her rot in there.

Just like that, she was gone.

Eventually Siro and Darren were forced to give up on their hunt for the alraune through the tunnels and returned to the others empty-handed. They had searched extensively through the darkness for around twenty minutes; any further or any longer and they might have messed up their bearings – gotten lost.

They met up together at the joining of a tunnel and not long after they found Ravendor waiting for them at the entrance to the caves, leaning tiredly against the wall. He had a cigarette lit but he wasn't actively smoking it, he was just letting it burn down to the filter as he stared absently at the ceiling.

"Did you find her?" Siro asked as he approached with Darren, slowing down.

"Did I find who?" Ravendor echoed politely, inquiring.

"The alraune." He responded. It looked like the other man's head injuries had finally caught up with him.

"Oh." He said, waited a second, and then added; "Yes. Indeed. She got away."

Darren groaned. "But we were so close! We had her! What if she comes back?"

Ravendor tiredly dropped his cigarette and ground the ashes out in the dirt. "I doubt she will be coming back any time soon. It does not matter. All that matters is that we are still alive and Magi is safe."

Siro supposed that Ravendor made a good point. Two out of three wasn't bad. The blond swordsman ran a hand through his short hair wearily. "We should go see how Magi and Warren are doing. It should be fine, but I don't like the idea of Warren being alone with him for too long."

"How come?" Darren asked, curious.

"Darren, Magi tried to stab and then strangle you, remember?" Siro told him, incredulous.

The rogue made a face at him. "Yeah, let's go check on Warren." He agreed.

But Warren was fine. While the others had been busy driving away the alraune he had set up kind of a temporary triage in the midst of the vacated cavern, safely away from the burning vines. It made the air a little smoky to breathe but there was plenty of oxygen in the Underwood and Warren didn't feel ready trying to move Magi right away. The archer hadn't stirred yet, he was still as quiet as a corpse, but he hadn't struggled when Warren had examined him so that was a bonus.

Warren climbed to his feet to greet his friends when they returned, wiping something from his hands with what looked like a damp washcloth. "How did it go?" He asked hopefully.

Siro told him. He didn't seem too happy about the news but in the end he was more concerned about their friend than the monster that had corrupted him. Warren had assembled a small stretcher and had laid the archer carefully upon it, covering him with a soft blanket for his modesty. There really weren't much of his clothes left to save anyway. He looked a lot better this way, less like a casualty and more like a patient receiving treatment.

The vines from Magi's arms hung limply around him and his makeshift stretcher. Warren cleared his throat in an anxious manner. "He's still, uh… growing." He said.

Darren folded his legs and sat down heavily on the floor. He was bushed. "What do you mean?" He asked.

Warren turned away and stepped over Magi to get around him, then crouched, picking up one of his vines. It was inanimate, lifeless, like a length of rope. The doctor indicated a part of the vine that had an imperfection in it, a small offshoot that hadn't been there before but had grown in the interim. The other vine was growing similar offshoots as well. "Do you see these? He's still transforming into an alraune. If we don't do something about this soon I don't know what will happen to him."

"What? But the alraune queen has fled." Ravendor protested, upset. "That cannot be."

The brown-haired man removed his glasses momentarily to rub at his tired eyes. "What can I say? I'm still mostly in the dark about all this. Logically, without the alraune around to groom him he should return to normal, but…"

He abruptly changed the subject. He didn't have any idea how to broach it otherwise. Warren's voice was a little shaky as he spoke. "Everybody… he's been raped. Multiple times, from the looks of it." He said.

There was a long, drawn-out silence. It seemed to last forever. Nobody spoke.

Eventually, after far too long Darren murmured in a very small voice; "Will he be alright?"

Warren looked at him sadly. Darren was probably thinking about how that could have been him instead; could have been any one of them. "I think so. It's just… you know… I hate it. He didn't deserve it."

Without saying anything Ravendor turned and made to walk back toward the tunnels beyond the alraune's cavern. He walked past Siro to do this, and, concerned by this strange behavior the mayor of Adratea took him by the arm.

He jerked his arm away so hard that he nearly backhanded Siro across the face. Ravendor's own face was a mask of rage. "Don't touch me! What was I thinking? I should have killed her! I should have *burned* her! I will be right back!"

"Ravendor!" Warren scolded, trying to remain the rational one in the party. "Don't. It won't change anything; it won't help Magi to get better. Take a look at yourself; you can barely stand right now. What's done is done."

The older man glared at Warren. He was furious, yes, but only as a ward to keep the devastation at bay. He was supposed to be their team's leader; it had been his duty to protect his comrades from situations such as these. He had failed as both a leader and a friend, and he felt like dirt because of it.

He brought his hand up to his face for a moment, closing his eyes. For the first time in what felt like, god, *years*, Ravendor felt like he was about to cry, but soon the feeling passed. Warren was right. He was too tired for this bullshit. Like Darren he also sat down, saying nothing.

Warren let go of Magi and stood again, patting soil from his knees. Growing or not Magi was stable and not in any danger, but his friends were hurt and bleeding. He had to prioritize, picking up his supply bag.

Siro was healthy compared to the others, he'd sustained some scrapes and bruises while fighting the alraune but his armor had protected him from any serious injury. He helped Siro unbuckle the thick plates of heavy armor, leaving him in just his clothes underneath. The armor itself was wrecked though; Cassie back in town would probably throw a fit over it when his friend brought it back in for repairs.

Darren had skinned knees, a bite mark and bruises around his throat. It wasn't too serious and he could still breathe clearly enough to Warren's satisfaction, though the young adventurer complained about how much it hurt. "At least you're not into that kind of thing." He joked as he washed the blood and grit out of Darren's knees, using gauze and drinking water from his canteen.

The youth blinked at him. "Huh?"

"You were screaming something about that earlier. I thought-"

"Ah!" Darren exclaimed, going a dark shade of red in embarrassment. He played along, there wasn't really much else he could do. "Y-Yeah, I guess." He laughed nervously.

"How's that bite? How do you feel?" Warren asked, rolling up the rogue's sleeve to get a better look at it.

"It hurts. I can't believe Magi bit me!" Darren complained, then registered the tone in which Warren had asked him how he was. "Why? Is something wrong? Alraune aren't like werewolves, are they? If one bites you hard enough you don't turn *into* one, do you?" His breath caught in his throat. "Oh my god, is *that* what happened to Magi?"

"Hey, hey, hey," Warren interrupted, patting him gently on the leg, "don't be silly. It doesn't work that way. The book I got from Mina says so."

Darren relaxed. He could trust anything that came from Mina, he was sure of it. "Really?"

"Yeah. They're not like werewolves, but they *are* poisonous. I thought that maybe Magi had bitten you and he could have poisoned you that way."

He anticipated Darren's wail. He quickly grabbed the youth by his injured arm, stilling him. "But! Darren, wait! Look at this wound. He didn't even break the skin. You're probably fine. How do you feel?"

Actually he felt sick, but most likely not in the way Warren was looking out for. "I'll be okay." He said in a small voice.

Once he was patched up Darren wandered away in a vague attempt to make himself useful. He went to go and find all the machetes that had been dropped during the course of the battle and also to find his lost daggers. Maybe he might even find his hat.

Warren found that Ravendor had not moved since he had chosen to sit down. He'd left the gunman for last mostly because he thought that Ravendor might need the most serious treatment, but also because he was a little wary about getting close to him right now. He suspected that his friend was in a mild state of shock. Warren didn't blame him. They had gone through a lot in the past two days or so.

He knelt down next to Ravendor. "What about you? Any complaints?" He inquired.

The dark-haired man turned to glance at him. It looked like he needed sleep, or a stiff drink, or maybe both. "Would you like the short list or the long one?" He asked.

The doctor smiled and unscrewed his water canteen again, soaking another rag slightly for treatment. He passed it to Ravendor. "Here, wipe all the blood off your face. I won't be able to see anything with you looking like that." He instructed.

He did as he was told. His face was fine but it certainly felt like he had a ragged wound or something equally nasty somewhere past his hairline. He had been numb to it before but now that they were safe it was making itself known. "Warren?"

"Hm?" He was searching for something in his supply bag.

"I know that we are victorious, and I am aware that I should be grateful for nothing else, yet… why does this feel so hollow?" He mused out loud, then added in barely a whisper; "It should have been me instead."

"Don't say that, you're starting to sound like Darren." Warren observed, trying to lighten the mood. He wasn't as badly injured as he had thought. The gunman had a slight concussion and a gash on his head, a knife wound in his leg, but apart from some worries about back pain he was fine. Were they up on the surface in Adratea he would have suggested someone keep an eye on him for the next twenty-four hours because of the blunt force trauma he had sustained, but for now their resources were short.

In any case he was going to need stitches. Not many, but a few. Warren got out a needle and some surgical silk, but swore harshly when he realized he had forgotten something after all. "Damn it! The anesthetic! I forgot the anesthetic!" He moaned.

"You needn't worry about that," Ravendor reassured him, "I will not flinch." He'd been injured a lot worse in the past. He'd be fine.

For his own merits he didn't cringe or make any noise, though Warren suspected that he secretly wanted to. He was skilled with a needle but there must have been at least a bit of pain. The wound in his leg was smaller and easier to handle, despite the other man complaining that he had to drop trousers momentarily to have it fixed.

"I found my hat!" Darren called out from the far side of the cavern. When he returned he was wearing it happily, both his daggers back in their scabbards and two reclaimed machetes in his hands.

He didn't notice the spider sitting merrily on the brim until Siro pointed it out to him. He squealed and threw the hat on the ground, jumping up and down on the spider as it skittered away. Despite their exhaustion a couple of people laughed.

While everybody else was focused on Darren Magi at last sat up in his makeshift bed, the blanket covering him sliding down and pooling about his waist. He moved about like he had just come out of a very deep sleep, a coma, and he raised his hands to his face like a weeping woman, staring at them as if he had no idea what they were.

Warren heard the soft movement before anyone else and turned, halfway through packing up after treating Ravendor. "Magi," he began, "are you-"

The only way to describe the sound Magi made was a mourning cry; a great howl of loss. It startled everybody and the rescue party leapt to their feet simultaneously, nerves rattled by the sound.

They ran to him but when Warren tried to touch him on the shoulder he thrashed out at him angrily, trying to push the physician away. Warren wasn't thrown off too badly by this, but then one of Magi's vines swatted him in the chest and that really stung.

Ravendor tried to grab the archer by the upper arms. Magi hollered and tore himself away. He grabbed again, trying to prevent him from struggling. "What is wrong with him?" He demanded, looking to Warren for advice.

"I-I don't know. I think he's just disoriented or confused." Warren stammered and then turned to Siro beside him. "Can you pin his legs down? I think he's going to-"

Too late. Magi's leg jerked under a nasty convulsion and connected with Warren somewhere most unpleasant beneath the belt. The young swordsman groaned lowly. "Ah... ow…"

"Don't let him bite you!" Darren announced, hovering nervously. "He'll poison you!" The rogue took a step back, noticing something the others hadn't yet. His eyes widened. "His vines have gone into the ground! He's taking root!"

The rescue party looked down. Darren was right. His vines had branched out considerably since the last time Warren had examined them and they had dug into the ground suddenly, pinning Magi against the floor. This could have been a part of the alraune's survival mechanism, trying to connect itself to a source of continued growth instead of shriveling up and dying. It could also be that Magi was intending to take the old alraune's place, Warren didn't know.

Caught hunched-over and unable to do anything for the moment he called to Darren and Ravendor; "Try to pull them out. Quickly!"

Darren hesitated. He didn't want to be grabbed or bitten again, *especially* knowing how Magi might be poisonous. Ravendor clutched at the vine closest to him and tugged ineffectually. He was afraid that if he pulled too hard he might injure Magi, and his friend had already been hurt enough that day. "I can't… get it out…" He growled. He had never been any good at gardening.

After seeing that nothing bad had happened to Ravendor Darren manned up a little and grabbed Magi's other vine, just above where it branched off into the dirt. He yanked with a lot more force and conviction, trusting his weight on both his ankles and his wrists. Magi cried out at him and kicked at Siro, but if it was in anger or pain he didn't know. "He's in there good." Darren sweated, unable to budge him an inch.

"Warren!" Siro yelled, concerned. In the absence of any real knowledge he had become their leader.

Warren tried to think fast, raising himself up on shaky legs. He adjusted his glasses worriedly. "Okay, uh, just keep him pinned down for a while. Someone hold him on his back and make sure he doesn't hurt himself. I gotta get Mina's book."

"*Warren*!" Siro echoed a little more urgently this time, barely avoiding being kneed in the throat. It looked like his partner was grasping at straws and that didn't make him feel too confident. They couldn't just hold onto him forever.

"It'll only take a minute! I promise!" He heard Warren exclaim as he disappeared behind them.

So there they were, two men on top of another man thrashing about and wailing like he was having the worst nightmare in the world. Siro could hear Magi being pressed against his stretcher and realized that

Ravendor had pinned him, which seemed to take a lot of attention away from Magi's legs. He could relax a bit, now. "You're close with Magi, aren't you Ravendor?" Siro asked, unable to see him but directing the question anyway.

The other man seemed surprised by the implication. "Well, yes. I suppose so." He replied.

"Try talking to him. See if you can calm him down." He suggested. It had almost worked when Magi had been attacking Darren, maybe it would work again.

But Ravendor had no idea what he was supposed to say. Usually he was actually quite good at coming up with stuff on the fly (his father had told him once that he should just get it over with and become a politician), but since he had been smacked into that wall he had been having trouble thinking straight. What could he say to Magi, especially in these circumstances? He probably couldn't even understand them.

"Magi… Magi damn it, stop struggling." He grumbled, having trouble keeping him on the floor. "Nobody is going to hurt you. You are safe." He told him.

The plea seemed to fall on deaf ears. Darren finally let go of the vine he was trying to dig up and moved to Magi's other side, hoping his left vine was looser in the soil. There wasn't really much else he could do right now. It would be easier if he had a shovel.

Ravendor adjusted his position on the ground a little to prevent the arm he was leaning against from going numb. A thought came to him from nowhere. "Magi, do you remember Mara? Surely you remember Mara. She is waiting to see you again in Adratea. You have to let go of all this, of this place so you can return and see her again."

For the first time since he had awoken Magi ceased the cries and animalistic growls coming from his mouth. He looked at Ravendor as if in a haze, but he could not speak. Maybe he *did* remember Mara. There could be hope for him after all.

He continued. "I made a promise to her that I would bring you back alive and well. I'd appreciate it if you did not make me a liar."

"Is it working?" Darren piped up.

"Shh. Don't interrupt him." Siro hushed.

"And… and… regardless," Ravendor added, flailing mentally for a moment, "you do not want to be here. You don't want to be a monster.

You belong back up there on the surface with those who care about you and can I stop this now, please? I don't know what to say!"

But even if the words meant nothing to Magi, Ravendor's familiar voice seemed to be doing the trick. The archer relaxed. His body was still as tense as a drawn bowstring and trembling with emotion, overwhelming sadness, but he went quiet. Siro and Darren sighed in relief when Warren came back.

But he did not come back with confidence. The expression on his face was like one who had been told some seriously bad news. Siro could read him like a book. He prepared for the worst. "What is it, Warren?" He asked softly.

"Guys, I need you to hold onto him for a little while longer." Warren said in resignation, arms folded protectively at his elbows – a gesture of uncertainty. "I have to, uh, perform surgery on him."

"Surgery?" Ravendor repeated. Now that Magi wasn't struggling anymore he had moved his arm to unconsciously cradle his friend's head. He didn't like the sound of that.

"Yeah. The book says he's not going to get any better with those vines attached to him and we can't move him until they're gone. I'm going to have to cut them off."

"You mean *right now*?"

"Of course right now! What other time is there?" Warren snapped, irritated and frightened at the prospect but he caught himself afterwards. He sighed. "… Sorry. I'm sorry. Let's just do this. Siro and Ravendor can stay where you are, but Darren can you help me?"

The youth paled. "I don't have to cut him or anything, do I?"

"No, but do exactly as I say."

He had a long list of demands, but only few supplies. Rags, water, gauze, bandages – a lot of them – and cutting instruments. He had brought a small scalpel with him just in case, but it wouldn't be large enough to slice through the vine and not cause Magi utter agony. Warren wanted this to be over quickly, but on the other hand the machetes Trina had made for them to use in the dungeon were just *too* big. They were for hacking, not surgical precision, and Warren didn't feel right using a weapon he had swung at an enemy so carelessly on his friend.

The only middle ground he had was one of Darren's daggers which he accepted without a word. Hopefully it would be sharp enough.

Another thing he wanted, and had surprised what was rapidly becoming Nurse Darren, was fire. He asked for Darren to hold one of the torches close to him for easy access. "Why?" Darren had ventured.

"You'll see." The doctor responded in a flat tone.

Even more than he had before Warren was kicking himself for forgetting to bring anesthetic. A few raw stitches were fine, whatever, but this? This was going to be *surgery*. This was going to *hurt*, and there was nothing he could do about it now.

Warren made his final preparations around Magi and his friends. It was almost like he could smell the anxiety coming off them in waves, and he most likely was no different. The brown-haired physician briefly sterilized Darren's dagger in the rogue's fire. He got to his knees beside Magi, wrapped the tourniquet around his arm, tightened, held the dagger carefully, made sure there were enough rags underneath the archer's arm to soak up all the blood that would come…

"Warren." Siro interrupted him. He looked understandably concerned. His lover's hands were shaking a little. "Are you okay?"

"No." He muttered like a child about to admit to some great sin. "I'm terrified. What if I do this wrong?"

Siro couldn't answer him. There wasn't anything he could say that would help. Ravendor leaned closer to Magi and took him by the hand. If this happened correctly he was going to squeeze, and he might as well squeeze him instead of hurting himself. Poor Magi didn't even seem to be aware of what was about to happen to him.

"Alright," Warren breathed, trying to keep himself steady, "hold onto him as tightly as you can, he's going to *buck*. Three, two, one…"

The knife came down in one smooth motion. There was no pussyfooting around. He was either going to cut, or not. He cut.

Magi screamed as the vine came free. Warren had amputated as closely to his human flesh as he could, doing it in one great slice, but initially only alraune's blood flowed from the wound. Soon that strange, thick, ichorous blood turned red. That was good. The severed vine immediately went dead, it didn't squirm like a dropped lizard's tail in self-defense which was kind of what Warren had been expecting, but Magi thrashed around enough to make up for the loss.

The archer reacted as if he had been stabbed. There was no bravery to his scream, no chance that he was going to bear with it with his friends;

he was just an animal that had been wounded and was too stupid to figure out why. It was a bewildering scream, and if Magi could talk maybe he would have asked; *'Why? Why are you doing this to me?'*

Ravendor grunted in pain as Magi almost crushed his hand. Siro braced himself and accepted the knee to the collarbone silently. Darren looked on, unable to do anything but feel faint.

Warren kept it together. "Fire!" He demanded, holding out an empty hand.

Darren didn't understand. "Wh-What?"

"The torch! Give it to me!"

Once he realized what Warren wanted he handed it over without question, though he didn't understand why he needed it. The unspoken question melted on his tongue, perhaps in horror as his friend took Magi by the bleeding arm and brought the torch down upon the wound, burning the incision closed with the flames.

Magi screamed again but it wasn't the thin, high-pitched scream of the amputation and surprise; it was a low, raw, somehow worse sound. It was burning. *He* was burning.

The alraune feared fire.

"Warren!" Ravendor shouted, aghast. "What in the *blue fuck* are you doing?"

He felt that he was too damn busy to be able to justify himself right now. Warren gritted his teeth as he held the torch steady despite Magi's protests. "I have to cauterize the wound! Magi's vines will grow back if I don't!"

"Can't you just sew him up or something else?" Siro suggested, hugging Magi's legs. He could almost *feel* the suffering coming off the other man and it wasn't right.

"No, they'll just grow back. Trust me on this. The book says-"

"Stop it." Darren whimpered. "You're killing him."

Warren didn't stop. Now that he had started there was no way he could stop. Leaving it halfway was worse than not doing it at all. The cauterization process would quickly seal the wound and shut down the veins that had been supplying blood to his new limbs, but it *was* going to give him scars. There was nothing he could do about that, and the pain? It would be temporary.

But Warren pitied him. His heart went out to him regardless. "I'm sorry." He cried, tears building behind his glasses.

For far too long he attempted to scorch the alraune's curse out of Magi's arm. After what felt like hours but was probably no more than several seconds he pulled the fire away and inspected the wound. It was ugly, an angry pink mixed with black, blue and green, but it had drained. Warren popped the tourniquet and delicately laid Magi's traumatized arm down on the bloody rags.

"Are you done?" Ravendor asked, wincing from the soreness in his hand and having trouble keeping Magi down. Now that it was over the injured man had begun to sob.

"Halfway finished. I have to do the other arm now." Warren muttered, picking up his tools and preparing to switch to the other side.

"Please hurry."

The second time was no easier, at least for Warren, but Magi was granted a slight reprieve. When the slicing pain got to be too much, when the rolling, gnawing fire became too intense to handle…

He couldn't take it. Much to the relief of his party, soon after the second cauterization had begun, Magi passed out.

And all he knew was darkness.

Now that Magi was unconscious Warren worked faster and harder to make every painless minute count. He finished burning the archer's final amputation with a little more care this time; with a steadier hand. When that was done he checked the wound for anything he might have missed and then slathered the affected areas with a heavy-duty burn salve (one of the first things he had packed the night before, immediately after Darren had come to him and told him that BW was planning on giving them the fire spell the next day).

It wouldn't really do that much but it would act as a buffer between the traumatized or missing skin and the bandages. It would also numb some of the pain. Warren gently bandaged each of Magi's arms from the wrist to the elbow, trying to keep the pressure as light as possible but the bindings firm. He thanked god once again that Magi had fainted; there would have been *no way* his friends would have kept him still enough for the dressing otherwise.

As he wasn't being kicked in various uncomfortable places anymore Siro finally let go of Magi's legs and moved to sit against the cavern's wall, rubbing the side of his neck in mild discomfort. Ravendor was able to stop pinning Magi against the stretcher as well, though he had opted to stay where he was by his side and just let Warren work without interruption. The doctor thought it was actually rather sweet of him, though he wouldn't have said it out loud.

There was one last thing he could do. Warren took Magi by one of his bandaged arms, touching lightly as if he were made of glass, and focused on his friend's aura much in the same way he had repaired his own wound earlier during the alraune battle. It wore him out something awful but if it could help, if it could make even a small difference in Magi's recovery then it was worth a try.

While Warren was focused on his healing magic Darren, who had been idly standing by suddenly had an idea. He didn't feel right doing nothing, but because Warren was temporarily indisposed with whatever it was he was doing to Magi he turned to Ravendor instead. "Hey, I was thinking… uh, now that it's all over we'll have to come back here someday to keep going forward in the dungeon. This is only one of the stops, right?" He murmured, not sure of what he was trying to say.

The other man didn't say anything; he just waited patiently for Darren to continue. This actually made the young rogue even antsier than if he had said anything at all. Darren sighed, turning a bit to look at the burning alraune's bramble far away from them. It was dead now, severed from its host, just a huge heap of discarded flesh. "Maybe we should get rid of the alraune's roots, burn it back a little so it'll be easier to find our way around next time."

"How do you propose we do that?" Ravendor asked him, but he already had a fair idea of the answer. He was just somewhat interested in seeing Darren trying to take the initiative for once.

Darren's hand automatically went to the pouch BW had given to him on his belt. She had made far too many for him, only a small handful had been enough to scare the alraune away. There were plenty left. He rolled a single fire gem delicately between his fingertips. "BW said that she made these only for me to use but what she doesn't know can't hurt her." He explained. "Want to do some deforestation?"

The older man smiled slightly at the prospect and then looked down at Magi lying silently in his stretcher. He was okay now; Warren was taking care of him. "It sounds quite therapeutic, actually." He said.

They moved away to the other side of the cavern where the alraune's vine tangle was at its worst. Part of it was already on fire but it wasn't enough; it wasn't spreading fast enough for the adventurers to be certain that it wouldn't just burn itself out. Darren showed Ravendor how to use the fire gems, it was simple really, and soon more bursts of fire erupted in the cavern as the flames spread. They were hardly fire-fighters. Hopefully they knew what they were doing.

Warren couldn't quite see if his healing magic had done the trick or not, with the bandages over the wounds it was too difficult to tell. Magi's color seemed to have improved a little through the contact of auras however, which was better than nothing. The doctor thought about Magi's severed, dead vines. What to do with them? They had been a part of his friend's body. Shouldn't he bury them or something?

But he was too tired for that and Warren probably wouldn't have been able to dig them out of the ground even if he tried. He cleaned himself and the area up, washing the blood from his hands, then moved over to where Siro was waiting patiently for him and sat down, arms around his legs. He tilted his head back against the wall and sighed. He was done.

They were quiet for some time, but then Siro heard Warren sniff as if he had a cold and realized that the other man had been crying. The swordsman turned to him just as Warren was cleaning the lenses of his glasses with the sleeve of his coat. Warren… he was a big guy, and surprisingly strong, but in many other ways he was pretty fragile.

"Is everything okay?" He asked lamely. Of course everything wasn't okay.

Warren laughed gently and wiped at his eyes. "That was the first time I've ever done an amputation without anesthesia. Poor Magi… did you hear the sounds he was making? *I* made him hurt like that. I hope I never have to do that again."

"It had to be done. You weren't just cutting him for the sake of cutting, you were helping him." Siro reasoned, but Warren turned away; unconvinced. The mayor of Adratea let out a sigh of his own, of endearment to the sensitivity of his lover and scooted closer to him, trying to wrap a friendly arm around his shoulders.

He resisted, a little annoyed but wanting nothing more than to be able to lean into the hug. Warren moved away, sliding against the wall and pushing against Siro with his forearm. "Hey, cut it out. Darren or Ravendor might see us." He whined.

"So what if they do? We can't just hide this forever, Warren." Siro said kindly, undaunted and making up the slight distance Warren had put between them. He could see the other two carelessly throwing the remainder of the fire gems at the vines.

He could hear them a little too, it sounded something like; "You know, I used to be really good at darts when I was in school. No one could beat me."

"Is that so?"

"Yeah, they used to call me Deadeye Darren."

"Oh, come off it. They did not."

"They did! They really did!"

"Well, I am not too bad if I do say so myself. We should have a game during the next guild meeting."

Darren laughed. "And you can buy me a drink." He suggested.

"They're not even paying any attention to us." Siro cajoled slyly. "Come on, just for a minute. You need it."

Warren blushed, stretching out his legs on the ground and staring at his shoes. He could feel his determination slipping. "Alright, but *just* for a minute. I don't want to have to explain all this to the others if I can help it. At least not today."

Siro smirked in a self-satisfied manner at getting his way and snuggled up against Warren, pulling him into a loose hug. Warren allowed himself to be roped into it with a shy smile and didn't resist as Siro kissed him tenderly on the cheek, just under the jaw. He could feel slight stubble prickling his lips; his friend was going to need to shave soon. He'd probably neglected to do it that morning. Warren was so forgetful.

He leaned his head against Siro's unarmored shoulder. He really *did* need this. Warren was beginning to feel a bit better already; a little more like himself. He sniffed again but the tears had already dried up earlier. "If Magi recovers and regains his lucidity, and I really hope he does, I'll have to do something special for him. Something to apologize for hurting him so much."

"I'm sure he'll understand." Siro reassured him, but then he remembered the way that Magi had looked at his alraune queen. The longing. The despair when he realized they had been separated. The swordsman pushed the thoughts from his mind. "Hold on. '*If*' Magi recovers his lucidity? He might not?"

"It all depends on how deeply the alraune had changed him. He still bleeds red, still has his legs; still has a heartbeat and a pulse. I'm confident of his chances." Warren explained. A silly idea came to him and he chuckled, recalling the conversation they had had on the way to the Underwood. "Legs. Magi almost found out what it would be like to live without them." He added.

Siro squeezed him again, running his fingers through the messy short hair at the back of Warren's neck. "I don't think I could live without you." He said.

That was possibly the sappiest thing Siro had ever said to him. It was so bad, in fact, that even though he was being sincere Warren couldn't take him seriously. He pushed his partner away with a little laugh and made to stand. "That's it, hug time is over now. Why don't you go and help Ravendor and Darren with the back-burning? I just want to check Magi one last time and make sure he's safe enough for travel. We might as well get out of here."

He offered Siro his hand. The other man looked at it for a second and then took it, squeezing warmly. What the others were doing *did* kind of look like fun. Warren helped him onto his feet. "All right. It'll be nice to finally get home." He agreed.

The two dark-haired men had already made considerable progress on the alraune's vine tangle when Siro joined in. Warren watched them for a while quietly. Siro was sweet, and he was beginning to believe that he loved the big softie with all of his heart, but Warren was a practical man. A private man. Siro was his secret and he liked it that way. When he had been dating Mieus (that felt like so long ago now) she had said that he probably got off on keeping secrets, something that she just could not relate with. Maybe she was right.

Or maybe he was just worried that if he told the world about his love for Siro he might lose him, or instead lose his friends. He didn't want to lose either. Adratea had become his home.

Warren brought his attention back to Magi. The archer looked so peaceful lying there in his stretcher; head tilted to the side in unconsciousness while his long, pale green hair spilled out around him like an unkempt mane. He wouldn't be able to walk, they'd have to carry him all the way from the Underwood to the surface and that would take at minimum two people to do. They'd just have to hope like hell that they wouldn't run into too many monsters.

As Warren was contemplating this Magi unexpectedly made a sound. It wasn't a scream or anything as bad as last time, but his brow furrowed as if he had been bothered by something and he emitted a soft grunt. Not long after that the youth opened his eyes.

Immediately he entered suffering, raw blazing fire from the burns on his arms, but this time he seemed to be able to endure it. Upon seeing this Warren approached him but he did not get too close. He didn't want another knee to the groin like last time. "Magi?" He asked carefully.

Warren was surprised when Magi seemed to react to his name. He turned to look at him, dumbly, perhaps, but it was better than being completely dead to his surroundings. Could his lucidity have come back so quickly? That would be excellent news!

He took a chance and knelt beside his friend. "I know you probably can't speak right now, but can you make any indication that you know what I'm saying? A nod will do. Magi, can you nod 'yes' for me?"

Magi just looked back at him passively. He didn't nod, but he did reach his bandaged arms out to Warren, as if he were silently asking him what had happened, why his arms and everything else were hurting so much. He could be missing his vines. Warren idly wondered if Magi would get phantom pains from the amputation, or if it had been too early for such a thing.

It was then that Warren realized Magi wasn't just trying to show him his arms; he was reaching out to him like he wanted to take him by the hands. He felt uneasy about that. Magi was ambiguous right now, he could have gone back to being a friend or he still might be their enemy. If Warren touched him while he was conscious there was no telling if Magi would try to tear his head off or not.

But he wouldn't find out if he didn't take a chance, right? Warren would just have to trust him.

Famous last words.

What had actually transpired was that Magi's self-defense mechanism had clicked over from 'defend his queen at all costs' to 'preserve yourself, you are dying'. The part of him that was alraune, the part that had been gifted to him was finally starting to dwindle and fall away. He had to protect himself; he had to keep the alraune's curse alive in his body somehow, like an addict just starting to come down from his high. Without the alraune's nectar to support him all he could hope to do was spread the curse in his own way.

Magi lashed out and grabbed Warren all of a sudden by his wrists, pulling the man roughly down on top of him. The doctor hadn't been expecting this so this was easy even in his weakened state. Warren let out a loud, startled yelp, toppling forward but bracing his hands around the stretcher so he wouldn't accidentally crush Magi. The noise he made was abruptly cut short when the archer leaned up and kissed him, deeply, on the mouth.

Warren was too surprised to resist. Without warning he had a pair of arms wrapping around his sides and a strange tongue in his mouth, kissing, coaxing, gentle but hungry. Desperate. A peculiar taste filled his mouth as well, it was hot, heavy and bitter, almost like the disgusting medicines he had used to take long ago when he had been a sickly child. It was foul, but palatable. The sweetness of the kiss itself made up for that.

He made a muffled sound around Magi's lips. The bitterness… it was making him feel numb. He closed his eyes for a moment. Despite not wanting this, despite the fact that this tasted so weird, so wrong…

God *damn* Magi was a good kisser.

"Warren? Warren!"

Somebody called for him. It kicked him back into his senses. All at once he realized what he was doing and tried to pull himself away but Magi resisted him, clinging with all his might. A part of Warren wanted to kiss back, but an even larger part of him (read: most of him) loved Siro and nobody else and this was just, well, a horrible betrayal of his trust. He grunted in protest and pulled away a second time, much harder than the first, a hand going to hold his glasses steady so they wouldn't slip off his nose.

Magi let go of him and he got free at last, letting in a frantic breath and tasting clean air. Warren ended up falling back onto the seat of his pants in surprise, dazed, wondering what the hell had just happened to him. It had been so *fast* and unexpected; he hadn't been able to keep up.

He heard his other three comrades close in on him and Magi, felt Siro place a hand on his shoulder in concern. He blinked. "Warren, what just happened?" He heard Siro ask.

"Magi kissed me."

"What?"

"He *kissed* me. I don't know why." Warren repeated.

They glanced at Magi lying placidly beside him. He was watching them all with a very small, odd smile on his face. Siro didn't seem to be so concerned with the knowledge that Warren had kissed another man so much that he was worried if he was okay. He shouldn't have left him on his own like that. "Did he hurt you?"

"No, I'm alright…" Warren began to say, and then it looked like a very serious idea just hit him. The doctor's eyes went wide and all the color drained from his face. "… Oh no. *Oh no*."

Darren folded his arms nervously. Warren was their expert on the alraune and if something was panicking him then it might be something they *all* had to worry about. "What is it? Did he bite you?"

Warren didn't seem to hear the question at first, pausing for the longest of moments and thinking very carefully, but then he looked up at the young rogue and smiled. He still seemed a little white but he had composed himself somewhat. "Ah, it's nothing. I was just worried about something for a second but it turns out it's nothing. Magi might have just gotten confused. Maybe he was having a dream."

"Perhaps he mistook you for Mara." Ravendor suggested, and smirked.

That idea passed through the minds of everybody in the rescue party to varying degrees of amusement. The only one who didn't find it funny was Warren, but he smiled anyway. He climbed back up on shaky, kind of wobbly legs and went for his water canteen, taking a swig, swishing the liquid around in his mouth and then spitting it out. No good, the taste was still there. Medicine. Or poison.

"Darren and Ravendor, could you two go wait at the mouth of the cavern for Siro and I to catch up? I just need to talk to him privately for a minute. We'll carry Magi up there to join you guys so don't worry about us." Warren asked politely.

He could feel the other men scrutinizing him silently. He wasn't sure if Darren had bought it but Ravendor didn't seem convinced, but Warren had expected that. He'd known Ravendor for a long time, back when he had been that sick kid puking up his medicine each and every day. He knew that Warren was a terrible liar, despite his desire to keep secrets secret.

Even though he could tell Warren was lying about being alright the older man didn't dispute him; he probably had his reasons and if it turned out to be something deadly serious he was certain they'd hear all about it soon enough. He trusted Warren. "Very well, if that is what you wish. Don't take too long, I'd like to get back to the inn before the evening if that is possible. Come on, Darren." He turned, making a gesture for the young rogue to follow him.

Darren hesitated, staring anxiously at the two swordsmen. "Are you sure you're okay?" He questioned.

Warren nodded, trying not to show his impatience. "I really am okay. Don't worry about it. We'll be right behind you."

Once they were gone Warren sighed and put his head in his hands. He moaned. "Oh Siro. Oh god Siro. I'm *such* an idiot. I *can't believe* I forgot about what Magi could do to me. Why did I get so close to him? I'm an idiot!"

Siro was utterly in the dark and had no idea what Warren was rambling about. He always did this, talking about stuff he hadn't explained yet and expecting the other party to know exactly what he was mumbling about. He would have been annoyed if he wasn't so confused and worried about him. Siro moved beside him and took him by the shoulder. "Warren, you're going to have to explain it to me because I have no clue what you're saying." He said.

Without looking up at his friend Warren fumbled his hand around on the floor beside him, searching for the book he had taken from the library the night before. It wasn't very far away, already open, and he pulled it possessively into his lap. "Do you know why I've been constantly referencing information from a book called; 'sexual explorations through crypto-zoology; a gentleman's guide'?" He asked.

He hadn't actually known the title of the book until Warren had mentioned it. "Not really, no."

"Remember how I told you about how alraune can reproduce? How they capture humans of the opposite gender to themselves and try to transmute them so they can take their unique genetic material and produce offspring? Do you know how they do that? How they make captured humans *want* to have sex with them?"

"Warren, I-"

"The first few times Magi probably *was* raped. I can't see anybody being okay with that the first or second time around unless you were the author of this book or something." Warren laughed. "The rest of the time he probably *wanted* it. Begged for it." He glanced over at Magi who was watching them but not saying anything, as obedient as can be. "Isn't that right, Magi? You probably begged for the alraune to have its way with you, didn't you?"

Magi said nothing, but this was making Siro feel pretty damn apprehensive. He'd never heard Warren speaking like this before.

"Alraune are like succubi, that's why they have such a thorough chapter dedicated to them in this book. If you can get close enough to one to kiss it, or kill one to extract its saliva glands you'll end up in possession of a poison so valuable it is worth more than its weight in gold to chemists or alchemists. A poison, I need to add, I just got a really good taste of thanks to Magi's wandering tongue. I've been poisoned, Siro." The doctor explained.

A cold chill went through the blond swordsman. After all of Darren's worries about being bitten and infected and *Warren* had been the one to suffer it instead. A horrible, terrible notion came to him. "It's not deadly, right? Tell me it's not deadly." He couldn't lose Warren; he'd only just told him how he couldn't live without him.

Warren shook his head. "I won't *die*. You don't have to worry about that."

Siro let out a deep breath in relief. "Thank goodness."

"Alraune poison is a powerful aphrodisiac. That's why it's so sought-after. In a little while, I don't know when and I don't know for how long, but soon… I might not be myself." He laughed again, nervously. "I might go a bit crazy."

All the pieces of the puzzle Warren had been hinting about from the very beginning clicked together in Siro's mind. The alraune hadn't entirely been about killing and eating human flesh; she had also wanted to breed. It was a good thing they had stopped her before they would have to deal with a hundred, smaller monsterized Magis running about. That thought amused him, but then he remembered Warren's predicament. "You… you might… *huh.* Just how crazy are we talking about here?"

It was enough for Warren to be afraid of what was going to happen in the immediate future. The book made it sound pretty severe. He blushed. "I don't know. I just know that I need to get home to my clinic as soon as possible, before something happens that I'll regret. Maybe I can put together an antidote or something."

That sounded like a stretch. "Can you make it that far?"

"We'll just have to find out."

Despite Warren's desire to keep his affliction a secret Siro felt it would be bad leadership for him to tell his other two friends nothing, especially if Warren *did* freak out and he'd have to come up with an explanation for him very fast. When he and his lover brought Magi up to the mouth of the cavern and met with Darren and Ravendor Siro discreetly took them aside while Warren was making sure Magi was comfortable, an arm around each man in sort of a conspirator's huddle.

They had been waiting for this. You didn't just send your friends away after making an expression like *that* and expect everything to be alright. They might have been tired and injured, but they weren't stupid. "So, what is it?" Ravendor asked, speaking for himself and Darren. "What has Warren done to himself this time?"

Warren had a bit of a reputation for being both forgetful and clumsy. His skills as a doctor or healer were palpable, but he just tended to break things. Or clumsily hurt himself. On others he was delicate and sure handed; Siro couldn't understand why he wasn't able to use the same level of care on himself.

He'd had a bit of time to come up with a good explanation; he thought it sounded well all things considered. "Warren's been infected with the alraune's poison. He says it's not going to kill him, but it is going to make him pretty sick for a while. He didn't want to say anything to worry anybody, but I *have* to tell you both. It wouldn't be right otherwise." Siro explained.

Upon hearing this Ravendor sighed in a 'here we go' kind of fashion and Darren looked just as concerned as Siro expected him to be. The rogue kept getting out of danger by the very skin of his teeth and having other people take the punishment for him instead. "Is there anything we can do for him?" He asked, wanting to help.

"He says that if he can get to his clinic right away he might be able to figure something out." The mayor continued, finding the little white lie was getting a bit heavier the more he added to it. "I think what we need to do for him is just don't panic if he starts acting strange. That'll just panic him more and he'll know I broke my promise and told you two."

"Siro, this is ridiculous-" Ravendor began.

"I know it is, but think about it for a minute. He went through a lot treating Magi and now he's really scared. Please don't make it worse for him. All we have to do now is just get home." Okay, maybe it wasn't *entirely* a lie. It was more of an omission of facts. Of sorts.

Ravendor considered the proposition. There wasn't really anything he could do about it, but it didn't quite sit right with him. Frankly he was a little offended that Warren hadn't felt he could be trusted with the truth. "It will still be hours until we reach Adratea and the clinic, even if we rush. We cannot handle *two* people who cannot walk."

"He'll walk. He'll try his best."

"Um," Darren interrupted, "do you know what makes me feel a whole lot better when I'm really sick? A nice glass of warm milk."

The other two adventurers looked at him, one with incredulity. "Thank you for your input, Darren." Ravendor said, his voice dripping with sarcasm. "If we happen to come across some comfortably heated cows on the way back to the surface I will be certain to pull up a bucket and stool."

"I'm just saying." Darren replied, hurt.

"What are you all talking about?" Warren asked the rest of his companions, approaching from behind. At the moment he didn't sound sick at all, but the others knew that would change. He actually sounded pretty upbeat all things considered, but it could have been nothing more than a show. "I just checked on Magi. He's hurting but he's not being any trouble anymore. I think we should be able to move him long distances if we take turns carrying the stretcher."

His expression changed from optimism to suspicion when he watched Siro slowly remove his arms from the shoulders of the two men. "Er… am I interrupting anything?" He inquired, getting three different variations of 'no' as a response. Immediately he knew that Siro had told, but the fact that they weren't all laughing at him must have meant that he hadn't told *everything*. Damn it, Siro! He was just as bad as Mieus!

But the only thing he could really do in the end was just get on with it. Warren and Siro elected themselves as the first to carry Magi (Siro because he still felt relatively lively and Warren because he wanted to do all he could while he still had the wits to do so) and Ravendor and Darren followed beside them, acting as the forward guard if necessary. Magi was a lot lighter than they had expected. Well, he wasn't a particularly tall man but he was easy to carry. That was a relief.

Magi himself just lay there quietly in the stretcher, frequently slipping in and out of consciousness or sleep. When he was awake sometimes he would make pained noises, or cry a bit, but his teammates tried to ignore him. There wasn't anything else they could do for him until they were back in town, and *nobody* wanted to risk getting a dose of what Warren had just experienced.

And Warren, for his part, didn't begin to show symptoms of the alraune's poison until much later than he had expected. They were almost out of the Underwood entirely and had had a couple of encounters with hostile wildlife, but thankfully Darren had saved a few fire gems left over from the back-burning. They weren't hindered for very long.

At first Warren had thought he was feeling a little overheated from the rogue's zealous fires, but then he pressed a hand to his forehead and realized his temperature was up. It had begun. He wondered what was to come next. Warren looked down at Magi lying down in his stretcher, for now at peace and cursed him silently.

He had never been under an aphrodisiac before. He'd never really needed one, the right person at the right time had never failed to get his motor running and Warren was the kind of man with such a medical history that he wouldn't take drugs unless he needed it, so doing anything recreationally was out of the question. Maybe it was like being drunk? He could understand something like that. Like being drunk… only you wanted to bone everything in sight instead of expecting everyone to listen to you and needing a quiet alley to throw up in afterwards.

No, that wasn't right. It would probably be like the time when he was at his very horniest, let's be reasonable here. Warren tried to remember when that time had been, but found he couldn't quite decide. Had it been during his first time, the virginity taker? He decided not, the first time was rarely the best time, but the most memorable. It could have been the first time Mieus had taken her top off for him, or the first time he had been able to touch Siro, fully naked, not as his doctor but instead as his lover…

Warren suddenly realized that for the past five consecutive minutes he had been thinking about nothing but boobs and sex. He blamed the aphrodisiac, but also wondered if it was because he just wasn't getting enough of it lately. Though he and Siro had shared a bed the night before they hadn't done anything; Warren had been too tired. He sort of regretted it now, it wasn't often he got a chance to do it unrestricted in Siro's house, in Siro's own bed. The clinic kept him too busy, so late-night rendezvous were always held there and his own bed was kind of old and frankly kind of crappy.

Actually they hadn't done it in days. *Days*. Maybe even a week! Not a long time for your average person, he guessed, but he and Siro were freshly in love. You… expected things. Dirty things. Sometimes.

The doctor swallowed hard. His throat felt dry. Siro really was the best kind of person he ever could have hoped for. He was handsome, kind, cared about everybody equally and was just so sweet. There was also a great deal of strength in him too, a strength that Warren both admired and envied and yet it contained a core of vulnerability that he as his partner had only recently discovered. It could have been that vulnerability that had drawn him to him. He didn't know. It was a romantic thought nonetheless.

Ah, the last time they had done it. That was probably it. He'd been kind of drunk and Siro had been kind of drunk, just enough to take the awkward edge off and he'd had his face in the pillow to keep himself from making too much noise because for *some reason* everybody said he was far too noisy during sex even though he didn't know *why* there was a benchmark for that kind of thing. It had been *that* kind of experience, the sort of feel-good bliss where if you died in that very moment, that very second it would have been the best time to go. He had certainly been pleased that night. At least more than once.

"Siro…" Warren said quietly to the other man, wondering why he didn't feel more ashamed. He should be. "I think it's started now."

Siro couldn't turn around to look at him, he was carrying the other end of the stretcher behind him to keep from having to walk backwards and that sort of put him in a bad position for discussion. He looked serious. "Do you need to switch with somebody else?" He asked.

Warren thought about it. He didn't feel any weaker, just distracted. He stared unsteadily at Siro's broad back. "I'm alright for now."

"If you're sure."

They made some real progression after that point and Warren held on for as long as his arms would allow him. There were more interruptions, of course, Ravendor ended up having to exhaust his six-gun for a second time that day but nobody was seriously injured. The entire party was grateful for that most of all.

Time passed. Warren got worse. He started to feel uncomfortable in his clothes, his skin felt super sensitive and he couldn't stand the feeling of the cloth rubbing against him, it was both awful and yet felt so strangely good. It was also getting too hot in the dungeon, he wanted to take his shirt off, and he was pretty certain he was sweating a little more than was normal. The taste of Magi's kiss in his mouth didn't seem to want to go away either.

His breathing grew heavier as he wondered how much longer he could last. Would Siro spend the night with him tonight, especially when he was like… this? That might not be a good idea; it might be a little too much like being locked in a bedroom with a hungry lion. If he got the chance he might just eat his partner up. But *man* it would be so good to just grab him, slide his hand up Siro's shirt, feel those toned abs, kiss that neck…

Warren stopped walking. Because he was at the back of the party and carrying half of the stretcher this had the chain effect of forcing everybody else to stop as well. Everyone turned to look at him; the doctor couldn't help but blush. He was almost afraid that they could read his thoughts, and if they could do that what must they think of him? They would probably think he was a pervert. "Nngh." He said, as if that would explain everything.

As one the party paused. Siro was afraid Warren was about to lose it, while Darren and Ravendor were just worried that Warren was about to collapse or throw up on Magi or worse. Ravendor spoke first. "It may be a good idea to switch places. Can you put Magi down for a moment? Darren and I will take over."

"I don't feel right." Warren pleaded to his friends, but did as was told and put Magi down. Siro did the same.

They made the switch. Darren and Ravendor were as tired as well and not as strong as the two swordsmen were but they had to be fair; everybody had to do their part. Warren found himself walking unsteadily beside Siro, hoping for this march to end. He knew there was still a way to go, but he wasn't going to last. He just wasn't. At least he had his hands free now so he could properly fix his pants; make his problem not seem so… *obvious*.

Siro felt Warren take him by the hand, he was wearing gloves so he couldn't feel how hot and sweaty his palms were, but he still squeezed back nevertheless. Just touching him made Warren feel much better, but he wanted more. A lot more. It was bad enough that the alraune's aphrodisiac seemed to eat away at propriety; at shame.

He wasn't entirely surprised when Warren leaned closer to him in a conspiratorial way, so their friends couldn't hear him and whispered softly into his ear; "Siro… I want to fuck your brains out. Right now." He murmured.

A light blush tinted Siro's cheeks slightly pink as well. He tried not to react, but that wasn't the sort of thing that Warren told him every day. He was usually quite shy when it came to sex and dirty talk. "Uh…" He stammered back. "I don't think the others would like it that much."

"I can't stand it. You're right here and I'm like this and I… ugh…" He continued in a low voice, his hand moving from Siro's to the small of the swordsman's back, slipping just beneath the hem of his shirt. His skin was soft, smooth and *oh* so warm.

"Just think about something else. Think of the unsexiest thing in the world."

"I just- I can't-"

"Try it."

Warren groaned in impatience. He was having trouble thinking clearly at all, let alone on something unsexy or wrong. He found himself focusing on Darren. He was a skinny, weedy little thing, nervous and awkward. He was pretty young too, Warren wondered if he was still a virgin, and if not then what poor girl must have taken pity on him.

Well… maybe there was a kind of odd aesthetic to his weediness. He couldn't really describe why, but he was a rogue, he was pretty flexible. Warren had seen him do some amazing stunts since Darren had become a permanent addition to their party. In a way he was almost feminine, with his semi-long hair and thin hips. Put him in a dress; ignore the cock and maybe-

The brown-haired man made a strangled sound in his throat. What the hell was wrong with him? *At what point of mental breakdown was he in when he could imagine Darren in a dress and that idea sounded* ***good*** *to him?* He was surely losing his mind.

Okay. Okay. Try again. What about Ravendor? He had known the older man for forever. He was almost like a childhood friend, even though there was almost a decade of age between them. It'd be creepy. Beyond creepy actually, like doing it with your uncle. He was far too old, even if he *was* somewhat handsome in an older man kind of way. It could be because he had some experience on his side he might be better in bed, better than Darren anyway.

He didn't really know much about Ravendor's love life. Hadn't he said once that he was divorced? He briefly recalled something like that. There was an ex-wife out there somewhere, and probably a bunch of former girlfriends to boot. How would he react if Warren himself came onto him? Horror and ridicule, most likely. But maybe not…

Warren let out a small scream, paralyzing the caravan. He had almost traumatized himself and it *still* had not been enough to kill his raging boner, not enough to make him stop wondering what it would be like to sleep with his friends. While fiercely aware of himself Warren ran a hand through his sweaty hair. He feared his glasses would fog up so he took them off for now. “S-Sorry. Let’s keep moving.” He apologized bashfully.

“I guess it didn’t work.” Siro commented once they were on the move again.

“You’re trying to kill me.” Warren complained, leaning against the other man. It could have been a tired, loving gesture, but it also could have been an exhausted comrade being supported by another and not suspicious at all. “I imagined Darren in a dress.”

The other man couldn’t help but chuckle. “What kind of dress?”

“Have you ever read ‘Alice in Wonderland’? Something like that.” He didn’t know why he had thought of it, but it had been one of his favorite books as a child.

“There’s something wrong with you.”

“I know. I know.”

He took a risk, leaning over even further and kissing Siro gently behind the ear. He wanted to do more, *much* more, wanted to shove him against the dungeon wall and tear his clothes off and fuck him in front of everybody who cared to see and damn the consequences, but he didn’t. Not because he had willpower, if it had just been the four of them he *would* have, but because of Magi. It was all about Magi. They had to get him out of there safely, first.

Eventually they came to a large crossroads in the dungeon, somewhat of a hub area with different paths branching off into other sectors of the labyrinth. The Underwood they had been exploring was only a small part of it and it was a good place to take a break; there was even a signpost stuck into the ground at the crossroads pointing the way. Zagtakh had likely built it; it looked like his handiwork and shaky, harsh writing.

They had rested there earlier in the day on the way to rescue Magi and although they needed a break more than ever now to stop and catch their breath there wasn’t any time. Warren and Magi wouldn’t benefit from a break so Siro, Darren and Ravendor would just have to soldier on. They could rest when they were at home.

However, they had to stop all the same.

“Hey! Hey you guys!”

A familiar yet unexpected voice echoed throughout the dungeon. Somebody had been sitting down on a rock close to the crossroads and stood when he had seen the party approach, waving an arm in greeting.

His other hand had been on the hilt of his sword, in the chances that the people he was greeting were not people at all but monsters. He didn't have to worry.

"Reiyu?" Darren called, surprised.

Reiyu had not been present at the town meeting the night before, he had been absent; presumed camping out somewhere in the dungeon. The large satchel he was carrying on his back seemed to support this theory and he quickly jogged over to the party of men, interested in why they were carrying one of their own. He leant over the stretcher to study Magi, a little perplexed at how strange he looked now. "Yikes," he uttered, glancing at the rest of them, "what happened to him?"

"It is a long story." Ravendor said wearily.

"Yeah? I'm actually just on my way back to the inn, why don't I follow you and you can tell me all about it on the way? I haven't talked to anybody for a couple of days; it'd be nice to have some company." He smiled broadly, brightly; a winning smile and touched the sleeping Magi gently on the forehead in concern.

"Can we put the stretcher down for a second? My arms are getting tired." Darren complained, wanting to roll his shoulders more than anything in the world right now.

Ravendor could actually feel the rogue struggling with the stretcher and he acquiesced, lowering Magi carefully to the ground. Reiyu was a tenant at his inn, he knew him well enough and it was almost a bit of a relief to see a friendly face after so many hostile encounters. "I suppose a ten minute break would not be so unreasonable. I could do with a smoke."

Warren was initially horrified at that prospect, he felt like he was on his last legs as it was, but then an idea came to him in a wicked flash of dirty perversion. The normal, sensible Warren would never in a million years have thought about it but this Warren was sick, as desperate as Magi's kiss had been. He pressed himself suggestively against Siro, grinding his erection into him. The way the other man tensed against him made it pretty obvious he could feel it too.

"Tell everybody I'm sick and about to throw up." He whispered harshly and heavily into Siro's ear. "I can't take this anymore; *I need to fuck you now.* We'll duck out while Ravendor is talking."

Siro could hardly believe what he was hearing, but he could feel how warm Warren was. He was panting like a dog and Siro was almost afraid for him. "You're crazy, we can't do that." He pleaded.

"If you don't do what I say I'm going to start taking your clothes off in front of everybody." He hummed and Siro could hear exactly how serious he was. As if to convince him further Warren inconspicuously slid his hand down the other swordsman's pants and smiled. This wasn't like him but he didn't care anymore; didn't care about anything but this.

The rest of the party had sat down near the crossroads beside Magi, Ravendor and Reiyu were sitting together talking and Darren was a little off to the side, eating an apple he had managed to keep hidden until then. Magi was still asleep. Siro cleared his throat.

"Uh, Ravendor?"

The gunman glanced at him. He had barely begun the story, he hadn't even gotten up to the part when Darren was kidnapped yet and one of the things he hated most of all was being interrupted in the middle of a tale he could potentially embellish. Reiyu hadn't heard any of it yet and he was interested, so this was an open invitation for him. Besides, the other adventurer was too amusingly polite to complain about the smoke. "Yes? May I help you?" He asked graciously, a throwback from working at his inn.

Siro realized that while omitting some parts or bending the truth was a simple and easy process outright lying was a little beyond him. He had to try anyway; Warren's hand was already in a delicate place and his friend wasn't bluffing; he was too delirious to be bluffing. "Wa-Warren isn't feeling too well. I'm just going to take him down one of the tunnels for a few minutes so he can get some of the sickness out of his system. Is that alright?" That was the closest he could get without lying. It sounded close enough.

Reiyu was the one who answered him instead. "Is Warren sick? What's wrong with him?" He asked, curious.

"... Must have been something I put in my mouth..." Warren muttered unevenly to the rest of his party. He tried to look convincingly sick. It didn't take much effort; he was already thoroughly sick in the head.

They were already resting and for the moment Magi was in no pain. Ravendor didn't care, for now Warren was the one who needed to be worried about and if Siro wanted to do that for him he had no qualms with it. He breathed out a stream of smoke, prompting Reiyu to move a little ways away from him. "Take your time, Siro. We will wait for you." He said.

The smile Warren gave him was not innocent. It was almost a little scary.

"Thank you." He said.

Siro wasn't able to get Warren very far before he was attacked. He got him out of shouting distance at least, down a tunnel that led to another, unrelated section of the dungeon. He'd been down there before several times; it connected to some ruins he was quite fond of. He doubted Warren would last that far. The tunnel would have to do.

He helped to support his friend, an arm around his back, almost as if he really *was* sick and about to lose his lunch. He turned to him, like he was about to ask a question and before he knew it Siro was shoved against the rocky foundation of the tunnel, uneven rocks poking into his back and Warren was against him, lips against lips, clenched hands against unresisting wrists. He had never been kissed like this before.

For the first time since Siro had met him he felt Warren's true strength. He was always so gentle, so submissive that he had never realized his partner could totally overpower him; hold him steady, firm and unable to resist. He thought that maybe he should be afraid, Warren wasn't acting like himself and he could do anything, *anything* to him without much resistance, but, well… Warren was still Warren, even under the power of the aphrodisiac. He trusted him.

That was why Siro kissed back. He wasn't made of stone, seeing, feeling; sensing his lover so turned on and desperate for him did something to the swordsman as well, made him want to justify the other man's lust. Warren's mouth tasted a little strange but it was mild and didn't bother him that much. It was likely he was detecting the poison that had invigorated him. Would it pass over one more time? Would he go just as crazy as his friend had?

If so it was about to make what would come next a whole lot better. Warren pulled his hands away only for a second and went for Siro's clothes, went under them, touching and caressing the hard muscles he knew so well. He seemed to like what he found, breaking their kiss just long enough to breathe out his name; “Siro…”

There was so much desire in just that one word that it prompted Siro to push himself up from against the wall and wrap his arms around the doctor’s back, kissing Warren again on his own terms. Warren held him easily and Siro’s hands clenched a bit in the fabric of Warren’s shirt as he ground against him one more time, letting the obvious bulge in his pants be known.

“I’m really sorry about this… making you lie to the others…” Warren murmured breathlessly to him as he pressed his lips against Siro’s neck. He could feel a strong pulse beating there, Siro’s heart must be going hard and fast but whether it was from anxiety or arousal he didn’t know. His words were actually pretty empty, at the moment he didn’t give a damn about forcing Siro to lie to his friends, but he *needed* his lover to stay compliant; needed Siro to forgive him. He’d say anything. Sincerity could come later.

Siro was still a little apprehensive about Warren’s dirty plan for a quick fuck in the dungeon while nobody was looking. Sure he loved the guy, and under the right circumstances he’d gladly sleep with him any day of the week, but to do it like animals in heat in a cave somewhere in the middle of nowhere wasn’t loving at all. It didn’t have any real meaning behind it.

But he supposed there didn’t *have* to be any meaning. Warren was being manipulated by outside forces; it wasn’t like this was the doctor’s true idea of romance. If getting his rocks off would bring him back to some semblance of normality then it was worth doing just so long as the others didn’t find out. He was okay with *telling* people about their relationship, but being caught literally with his pants down was a different matter entirely.

The way his friend was touching him was making it harder to say no, and when Warren started to undo the buttons of his shirt to reveal Siro’s chest underneath he let out a small sigh of defeat. He couldn’t deny that this wasn’t turning him on as well. “You’re impossible.” He said, seemingly annoyed. “You know we can’t do this.”

Warren barely heard him; he was in too much of a daze to care about anything Siro was saying. Once he was done with the shirt he quickly moved onto Siro’s belt, working the buckle. Warren’s words were uneven, humoring him. "Sure we can. I'm going to lean against this wall right here and you are going to *fuck me so hard* that I won't be able to stand up anymore. That's what we're going to do. Or, if you prefer I could do it to you instead – I don't care. It's up to you."

"You don't have any idea what you're saying, do you?" Siro ventured, fiercely aware of how red his face was getting from being talked at in such a way but also somehow liking it as well. He wanted to be stern, he was trying to be, but it was just so difficult.

The other man laughed. "I know exactly what I'm saying. You're the sexiest fucking man in the world Siro and if I don't get you inside of me in the next few minutes this poison really *is* going to kill me dead. You don't understand… just how bad this is…"

Warren got the blond swordsman's belt undone and didn't waste a second to slide a hand in, grasping what he already knew to be there and waiting for him. He smirked in a perverse manner, but somewhere behind those grey eyes there was also tenderness. Love. "You don't understand how much this hurts."

Siro groaned as Warren gently squeezed him. Maybe he couldn't understand how he felt, not without having to make out with Magi himself, but if Warren was being honest with him then he had no other choice. It wouldn't be that bad. It wouldn't be *bad* at all. Why was he trying to resist it anyway?

Oh yeah. Common sense. They weren't in the least bit prepared and a quick ten minute break wasn't nearly enough time to satisfy his friend in the manner that he seemed to want it. If someone came looking for them it would be over. Siro's mind raced to think up an excuse, one that would make it through Warren's thick skull. "We, uh, don't have any lube…" He began.

Warren gave him a 'don't try to worm out of this' smile. It was almost condescending. "Siro, I'm a *doctor*. I usually have my hand up something or other on a bi-weekly basis. Do you think I don't carry some with me at all times?" He quipped, and then kissed him again.

He made a good point, and the tandem feel of being both kissed passionately and stroked by his lover just gnawed away at his resolve. He could feel himself weakening and when Warren pulled away all he could do was find himself murmuring; "… Well then, what about protection?"

He sensed the other man hesitate. Ah, so he had hit upon something there. Medical supplies were one thing, but bringing some condoms along to a dungeon crawl didn't seem nearly as normal unless Warren had been intending to use that monster sex guide sometime in the future. Siro almost smiled at that thought.

However, in the end all Warren did was just shake his head. "No, it's okay. I don't need it. I love you, Siro." He said.

Oh *come on.* Siro suddenly reached out and grabbed Warren by the shoulders. The brown-haired man let him, but he looked confused and above all impatient. He wasn't going to let Siro try to reason with him forever; it would cut too far into their precious sex time. They had wasted too many minutes already. If Siro wanted to get his way he would have to think and talk fast.

"Warren, *listen* to me for a second. Just a second." He ordered.

Even that was a tall order by this point. "Wh-what?"

"I'm not going to have sex with you here. We don't have time, not even for a quickie. Besides, if we do this I know you will end up regretting it. I know you too well, Warren. You'll guilt yourself for weeks, and I don't want that."

He knew Warren was going to resist him both physically and verbally and Siro had prepared himself for that. He held firm against him even as Warren growled in frustration and tried to shove him away. This wasn't what he wanted to hear; it hadn't been a part of his devious plan at all. Siro was supposed to love him; it had never even occurred to him that his partner might say no.

A dark, unwelcome thought entered Warren's aphrodisiac-addled mind. Just because Siro said no, it didn't mean he had to *listen.*

No, it didn't.

Poisoned or not Warren squashed that idea without a second thought. He was a little frightened of himself for even thinking about it in the first place. "But I," he whined, looking like he was about to cry, "I… can't go on like this…"

Siro nodded in understanding and smiled compassionately. He squeezed Warren's shoulders gently, guiding both of them with careful steps to the other side of the tunnel's wall. "I know. That's why I'm willing to compromise. If you let me do this one thing for you, and if it's enough to keep you sane until we get you back to your clinic… I'll let you do whatever you want to me for the rest of the night. I'll be all yours." He proposed, blushing as he said it. It felt a little too much like he was trying to sell himself to him.

At last it was Warren's turn to be utterly lost by what Siro was trying to tell him. "… I don't… what one thing?" He asked, and then felt his back touch the wall of the dungeon. The coldness of the stones seemed to quell the burning, raging heat in his body, but only for a moment.

The mayor of Adratea only managed to half-hide a look of brief shyness. He was a fully-grown man but it wasn't like he had been interested in other men for forever. Warren had actually been his first, and in many ways he was still pretty virginal in the whole bisexuality thing. It didn't mean he wasn't curious, though. "Here, I'll show you…" He said softly, dropping down to his knees.

When Siro went to loosen his belt Warren finally got the hint. *Oh.* That. He could definitely get behind something like that. It wouldn't be as good as clinging to the dungeon's wall and moaning like a whore as his partner railed him as rough and hard as humanly possible (he felt his cock twitch in his pants just thinking about that) but it was better than being left entirely in the cold. He relaxed, sagging against the stones.

Warren obligingly pulled his shirt up a little for him and dropped his pants down to his knees. He felt kind of vulnerable leaning against the wall like that, exposed, but the very sight and concept of having Siro between his legs and willing to service him was more than enough to make up for it. It was actually pretty fucking hot the more and more he thought about it.

"You weren't kidding about later tonight, right? You'll stay with me?" He asked just as Siro began to tug down the waistband of his briefs. Maybe if he had something to look forward to he could fight the poison to the very end.

Siro paused in the process of getting his friend's cock free. Warren was… evenly proportionate and he had never done this before. It was a little scary, but the swordsman smiled up at him anyway. There was a first time for everything. "I promise. I won't leave you until you return to normal."

Warren swallowed hard as he felt his lover's breath gently caress his rigid member. Aah, even that felt good. "Okay. Th-thanks."

"Just do me a favor and don't make too much noise. I know you do that."

"Uh…"

"Because if somebody comes running and finds us you are going to have a lot of explaining to do. I'll have my mouth full." Was that a joke? It had sounded like a joke.

Warren laughed, trying to resist the urge to take him by the chin and just shove it in. That wouldn't be so courteous, especially after Siro was being so patient with him. "Just fucking hurry up, Siro. Please." He begged.

The aphrodisiac was certainly doing its job, just by touching him Siro could tell that he was *ready*, a thin dribble of pre-come already beginning to drip down the shaft. He supposed it was a bonus that Warren wasn't going to last very long, so maybe that way they could finish up and return to the others with a few minutes to spare. He leaned forward.

Warren let out a low moan as he felt tongue, felt Siro clean off that drip like a cat that had just gotten the first drop of the cream. He had to physically stop himself from just thrusting his hips at him, he had to just let Siro do what he liked and then maybe he would keep his promise to him. Warren heard his own moan echo in the tunnel and he slapped a hand over his mouth. Can't be too noisy; had to have willpower. Just have to *feel.*

He made a small noise around his fingers anyway as Siro engulfed him with his mouth. *God* that felt so good, so warm and wet almost like a pussy, only Siro with his mouth full and his eyes closed was a lot more attractive to look at. The blond swordsman reached up with a hand and grasped Warren by the side of his hip, to hold him steady, while the other hand carefully held the base of his shaft, squeezing gently as he worked.

Siro had thought that this would be a little more difficult than it actually was, but from the sounds Warren was making above him he guessed he was doing a good job of it. He had worried that he might choke, but if he breathed steadily it would be okay; like the breathing exercises he had learned when first starting out on the path of the sword. Perhaps it was a bit uncomfortable but if it made his friend feel better it was worth it. He would suck out all the poison himself.

He felt the palm of Warren's hand hover at the nape of his neck for a few seconds, detecting it through the hackles that were automatically raised when he was either alert or aroused. It pressed and Siro thought for a moment that Warren was trying to guide him, but no. He just wanted to touch him in any way that he could. His fingers entwined in Siro's short hair. He sighed.

"Oh god, Siro…" Warren groaned, but it also sounded strangely like a sob. "I don't deserve you…"

He was too busy to answer, and beyond that he didn't want to lose his focus. Siro knew that this would feel good for anybody, Warren and a couple of old girlfriends had done this for him before, but he hadn't quite expected that sucking cock and feeling his lover's pulse all the way down to the root would turn him on so much as well. He could feel his own cock straining angrily at the front of his pants, demanding to be released. Perhaps he should do this more often. He might develop a taste for it.

Siro found that one of his hands had unconsciously snuck to the front of his pants, rubbing himself through the fabric as he hungrily bobbed his head against Warren's crotch. He stopped as soon as he realized he was doing it, if he wanted to have any energy for the night ahead he would just have to keep it in his pants until then. He wasn't infected; he could wait… even if it ached like a bitch to do so.

Warren didn't have that liberty and it sounded like he had given up trying to be quiet. He was gasping and trembling all the way to his toes, his cock throbbing halfway down Siro's throat and not far off from the end. He could tell.

"I, ngh… I think I'm gonna come…" He warned, a bead of sweat running down his just slightly stubbly chin. He didn't know how Siro wanted it so he felt it safer to simply tell him, in order to be sure.

Siro pulled away just long enough to get a few words in edgeways. His voice had roughened somewhat, his eyes half-lidded with lust. "Then come." He suggested, though a part of him now wished he had taken Warren up on his offer earlier. Bending him up against the wall was sounding more and more appetizing as time went on…

But he wouldn't get that chance. Warren was too obedient. He felt his lover jerk suddenly, felt his balls contract and he only had about a second to prepare himself before he was choking on a flood of semen that poured down his throat, more than what he had been expecting. He swallowed most of it, completely on reflex, but he also pulled away at the same time in surprise and some of it ran out of his mouth. The rest was spattered on his face and chin.

He began to cough, bringing his hands to his face and then realizing that they came back sticky. Siro was perplexed for a moment until he realized what had just happened. His mouth tasted bitter, but not from something as alarming as the alraune's poison; just from his friend's seed. The swordsman glanced up at Warren, wiping his mouth and panting. It didn't just look like the other man had come; it looked like someone had slapped him at the same time. He wondered if Warren was okay.

"Damn it," Siro muttered, still breathing a little hard, "you missed. It's everywhere." It was a bit of an overstatement, but Siro was wearing dark clothes and he feared they would show. He didn't really care about staining a single set of clothes but come-stains on his collar would be quite difficult to explain to his friends.

He heard Warren whisper faintly; "Sorry. Couldn't help it."

Truth be told Siro could hardly believe he had just done that; it hadn't really been on his list of things to do that day. He thought it should have been demeaning… but he had liked it, a little.

He didn't move away when Warren eventually pulled himself out of his post-orgasm high and fixed his pants, then he crouched down to kneel beside his friend. Siro looked so adorable like that, as if he had no idea what had just happened to him. The doctor reached for a clean handkerchief he kept in his pocket.

"I'm such a bastard. I'm so sorry." He apologized bashfully, but instead of offering it to him he instead took Siro by the chin and did it himself, like a parent cleaning up a grubby child. The mayor allowed him to do this for only a few seconds or so before he got impatient and grabbed the cloth from Warren, showing that he needed no help.

"No, it's alright. You don't have anything to be sorry for." Siro reassured him from behind the handkerchief. When he pulled it away he was smiling. "I said I would take care of you. How are you feeling now? Not so crazy?"

The fact that Warren was able to pause to consider this was in itself a good sign. Beforehand he might have just wanted to hump him silly, but the blowjob had taken the edge off. It hadn't cured him, but it had helped. He could still taste the poison, and for as long as he did he guessed he was trapped under Magi's spell. "I feel like… like you just blew my mind a little, Siro." He explained and then felt the embarrassment and shame rush to catch up with him. Warren looked away. "I'm sorry I said all those nasty things. Usually I'm not like that."

Nasty things? Oh, he must have meant the swearing. It would probably blow the young doctor's own mind to learn that hearing him say all those nasty things had excited him almost as much as the kisses had. Siro shook his head and stood. His friend followed him. "I understand. Do you think you can make it back to the surface without jumping all over me now?"

He still was all hot and bothered and continued to feel pretty horny for a man who had just shot a load onto his lover's face, but it also kind of felt like he had been rolled back to an earlier time, back to before the only thought in his head would be what it would feel like to be at home and fucking the only man that really mattered to him in the world. That sanity might melt away soon enough, just as it had before, but until then Siro and his comrades were safe.

Warren stepped forward and embraced him, not out of lust but of love and gratitude. He was pleased when Siro hugged him back. "The stuff you said earlier, it still... uh, stands?"

If anything it was standing even firmer than before. Warren might have been feeling a bit better but Siro was now suffering from a mild case of frustration. It'd go away in a while, it would aggravate him, but he had hoped they'd be able to resume later. "It does. I always keep my promises." He reassured him.

Warren grinned. He was just like a mule with a carrot to follow. "Well in that case I'll try my best."

It felt like it had been a little longer than ten minutes, but nobody had really been counting that hard. Ravendor had given Reiyu a condensed version of their adventure in the Underwood, barring some smaller details that he didn't quite feel like going into (like Magi being raped, stupidly letting the alraune go free, that sort of thing). He couldn't get technical, Warren was their guy for that with his curious little book, but Ravendor felt that he had covered everything as well as he was able.

Unfortunately Reiyu seemed more interested in the technical aspects than anything else. The adventurer was lying down on the rock he had been sitting on earlier, knees bent, back straight against the cold stone. It was comfortable and a good way to avoid the cigarette smoke from his friend. "So you're saying Magi started to *grow* vines? Like that monster? Like a... a pot plant?" He asked, raising his arms to nobody in particular.

Ravendor nodded. "I found it quite disconcerting myself. It was not what I had been expecting when Warren told us to prepare for the worst."

"They were really strong vines too." Darren chimed in from not that far away, sitting by the still-sleeping Magi. He rubbed at the sore spot around his throat. Being strangled twice in two days must be a new Adratean record or something. "I didn't think I was going to make it."

Reiyu shook his head in regret. "I wish I could have been there. That would have been something to see." And probably more exciting than what he had been doing at the time, which if he synched it up correctly was sometime just before lunch; frying eggs at his last campsite.

The eldest member of their party leant forward a bit from where he was sitting and peered down the tunnel Siro had dragged Warren into. He knew he wouldn't see or hear anything, but he was getting a little impatient. "Just how much longer do those two need? Surely Warren cannot be *that* sick." He complained.

"I dunno, just how much bile can he hold in his stomach?" Reiyu speculated, smirking.

Ravendor looked back at the other man. He half-smiled. "You would be surprised." He'd been out drinking many times with Warren before, mostly because Magi for some reason rarely touched the stuff. He didn't quite understand why.

"Hey," Reiyu asked, having another question for the party, "I just had a thought. If Warren is sick and too busy puking his guts up in order to do his job properly, who is going to take care of Magi once you guys get back to town? It doesn't look like he's going to be up and about any time soon." He didn't like to bring up such a problem but he wasn't sure if the others had considered this.

Darren and Ravendor hadn't, really. It was a rather sobering thought. Ravendor had just assumed that they'd be able to dump Magi into Warren's hands and have the doctor look after him for a couple of days at his clinic, but exactly how long did alraune poison last? The sick couldn't effectively tend to the even sicker; he hoped that when Warren returned he'd do so as a healthier person. Maybe if he threw up enough it'd purge the poison from his system.

When it came down to it they had no idea what level of care Magi was going to need. But he needed help; there was no doubt about that. Darren shifted uncomfortably in his seat. He lived in the boarding room right next door to Magi. He hoped it didn't have to be him. The rogue liked Magi, but he didn't want to have to risk changing his bandages or something and getting bitten for a second time. "It might be okay." He reassured them hopefully, with no real basis for his optimism.

Reiyu was Magi's other neighbor so he guessed he wasn't entirely free either. In any case he had just sort of wandered into the Underwood exploration team's problems, it didn't mean he was responsible for them, but he still kind of wanted to help. He liked to think that were he in that stretcher instead of the young archer at least one person would volunteer to help. "Warren really needs to hire a nurse." He said noncommittally. It was slightly odd that he didn't have one already.

"I'll do it."

Darren and Reiyu turned to look at Ravendor. "Er, what?" Reiyu said.

It took Ravendor a moment for him to realize what they were so confused about. He scowled. "What? No, not *that.* Idiots. I mean that I will care for Magi if Warren is unable to do so himself. This whole affair is partially my fault; I did not do a good enough job protecting him. It is the least I could do."

That was pretty unexpected. For the most part Ravendor rarely volunteered himself for anything unless there was something he could get out of the deal or there was somebody else more qualified to replace him. The other two hadn't entirely realized he cared about Magi that much. Still, the dark-haired man appeared serious about it. Reiyu seemed relieved. "I'm sure he'll thank you once he's well enough to speak again." He predicted.

"We shall see." Even though he had volunteered he wasn't exactly thrilled with the idea. He was injured too; what he wanted to do most of all was just go home and sleep off all of the aches and pains he was experiencing. He wouldn't be able to do that if Warren couldn't take Magi, but apart from Warren he didn't quite trust anybody else.

After all, Magi didn't really have anybody else in town to rely on. There was Mara, of course, and he was certain she was going to try and help him whether he liked it or not, but apart from that it was just him. He kept to himself a lot and it didn't seem like he had any family. He never received any letters from outside of town and Ravendor realized that he had no idea where Magi had come from. He wasn't one to pry, that was his own personal business, but it was curious.

Maybe he was just getting older and that instinct to parent some lost kid was taking over. Who knew?

While Ravendor was pondering this Reiyu reached around to his side and fished a small metal thermos out of his satchel. It was just something from his lunch earlier but it was still warm enough to be palatable, barely. Darren perked up immediately when he saw it. "Is… is that?" He murmured.

Reiyu unscrewed the lid. "Coffee? Yeah. It's black though, I didn't have any milk."

"Can I have some? I'm so tired."

Poor Darren. Reiyu smiled and got up, moving over to him and offering the flask. "Sure. Careful, it's pretty strong. Here you go."

It was at that 'meh' heat just before it would turn lukewarm, but Darren needed a pick-me-up quite badly and would try anything. He didn't drink coffee but it couldn't be that bad, could it?

He got about one or two mouthfuls down before the taste hit him and he recoiled, gagging on its bitter acidity. It tasted awful, and though this must be making him seem like an even bigger wuss than normal he didn't think he could get any more down. Darren coughed and grimaced, holding the thermos at an arm's length towards Reiyu and wiped at his mouth with the back of his wrist. "Th-thanks." He managed to say roughly.

It was the sight of him trying to be so nonchalant about it that almost made Reiyu laugh. He had a nearly full waterskin as well and thought about offering it to the rogue, but he didn't. The kind of coffee he liked really was something of an acquired taste, he guessed. He took the flask back and bagged it, then looked away down the pathway into the deeper dungeon. "But you know, it *has* been a while since Siro and Warren left. Maybe I should go and see if I can find them." He mused out loud. There was always the chance monsters could have ambushed them and the rest of their party would never know.

Ravendor wasn't paying attention to him now; instead he was looking at Magi. "He has been unconscious for some time. It does not seem natural." He said, as if in the middle of a conversation he had started by himself. It was probably just a stream of thought that had become external and he hadn't realized it yet. It had been at least an hour or two and in the very nature of moving him they hadn't been that gentle. It was best that Magi wasn't awake and in pain, he guessed, but it still worried him a little. What if he didn't wake up?

Reiyu took being ignored in stride. He turned back to Darren instead who was still trying to get the acidic taste of the coffee out of his mouth. "Well, what do you think?" He asked.

Darren seemed surprised that somebody was asking his opinion on something. It didn't happen often. "To be honest I think they're probably safer than we are right now. Siro is pretty tough." At least those two were still up and moving around. Darren wasn't certain if his legs were going to listen to him when he tried to stand later on.

The whole thing became a moot point anyway because not long after that the others came back. Warren was walking unassisted this time and he seemed a lot more balanced than before; a lot less flushed and feverish. Siro was with him and neither of them appeared like they had been harmed, though Reiyu casually noted that Siro looked a little embarrassed for some reason. His face was kind of red. The young adventurer never did realize that he was mistaking sexual frustration for embarrassment. Some things he was probably better off not knowing about.

"We're sorry we're so late!" Warren exclaimed as they rejoined the others. "You weren't waiting for too long, were you?"

"Are you feeling better?" Ravendor asked, though his mind was still on Magi.

The doctor smiled oddly, like he was enjoying something of a private joke. It was good to see the others had been too tired or too lazy to check on them. Maybe they could have had that quickie after all. Oh well. "You could say that. I think I'll be fine until I get home now. I, uh, I know Siro told you guys about it. I'm not a dummy you know." He didn't look unhappy about them knowing about his sickness, he was just relieved that he was feeling a little more like himself again. Besides, they still thought he had simple stomach troubles, *not* spontaneous sex problems.

"It's strange to think that a human can become poisonous." Reiyu commented off to the side, one hand shoved in his pocket. He wondered if there was any practical application for that in combat, or if Magi would just be limited to biting or kissing people. It wasn't the most glamorous ability to develop, he supposed.

But the truth was he was more dangerous now than he ever was before. Warren couldn't even imagine the sort of trouble Magi could cause with a kiss like that. One simple mouth-to-mouth dose and he had been on the very verge of *wanting* to rape Siro. If that ability lingered with him, stuck by him like the scars he was inevitably going to develop there was no telling how hazardous Magi may become. In his own professional opinion Warren was pretty sure his poison would atrophy and fade with time, but he couldn't be one hundred percent certain.

Best to keep his distance and stay quiet, so such a thing would never happen again.

"Um, Siro?" Darren interrupted, addressing the blond swordsman. He had a slight smile on his face.

"Yes?"

He watched Darren point to the lapel of his grey jacket, drawing attention to the front of Siro's own shirt, just below the clasp of his cape. "Your collar. You might want to fix that." He said softly, so the others couldn't hear.

What did he mea- Oh god. *Oh god.* He thought he had cleaned himself up thoroughly. Surely he hadn't left a painfully obvious stain on his clothes? Why hadn't Warren warned him about it earlier? Siro went a shade whiter than usual. "My… you mean…" He began, moving a gloved hand up to grasp at his neck self-consciously.

This confused Darren more than anything else. The mayor of Adratea had reacted as if he had told him his mother had just died. The rogue smiled at him in perplexed placation. "It's alright; I do that sometimes when I'm still half-asleep." He said.

*What in the hell was he talking about?* Siro touched his collar and finally understood. He relaxed, sighing. He didn't have semen on his clothes; he had just done the last few buttons of his shirt up incorrectly. He had redressed himself too quickly to notice it earlier. "Oh. Thank you Darren." He said to the youth and fixed himself up hastily before anyone else could take notice.

Now that they were all back together again Ravendor wasted no more time. It was kind of dark in the dungeon so he had been having trouble reading his watch, but he was pretty sure it was already well into the afternoon by now. He rose, stubbing out his cigarette and heading back to the stretcher. He felt that he could carry Magi the rest of the way to the surface provided somebody switched out with Darren. "We should get moving again." He suggested, his words just shy of an order.

It wasn't far to the surface now, maybe one more hour or so. Reiyu was happy to carry Magi, he had had a good night's sleep camping in the dungeon and compared to the others he was perfectly refreshed. Siro, Warren and Darren could just go ahead of them, so they did. It was unlikely they'd be attacked now in such a large group, especially so close to the entrance of the dungeon. All they really had to worry about from then on was the terrain.

It got a little tougher the closer they drew to the upper world. This was generally because a huge earthquake had unearthed the dungeon in the first place; splitting the side of the mountain right open into the caverns below. The dungeon refined itself as it went down and branched out into the stone. Before daylight and warmth and open air there was rubble and jagged stones. It took some time to get through it, even longer than usual with the stretcher to consider and all.

While they were walking Warren could feel the alraune's toxin slowly reverting him back to the way he had felt before Siro had 'fixed' him. It wasn't as bad this time but it *was* persistent, but this time he knew what to expect; he wouldn't let it sneak up on him unexpectedly like before. He kept his distance and stayed far at the back of the party, even away from Siro. Staying near the swordsman would only tempt him, and he had Siro's promise to consider after all. He would be okay. Warren bit his lip. It wouldn't be far now.

And then, at last, eventually…
Sunlight.

The heat struck them first. It was summer but it had been cool in the caves and it took a bit of time to adjust to the temperature and the change in the light. Darren found himself squinting, holding an arm across his face to block out the sun. "Nugh." He said, almost bumping into Siro walking in front of him.

Siro closed his eyes and took in a deep, relaxing breath. "Ah, the fresh air smells so good."

"What should we do now?" Reiyu asked, looking ahead to the others.

"The clinic is a lot closer than the inn. We should head there first. I'm sure Warren is eager to get home too." Siro explained, turning to his friend in question. The doctor didn't seem too good, flushed and anxious again, but he was still standing. The mayor's smile contained only the very slightest trace of something a little more devious than normal. He hadn't really been in the mood earlier. He kind of was now. "Right, Warren?"

He glanced up in reaction to the mention of his name. He had been off in his own little world, probably thinking perverted thoughts again. "Huh? Oh, sure. Yeah." He agreed, not really knowing what the question had been.

The sudden sunlight had not only jarred the human members of the Underwood exploration party; it did something strange to their recovered comrade as well. It could have been a combination of effects, the warmth or the light, but it seemed to knock Magi directly out of his sickly state of unconsciousness. He sat up in the stretcher while the others were carrying him, disoriented and eyes burning from the sun.

As a rule alraune typically weren't used to direct sunlight. They were a cave-dwelling species and while light would certainly help them to grow at a much faster and stronger rate, going from a dark cavern to the middle of summer was a little much. Magi's vision had been readjusted for low-light; he was temporarily blinded for a few moments and he whimpered in pain. But this… this was… he had been here before, hadn't he? He had known of a place before that wasn't just darkness and water and earth.

Oh *gods* his arms hurt.

Water. That was it. When had been the last time he'd... but he couldn't remember. He had a dreamlike memory of being desperate for it though, so very desperate that he'd been willing to whore himself out for a chance to slake his dire thirst.

Magi's stomach cramped abruptly. He made a pained noise in the back of his throat and hugged himself as if to push the tightening dehydration back, but that only put pressure on the bandages of his arms and he sobbed at that as well, knowing that it hurt but not really understanding why.

His friends stopped and set him back down in a hurry. They were on the outskirts of town by this point and *so* close to home, but Magi doing anything more than just lying there crying was definite progress. Most of the party was nervous of this, save for Reiyu who brightened considerably and smiled. "Hey, he's awake! I told you he was going to be fine." He announced.

Actually he wasn't fine at all. He felt like he was dying, but his throat was a desert and he didn't know what these creatures wanted from him. Magi found himself focusing on Reiyu kneeling before him with that dumb grin on his face, hands on his knees. Human... humans were full of fluid, weren't they? Blood and other things. He'd take anything.

*Protect yourself, you are dying.*

Several things happened at once and each member of the party reacted in a different way. Warren just stood there, dazed. He was far too out of it to do anything but stare. Darren startled but couldn't do anything in time, and Siro was too far away. Ravendor made to grab Magi as he tried to lunge forward at Reiyu, but his grip wasn't that good on the archer's bare shoulder and his hand slipped.

He leaned forward, diving at Reiyu and got through. The young adventurer reacted too late, flinching and recoiling backwards. His smile became a look of shock.

Magi didn't attack him. Not directly, anyway. He would have gone for the throat normally, naturally, the jugular, but at the very last second before his instincts could take over one fuzzy, almost human thought popped into his head. He recognized the small leather pouch Reiyu was carrying under one arm; it was a familiar shape to any traveler worth his salt. A waterskin; and it was nearly full, too. He grabbed at it wildly, not even bothering to ask for permission first; not that he could.

He wrenched at the carrying strap around Reiyu's shoulder and rather than let the other man drag him down with him Reiyu gasped in surprise and let him take it, twisting his arm to let the leather pouch come free. Magi didn't waste any time. He uncorked the waterskin and drank deeply for the first time in what felt like forever, the coolest and most satisfying drink of water he had ever had in his entire life. It felt like he could easily drink a gallon of the stuff, but there wasn't enough for that. When he was done and the waterskin was empty he flopped back down onto the stretcher, exhausted.

Warren slowly approached the others. His laugh was a little unbalanced, a little weird, but he did seem optimistic about what had just happened despite Reiyu's encounter. "I guess he was thirsty."

Reiyu stared at Warren and then at Magi. "I thought he was gonna tear my throat out. I could practically read it in his eyes." He breathed.

"No, this is actually a really good thing. If he's taking in water normally that must mean his organs are functioning properly, like a human's would. Otherwise he would just try to absorb water through the ground with his vines, like I'm sure he was doing before we found him. He doesn't have them any more so he might have no choice but to return to normal." Warren clarified. It was hard to explain and mostly just speculation but it was the best he could do while his thoughts kept getting interrupted by dirty daydreams of riding Siro like a pony.

The fact that Magi had also chosen a more calculated, non-violent option instead of just attacking was also an encouraging sight. If he could recognize what a waterskin looked like and what it contained maybe he could remember faces, or names. Maybe he would speak again, eventually.

They took Magi to the entrance of Warren's clinic, but didn't go inside. The Guildhouse was open and not very far away down the road, they had passed it on the way, but the streets of Adratea were quiet in the summer heat and nobody seemed to be around. It was better that way; there would be less nosy onlookers to bother them. All of them just wanted to get home.

And as for Warren he was home already, but he had a dilemma. It wasn't helped much that he could barely think straight; think sensibly.

Should he take Magi into the clinic with him or shouldn't he? Magi seemed to be getting better, bit by tiny bit. Maybe he would heal faster resting in his own bed at home. He could make a thorough examination of him in the morning, after he (both of them) had had time to heal. The bandages wouldn't have to be changed until the next day, too. That was reasonable, yes?

Hell no. It was selfish. He couldn't lie to himself, he knew he wanted the clinic nice and quiet and closed tonight so he could fuck Siro like crazy all night long without interruption. If Magi were there he'd have to keep checking on him or he might forget about it and *that* would be gross negligence and he didn't think he could focus on being a doctor any more that day; he had already done more than enough. He was sick. He was poisoned. He was a selfish prick. He could accept that.

But he *needed* to be, needed this just this once. If the others only could have kissed Magi too he was sure they'd understand.

Warren finally removed the heavy supply bag from his back. It was a huge relief. He gave the others a sheepish smile, pushing open the door to his home. "Well, I guess I'd better hurry and get started on that antidote." He lied, feeling like he was just simply bailing on them but not knowing what else to do.

He expected them to protest, and they did. Ravendor looked at Warren disapprovingly. He had been afraid of something like this; the brown-haired physician had been acting funny all afternoon. "You are not going to admit Magi?" He asked. He knew what that meant and wasn't really looking forward to it, but he had given his word. He couldn't go back on it now.

Regardless of his aphrodisiac-fuelled conviction Warren felt a twinge of guilt. It felt like he was going back on everything he had sworn to be when he had first chosen to become a doctor for something so trivial like… like sex. Even if he knew it was going to be *amazing* sex. He sighed, a little disappointed in himself. "I think what Magi needs most of all is time and plenty of bed rest. We really won't be able to tell if the alraune's influence is wearing off until some time has passed. Besides, he seems to be pretty stable right now. Do the rooms at your inn have locks, Ravendor?"

That was an odd question to ask. At first he didn't quite understand why Warren would ask that. "Of course they do. I cannot just have people wandering into the rooms taking things." He replied. It sounded like he might have had problems with something like that before.

"Do you have a master key, or at least a copy of Magi's key?"

He was the innkeeper. It was kind of a stupid question. "I do indeed."

That would make things a little safer for everyone involved, possibly even safer than if Warren had chosen to keep Magi at the clinic. The beds in the ward weren't separated by rooms, there would be no telling what Magi could get up to if left unsupervised, and there were a *lot* of dangerous instruments not under lock and key. "Put him to bed tonight and lock him inside his room. Be sure to check up on him a few times in the night just to be safe. You should be the one doing this Ravendor because you have a concussion and I don't want you sleeping for long periods of time either."

That way they could take care of each other. Warren was a little proud of thinking of it while in his state. Ravendor on the other hand didn't seem too happy, but Warren was the doctor and at least in this particular area he would have to do what the younger man said. It looked like he was going to have to play nurse after all. "Very well, if you are sure. I will come get you tomorrow morning regardless of if you are recovered or not."

Warren nodded. "That sounds good to me."

"And if Magi takes a turn for the worse in the night I will break in and wake you up. I don't care how sick you are." He added after a moment of thought.

The doctor chuckled nervously. That didn't sound quite as good. "Er, okay."

Siro cleared his throat. His home was on the way to the inn but he knew that Warren would kill him if he decided to leave. He didn't want to leave; he just wasn't sure how he was going to justify staying at the clinic when Warren wouldn't even take *Magi*. He'd been hanging around Warren a lot, it must be looking pretty suspicious to the others, or maybe he was seeing into things that just weren't there. "Warren is sick too. Maybe I should stay and make sure nothing bad happens to him." He suggested to the others.

"You don't have to do that…" Warren demurred, holding onto the doorframe with one hand to keep himself steady. It was another lie, Siro knew that he was counting on it; on him.

"You're not going to be busy?" Darren asked after not really saying anything for quite some time. He didn't really have much to say, he was too tired. To be honest he was beginning to wonder whether it would be worth it to stop by BW's place and see if she was home. Probably not, with his luck she'd most likely still be asleep.

Self-consciously Siro rubbed the back of his neck. "I'm sure there's a lot of work waiting for me at home and Mina might not like me shirking my duty for so long but Warren is a good friend. I'd feel bad if I don't help him, he's helped me out before countless times." In more ways than one.

So the party was breaking. It was finally over. It'd probably be a while until they banded up again, especially after an adventure like *that*. Warren took Siro by the arm and pulled him possessively into the threshold with him, almost a little too roughly for comfort. Now it just looked like he wanted them to leave. "Goodnight then. I'm sure everything will be okay. Just take care of yourselves and especially Magi."

"But what if Magi-"

"See you!"

"But-"

"*Goodnight!*"

Darren, Reiyu and Ravendor abruptly had the door slammed in their faces. They all wore the exact same expression; utter bafflement. That wasn't very polite but Warren had his reasons, they guessed.

"Uh..." Reiyu began, but didn't really know what to say. "So who's going to help me with the stretcher now?" It'd be the last leg before they could stop entirely. He was looking forward to it.

"I got it." Darren volunteered. His arms were feeling better now after such a break and he had more motivation now that they were closer to home.

As the three men turned to leave the clinic they were too occupied with themselves and their charge to hear the subtle wooden sound of someone being shoved against the door inside.

It didn't matter. Warren didn't need to make an antidote. He already had one right there, and Siro was a medicine he could *definitely* swallow without complaint. He'd take him until he was healthy again.

They had all night, after all.

They decided to take the roundabout, back-streets way through Adratea to reach the inn, avoiding the main road and anybody who could be wandering between. It took a little longer to get there because of this, but it also spared them the problem of being delayed by townsfolk while carrying an injured man through the village. They weren't hindered, luckily, and as eastern and then central Adratea parted way for the more familiar west Adratea the three men knew they were finally home.

The inn was empty, as was to be expected. Apart from the more permanent boarders who lived there they hadn't had any casual guests for quite some time. They tended to come, all gung-ho and eager for adventure and then the dungeon would simply eat them. Lots of people had disappeared, despite the warnings. It was one of the reasons why Ravendor would only accept payment for lodgings up front and nothing else.

Ravendor went over to the tag board near the entrance and flipped four of the nametags from 'out' to 'in', an easy way for people visiting the inn to know who was at home and who wasn't without having to knock on doors or ask. As he did this Fortinbras came barreling down the stairs, hearing with his acute doggy senses that somebody had at last shown up. He hadn't been fed all *day*, and he was lonely.

But he was a good dog and had been trained not to jump up on people carrying something like, say, a stretcher. A person without anything in his hands was fair game, however. He decided to jump up on Ravendor instead, but the older man had been expecting that and caught the huge afghan before he could knock him over. Fortinbras whined happily and tried to lick his face, but Ravendor wouldn't let him. He kind of hated that.

He knelt and patted the animal on the head instead. He wasn't particularly fond of dogs, but it was nice coming home to something that actually looked forward to seeing you there. While Fortinbras wagged his curly tail at him Ravendor searched his pockets for his master key. "Why don't you two take Magi up to his room while I feed Fortinbras and check my messages? I will only be a few minutes."

He found his key and tucked it into the pocket of Darren's jacket, as the rogue didn't have his hands free to accept it normally. He guessed he could have just given the key to Magi, who was still awake and not holding anything, but he might not relinquish the key when they tried to take it off him later.

"Alright, we can do that." Darren said. He hadn't ever been in Magi's room before. He wondered what it looked like. Magi seemed like the kind of person who collected hunting trophies or something.

"Once you are done you may leave him up there and do what you wish. I will take care of him from here." Ravendor instructed. He hesitated in front of Reiyu and Darren, as if he wasn't sure if he should continue or not. He did anyway, sincerely. "Thank you both for your assistance today. I have seen many people lost to the dungeon but I did not want that same fate for Magi. We would not have been able to save him without your help."

It was once in a blue moon when Ravendor thanked somebody like *that*. Darren had a feeling he wasn't ever going to see it again in his lifetime. As for Reiyu he had only just walked home with them, nothing more, so he thought the gratitude was a little misplaced. He smiled. "It was nothing, really. Magi would have done the same for any of us."

"Yeah." Darren agreed. Magi probably would have done it with a lot more finesse, too. When he was human he was a seriously competent adventurer, one of the best that Darren had ever known. In the here and now he was just kind of a quiet, docile presence, but at least he was conscious and nonviolent.

They parted ways at that point, saying good evening while Reiyu and Darren took Magi upstairs and Ravendor went to feed Fortinbras, giving the animal some leftovers that he hadn't really been intending on eating himself. Half the stuff he cooked tended to turn out that way, not because he cooked dog food but because he was such a bad chef that with most meals he could barely tell the difference. He'd gotten used to it a long time ago, though he supposed that someday he should marry someone who wasn't as horrific at cooking as he was.

He was glad that Fortinbras never complained, well… most of the time. Once the dog was fed he lost all interest in the humans of the inn and soon wandered out the front door, off to do whatever it was that afghans did in the late summer afternoon. As for messages he had received only one on his desk, and that was just a concerned note from Mara asking how everything had gone. She was close by, she practically lived down the road so he guessed that it would be courteous to go see her, but it had been a long day. He could do that tomorrow morning on the way to seeing Warren again.

When he got upstairs both Darren and Reiyu had already retreated to their respective rooms. Somebody had left his master key in the lock of Magi's door and when he retrieved it and went inside he could see that together the two adventurers had taken Magi from the stretcher and moved him into his bed. He was lying there now, staring disinterestedly at the wall and covered by the blankets. He didn't move nor make a sound when Ravendor entered; the stark whiteness of his arm bandages a contrast to the woven earth tones of his bed.

Magi's room… he hadn't been in here often, not since Magi had moved in even though he technically owned the building itself. He preferred to leave his more permanent tenants to their own devices, and he was happy to see that for the most part Magi kept everything clean. It was slightly spartan though, kind of empty; he didn't see any photographs or pictures or many personal effects. He mustn't have been that kind of person, he guessed.

It was actually a little sad. It wasn't like he had many friends or family either, but he had at least *one* old photo of his ex-wife and kid somewhere in his room. Well, the sooner he got Magi sorted out the sooner he could get some sleep for himself. He looked around for where Magi might have kept his clothes. "You don't mind if I search your drawers, do you?" He asked him, moving to do just that and not really expecting an answer.

It was just better than not saying anything at all, or else it might seem odd to be going through somebody else's things. Eventually he found a pair of clean pajamas and Magi's hairbrush and went back to the bed, sitting on the edge of it close to where the young archer was lying down. He looked at him carefully, then took Magi by the shoulder and gently hoisted him up into a sitting position, meeting no resistance.

"You are not going to attack me, right?"

Magi said nothing.

"I am just going to help you get dressed."

No response. Magi was watching him, but only with very vague interest. It was rather unnerving, especially knowing that he was poisonous and could try to bite him at any time, but for now it seemed like he was safe. Ravendor took that silence as a 'yes'.

He helped Magi into his clothes, which was a bit harder than expected because while the other man didn't resist he was also far from helpful. It was like trying to dress a child. Afterwards he brushed Magi's hair for him and that was significantly easier to do, though it did seem a lot longer than he remembered it to be. Maybe partially becoming an alraune had caused it to grow faster; he didn't know.

That seemed good enough. He could leave now and both he and Magi could get some sleep. Ravendor turned back to his friend and touched him lightly on the shoulder. "Goodnight, Magi. I will be back to check on you in a few hours." He said.

After going for so long while being completely passive what Magi did next was a shock to all; maybe even a shock to Magi himself. It certainly wasn't what Ravendor had been expecting from his sick friend.

The young archer crawled forward onto his knees on the bed and suddenly wrapped his sore arms around the other man, not to hurt, not to strangle, but just to hug. It was a hug. He leant his head against Ravendor's collarbone, silent.

The dark-haired man tensed up immediately, understandably, especially after what had happened to Warren and Reiyu after getting too close to him. He had taken a big risk already just staying within biting range of him, and this was *very* awkward. He could feel Magi's hands at the small of his back, clinging to him. His long, pale-green hair tickled the side of his neck.

And the most curious, strangest part of all was that it didn't feel too bad. It had been a long, long time since somebody had held him like this, and it felt good to have a pair of arms around him again even if they were just the arms of a friend. It took Ravendor a few moments for him to reciprocate but he did, eventually, even if it was a little bit stiffly.

Magi had been hurt so very badly by the alraune. Ravendor knew this, wanted to fix it, to fix *him*, but he didn't know how. This was really all he could do, but it still didn't quite feel like enough.

"I'm sorry." He said at last, barely above a whisper. It sounded like he had something stuck in his throat. "I really am."

For long minutes neither of them moved. Slowly Magi's grip on Ravendor seemed to weaken, and after a little while the older man realized Magi's breathing had changed in pitch and pace as well.

He had fallen asleep.

Ravendor took Magi by the upper arms and pulled him away. The archer resisted, not consciously, but like a sleeper who had found a comfortable spot and didn't want to be moved. It was actually rather endearing, but Ravendor couldn't just sit there forever for Magi's benefit; he had too many things to do. He put him back to bed as best as he could without waking his friend and stood, feeling a little strange himself. It was possible he was just overtired.

He locked Magi safely away in his room and then headed downstairs, back to his own room. It was good to be home, even though it really wasn't all that much. When he glanced out the window he noticed that the sun was already beginning to go down – was it that late already? Summer usually meant long, hot protracted sunsets. Maybe it was different in this country.

Though he was exhausted Ravendor didn't go to bed right away. He was a little worried about his concussion and that if he fell asleep he might not wake up again, or with parts of his memory missing. It *could* happen, but chances were he was probably fine. Still, he took his time cooking a proper dinner that didn't suck quite as badly as last time, got himself cleaned up and performed some routine maintenance on his six-gun, waiting for the sun to finish setting. It wouldn't feel right to sleep until then.

He tried reading, but couldn't quite focus on the words. Soon he resorted to his liquor cabinet and poured himself a drink, but he couldn't enjoy that either. He kept thinking back to Magi. It was all over and he was safe, but it didn't seem finished; somehow. There hadn't been any closure, and that hug-

Why had Magi held him like that, and *why* would he attack anybody in reach except for him? He didn't understand.

In the end Ravendor gave up and just collapsed onto his bed, not bothering to lock the door, not even caring enough to get under the blankets. It was too hot for that anyway.

Within two minutes he was already dead to the world.

He awoke suddenly and realized that he must have been jolted out of a dream.

Ravendor lifted his head from the pillow, groaned, then face planted back into it again. He couldn't remember what the dream had been, it more than likely wasn't important, but it was relieving to find he could sleep without the concussion getting in the way. His room was dark; the candle he had lit earlier had burnt itself down into a little stub and cast minimal light throughout the room. Outside the stars shone; it was either still evening or the middle of the night.

He hadn't fallen asleep under the blankets but for some reason one side of his body was warm. As he hadn't brought a woman home with him there was only one explanation and he muttered; "Fortinbras…" angrily, using a leg to shove the black afghan off the bed. Some of the other people staying at the inn tolerated that kind of behavior but Ravendor wasn't one of them. It didn't stop the animal from sneaking in and mooching now and then, however.

Fortinbras whined as he was kicked onto the rug but he didn't try to climb back up again. Ravendor got up, brushing his long, loose hair out of his face. He felt like death warmed over but it was quite a few steps up from before now that he had gotten a few hours of sleep. To be honest he just wanted to go right back to bed again, but he remembered Warren's instructions all too well. He had to go and check on Magi at least once.

He was in all likelihood just fine, still sleeping just like he had been only moments ago, but it was better to be safe than sorry. Ravendor got dressed again, pulling on his coat and buckling and holstering his gun. He was only going upstairs but he didn't feel right leaving his weapon behind, perhaps because he was paranoid, but the gunman was certain that the one time he'd need it most of all would be the one time he would forget.

He took the candle with him so he wouldn't trip over anything in the night. Upstairs was quiet and dark as well, with no light streaming in from under the doors of Darren and Reiyu's rooms. They must all be sensibly asleep as well. Lucky bastards.

Ravendor unlocked Magi's room and stepped inside, allowing the door to swing closed behind him. The place was just as he had left it earlier, but with one small exception.

Magi was up and out of his bed, awake and standing without assistance. He wasn't doing much, just loitering there, but he glanced up in the direction of the door as Ravendor entered the room, almost as if he had been anticipating the other man's arrival. Beforehand Magi had barely been able to stand up by himself; it looked like some bed rest had strengthened his legs during the night. That was good to see.

Good news or not Ravendor was quite surprised to see Magi up and about so early. He set the burning candle he was holding down on a nearby table, taking a few steps towards him, and then stopped. Even if he was up maybe he should be put back to bed anyway so he could rest, but if he could stand maybe he could do other things too, like speak.

"Magi, are you lucid?" Ravendor asked, taking a chance and hoping for something good to happen for once. He felt like they deserved it after all they had been through.

The archer didn't answer with words, though he did cock his head to the side slightly like a dog that recognized its name. It reminded Ravendor a bit of Fortinbras, actually.

It was better than a blank stare. The gunman pointed to himself, simply. "Do you know who I am?" He inquired instead. That might be a little easier for him to comprehend.

Magi opened his mouth as if he were preparing to say something, but then he stopped. He knew *exactly* who Ravendor was; he had been waiting for him patiently after all. With his alraune queen gone, lost forever, Ravendor seemed like the only person left in the world who still cared about him. He hadn't pushed him away earlier even though he had been expecting it, and… and…

He had saved his life, hadn't he? He was sure that he had.

For the first time since he had been captured Magi made an indication that he understood what the other man was saying. He nodded once, shortly, like he was unfamiliar with the motion but did it anyway. He walked forward, closing the distance between himself and Ravendor in a few unsteady steps.

Ravendor was pleased to see such a reaction but found himself stepping backwards carefully, up against the wall. "Magi…" He started to say, but then…

Magi finally gave in to the secret desire he had been harboring in his heart of hearts for, god, *months*. He'd hardly dared to let himself think about it until now, but the alraune's curse had brought a lot of things of his crashing back up to the surface. The poison killed inhibitions, even in one who was a little alraune himself.

The archer smiled and then lunged at Ravendor one last time. His arm came up to hold him, to choke him, to keep him steady. It pressed, and the other man had been too slow to get away.

The kiss was hard, firm, shoving him up against the wall with such reckless force that Ravendor smacked the back of his head against the flat surface. The brief exclamation of pain had been enough to give Magi a way to reach him and he fought him relentlessly, fuelled by an energy that had lain dormant beneath his ailing exterior. No, not dormant, just hidden; like a predator lying in patient wait for its prey.

It was a bitter kiss, in more ways than one, more of an attack rather than some kind of display of affection. Magi pressed up against him silently, firmly, even as he held his free arm sorely against Ravendor's throat. It became difficult to breathe, he wanted to gasp for air, but all he would be doing was gasping deeply into Magi's mouth and he was fairly certain he didn't want any of that. He tried to push against the younger man to get free, but this must have been misconstrued as something entirely different because Magi made a low sound in the back of his throat that could have been a moan, but just as easily could have been laughter.

This was *beyond* insane, and even a little bit frightening. Ravendor slowly slid his right arm down the wall from where it had been pinned over his head, and while Magi's hand had clamped over the wrist like a manacle he didn't seem to mind or care over this small adjustment. The innkeeper's mind reeled. Magi had struck like a viper coiled for battle, and while he had not been *entirely* off guard he had never expected anything like this. He continued to fight against Magi's arms but the youth kept on overpowering him. Somehow.

Perhaps he was getting weaker? He had been tired from the dungeon at the get-go and worrying about his friend hadn't been helping things either. The blond… or, well, green-haired archer did something subtle with his knee to Ravendor's inner thigh and he recoiled against it and let in a sharp breath; the slight moment of weakness enough for Magi to force his tongue deeper inside.

It was nothing at all like kissing a woman, even in the hardest of instances. There was no softness here, no warm luscious lips so full and unmistakably feminine… but that was to say it was not *bad.* Just… different, really. Like the difference between cotton and silk. The horrible thought that this didn't feel very horrible at all filled him with dread.

It was very possible that the hugest difference between the two was that Ravendor had never been out of control before, and losing that control to somebody else actually scared him a little. It reminded him of when he had been younger, or the very first time he had kissed someone like this, back when he had had a few less wrinkles and a lot more life ahead of him.

But still, he did not want this at all. That decidedly bitter kiss, lithe tongue and hot breath tasted far too much like poison. Moreover this was *Magi.* His *friend.* It was way too wrong.

He shoved against Magi again, hard enough this time so that there was no way for anyone to mistake what it was; an act of aggression. The kiss broke as Ravendor twisted in the hold and punched with his shoulder right into Magi's chest. If Magi didn't let up with his arm he would have choked, but the younger man pulled away in reflex. So, even in his animalistic, dumb stupor didn't want to hurt, or at least strangle him. That was somewhat reassuring.

So Ravendor pushed him away while shouting "Get off me!" in a restricted tone, and when he was free he bent over a bit with his hands on his knees, coughing and gasping for clean air. When he was done he shot an exceedingly dirty glare in Magi's direction. "What in the blazes was that all about?" He demanded angrily.

Magi just looked at him incomprehensibly. He didn't answer, couldn't, really, at least not in any language that Ravendor would be able to understand. He was a bare man, stripped of basic human faculties such as speech and tact and reasoning. He *was* a human, but the alraune's kiss and bitter blood were causing his membership to expire.

He was fine with that; a creature of hunger, of instinct… of *need.* Nothing else mattered.

Of course, memory did not fail him, even if the language of the mind could only translate into pictures and blurs of instinctual knowing. As a human, Magi had had a bit of a crush on two people in town. The first was Mara, the beautiful girl next door whom he often saw tending to her peach-coloured rose garden. The scent of the roses and her memory were interchangeable now; one begetting the other. The second crush was Ravendor himself, though the older man had had no idea of it up until now. Magi had always harbored a weakness towards older men, despite the self-analytical idea that he was searching for the approval he had lost from his father so long ago. Besides, Ravendor had shown him kindness and civility in a time when he had felt little more than an outcast. The fact that he was exceedingly handsome helped matters as well.

If the innkeeper could read his mind- well, look at the pictures and half-formed concepts of a man on the edge of humanity he would have both been worried for his own hide and supremely grateful that Mara was safely alone and out of Magi's reach. He steadied himself and straightened up, unable to read anything at all in Magi's blank green eyes. Having that forearm held against his throat had hurt, but it must have been nothing compared to the pain of putting such pressure on the bandaged burns.

The one thing that Ravendor hadn't realized yet was that he had already been poisoned, and that poison was rapidly dispersing in his body like a drop of ink within water.

Knowing that, Magi seemed to smile a bit. He tried to grab Ravendor again, this time by the upper arms, but the older man had been expecting it and shoved him away before he could kiss him again. Magi was strong now but also quite unsteady on his feet. He wobbled and fell back against the table, but held onto it to keep himself upright. Ravendor grabbed him by the front of his shirt, making a fist in the soft fabric.

"Have you lost your tongue? Answer me!" He barked. If Magi had lost *anything* it was fairly obvious where he had lost it in, but Ravendor would not have been amused by the joke. The younger archer just looked at him mutely, unable to give a response. A lamp would have been more talkative.

Magi looked to his right, away from him, and then glanced back at Ravendor slyly. All of a sudden he had all the time in the world to lean there and mire his friend in deeper confusion. Why? It almost seemed like he was waiting for something.

Surprise. Overpower. Infect. Retreat. Wait. Then strike.

The typical attack plan of the alraune.

When Ravendor's shoulders seemed to slump and he swayed just a bit on his feet, as if he were punch drunk he knew that the poison was starting to take effect, that it was reaching deeper still; working its way into his heart. Ravendor seemed to hardly notice, for now. "Listen, I have never held any qualms with people like you mainly because your preference has never bothered my lifestyle, but there *are* limitations. Don't you *ever* try to kiss me like that again!" He ordered.

A haze had fallen down upon him. It hadn't taken long, Warren had lasted almost half an hour before he had started to notice the ill effects, but Magi's desperation had tempered his kiss with a dangerous edge, and Ravendor's rapidly beating heart was doing nothing to slow it down. There was also something quite different in the toxicology of a man who was getting frequent and gratifying sex and another who had been single for far too long (and who could blame him when the only really attractive girl in town was Mieus and he hated her guts and besides she always wanted to do macabre things with a riding crop and that was waaaaaay too strange for him even if turning her ass a pretty little shade of red *had* been entertaining…).

The 'people like you' line might have bothered Magi if he still had his wits about him, but even if you changed a name the definition remained the same. Ravendor let go of Magi's shirt and stepped back, intent on getting to the door and leaving before the situation became any worse. The kiss had flustered him, because it had felt *good* it flustered him, and now from out of nowhere he felt both faint and weak, like the onset of anemia.

The door wouldn't open. It must have clicked shut when he'd entered the room not long ago. He didn't remember hearing that clicking sound upon entrance but he *did* know his inn quite well and how the lock on Magi's door was a little sticky. He'd been meaning to fix it in the coming week, and now…

A hand wound gently into his ponytail. Hot lips were now at his neck. He froze, hand on the doorknob. "Magi…" He growled lowly, trying to warn him off.

Magi made a sound that was more animal than human and spun him around. He was a little shorter than Ravendor but if he stood on the balls of his feet it made up the distance. He leaned forward to take another kiss, certain that with the aphrodisiac in his system he wouldn't resist this time, and then-

Ravendor didn't think he'd ever be able to strike Magi unless he had a *very* good reason. Now, this seemed good enough. He shot a fist out in a remarkably hard jab and smashed Magi right in the mouth, mashing his lips against his teeth. If he had been significantly stronger, like, say, Warren, he would have knocked out a few of the archer's teeth. However his strength was no greater than the average man and he wasn't actively *trying* to hurt him, so on the following day all the green-haired youth would have to remind him of it was a split lip and a nasty bruise down to his chin.

Magi hit the floor, nursing the wound with a soft, pained groan. Ravendor frowned. "I am *not* a poofter." He stated with disapproval, and then a rush of vertigo threatened to knock him off his feet as well. He withstood it, but not by much, and when Magi didn't get up again Ravendor all of a sudden worried that he might have hit his friend a whole lot harder than he intended, so he knelt down beside him in concern.

He took the younger man gently by the shoulder as if preparing to hoist him back up into a sitting position. He began to say; 'I am sorry', both for the punch *and* the offensive remark, but before he could properly recoil Magi was on him again like a mongoose upon a snake, grabbing and clutching and using his momentum combined with his weight to throw Ravendor onto his back.

He grunted in surprise as his back hit Magi's woven, earth-toned rug. It was immediately scratchy and uncomfortable, made from the wool of some kind of llama or alpaca-like animal. Ravendor made to get up in a hurry, pushing up off the floor with his hands, but uttered a low 'oof!' as Magi finally climbed on top of him, pinning his legs where they were.

He was heavy, but the weight was bearable. Even so he didn't think he'd be able to push the other man away this time without a significant adrenaline surge. Ravendor had been nervous before, yes, but that had been the kind of nervousness associated with trying to coax a drunken friend out of an extremely stupid idea or trying out a new sexual position for the first time (equal parts chance you were going to either ruin the encounter or throw your back out for half a week). Now, with Magi looming over him with the look of a carnivore on his face, pure, predatory hunger evident, the gravity of his predicament at last hit him like a ton of bricks.

He knew that Magi was bisexual. Magi could *rape* him right now if he really wanted to, and Ravendor didn't think he'd be able to stop it. He could struggle, oh yes, he was certain that he would, but short of shooting the man there wasn't much he could do besides yell for help. As utterly foolish as it was Ravendor didn't think he'd be able to cry rape like a bewildered maiden; he just had too much pride for that. He didn't think he could shoot Magi either; not unless his very life was threatened by the man.

Ravendor was able to prop himself up a little on his elbows. That was all Magi seemed to allow him. It felt like his senses had begun to dull somehow and he felt weak… as if… almost as if he had been drugged. How was that possible? The last thing he had put into his body had been a nightcap before bed and that had been hours ago.

He was starting to feel giddy, like a teenager hopped up on the first sight of a flash of bare breast, real flesh, silken, and the heart-racing memory of a naked, curvy silhouette shaded only by pale moonlight. Perhaps others would not have put it so poetically, but the alraune's kiss could only dredge up such memories as the dreamer was willing to part with. In a more succinct way another man in his situation would have said that they felt hornier than a goat in the rutting season, and all poetry aside were the two states really so different?

Even with the alraune's toxin in his system the older man still experienced abject horror as he felt as he felt himself harden against Magi Magemere's inner thigh. He had never really considered the idea that he might be bisexual himself, mainly because the thought had never completely crossed his mind before. Ravendor tried to pull himself away ineffectually, uttering ironically the very same words Magi had said to the alraune queen moments before he had been mercilessly raped. "Let me go…" He said softly, as if ashamed by the utter surrender in those words.

And Magi heeded them just as well as the alraune had, which was to say not at all. But it didn't matter much anymore. The older man had the dazed, flushed expression that spoke of the poison reaching his heart and words no longer held any real meaning for them. When Magi dipped down, leaning over his body, he didn't have to worry about the repercussions of the next kiss. Ravendor kissed back this time, obediently, passively; even if he hated himself for it. He closed his eyes, it was easier that way, not resisting as Magi planted a hand on his chest while the other held his chin so lightly, as if to keep him from turning away.

The bitterness and the coppery tang of blood wasn't so bad once he got used to it, an acquired taste, just as Magi got used to the fact that kissing Ravendor was a little bit like kissing an ashtray. Leaning over at such an angle caused his loose, long hair to spill over his shoulders and face, obscuring vision like the lazy overhanging strands of a willow bough. The younger man smelt different too, not so much like his usual cologne but more like the scent of the earth, like soil and rainwater; like freshly clipped grass. Magi felt Ravendor's hands come up to grasp at his shirt and his side, but not to push him away. To hold.

Magi would have smiled had his mouth not been occupied with other things. He pulled away, leaning back and breaking their kiss with a disappointed groan from his compatriot. This time Magi *did* smile, wiping gently at his bloody lip while the taste of the ashes still lingered on the tip of his tongue. Possibly *any* smoker he kissed from that point onward would remind him of his friend, but he was fine with that. Now, with his own need freshly awakened and throbbing restlessly in his pants he felt that there was no more time to waste.

The young archer clumsily and hurriedly pulled his white bed shirt over his head and threw it to the side, revealing the nicely-toned and slightly tanned musculature underneath. He was not a physical fighter like Siro or Warren, but he was in pretty good shape regardless. In the very back of his mind Ravendor probably would have felt that the sight was wasted on him, but it was hard to think about anything at all as Magi returned and resumed the kiss with renewed vigor, distracting him with his mouth while his hands got to the task of disarming Ravendor safely.

Even deep in the clutches of the alraune's curse, the gun Magi knew Ravendor kept in an underarm holster unnerved him greatly. He knew it was there; the innkeeper never left his room without it. He went for it now, fumbling and trying to work the holster's buckle with fingers that weren't entirely certain of what they were doing. Ravendor seemed to tense against him. "Magi, stop…" He began to say, out of breath, "don't touch…"

Magi answered by grinding his hips against his friend, pressing their erections hard against each other. The soft moan he received delighted him, and after a few moments more the shoulder holster came loose and he was able to move it away and out of arm's reach; throwing it safely onto his bed. Ravendor offered him a malevolent glare at being disarmed so easily, but it was a weak one with no real threat.

When Magi came forward again to help him pull off his coat Ravendor twisted to the side a little to get out of his reach, holding an arm out over his shoulder and head in the same way a gladiator would hold a shield to repel against a volley of arrows or a downward sword slash; a defenseless gesture of helplessness. He was well aware how wrong this was and how his body ached to do it, but it was wrong. His body was wrong. His mind was wrong. This was all wrong! "No…" He tried to say resolutely, but his voice was shaken, "no, no, get the hell away from me…"

He'd lost the cultured tone in his ever-present accent and now he just sounded, well, lost. Like there was no possible way he was going to avoid the terrible thing that was going to happen to him, but he was still trying anyway. This time Magi *did* pause, hands on the lapels of Ravendor's coat, just looking at him with quizzical, alien interest. Ravendor looked back at him as if he expected Magi to bite, and he was not disappointed.

And that was when things started to turn *violent*.

Magi pinned Ravendor to the floor and ripped at his clothes harshly, ripped at Ravendor himself if he tried to resist, and eventually got his way with only a minimum, single tear to the coat. If it was going to happen it was going to happen, and ripping up an expensive (and favored) piece of clothing seemed pointless, really. When Ravendor realized what Magi intentions were he stopped and willingly struggled out of his coat and his shirt, breathing heavily from the aphrodisiac and more.

Ravendor's body wasn't quite as impressive as Magi's was, he was older and thinner with a little less muscle tone, but he wasn't bad. The rational part of Magi's mind would have noticed the huge but faint scar-line running across the other man's chest, along with several other marks of battle and long-past conflicts. But that was to be expected, wasn't it? Ravendor had been a fully-fledged adventurer way back when Magi had still been too young to shave.

With the shirt and coat gone Magi shifted backwards a little from where he was sitting on folded knees and gave himself greater access to his friend's belt and pants. With long, rough fingertips so used to the bowstring he traced the outline of his friend's cock just *waiting* for him, if only he could just get past that one barrier…

He pressed himself into Magi's hand automatically, sighing as it became so much harder and harder to hate this. If things didn't get any worse he could probably stand it, could probably even *enjoy* it if he blocked out in his mind that Magi was another man. It felt good, better than good, really, and as the green-haired archer got his belt undone and worked on the fly of his jeans he wondered what the difference would be like to have a man's lips work on his cock instead of the norm.

Then, suddenly, as his fly was undone and the pressure against his crotch was released Magi climbed off him, wedged himself in-between Ravendor's legs and then hiked one of them over his shoulder. His train of thought stopped dead in his tracks. This wasn't the right position for… for…

"*No!*" He cried, fear pulling him out of his haze momentarily as he put two and two together. "God damn it Magi if you don't let me up this very second I swear I will break my foot off in your arse! *I will not let you make me into a woman!*"

That last part he had yelled almost loud enough for the neighbors to hear. He hoped not; he would never be able to live it down, but he also hoped so because then maybe someone might barge in and let him out of this godforsaken nightmare. So Magi liked to do things like these in his private time, well, whatever. That didn't mean he should assume the same about everybody else.

The expression on Magi's face was now blank, jade-green, horny anticipation. *This must be what it feels like,* he thought unexpectedly, *this was how he felt when that monster had its way with him...*

And just like that Ravendor was angry. Beyond angry, furious, it felt like a white hot laser had sliced him all the way down the middle; cleanly in two. One side was still infected with the alraune's poison and wanted nothing more than to fuck (or be fucked by?) his friend, while the other would have gladly given all the riches and treasures hidden in the dungeon for a chance to kick Magi in his lousy, perverted face.

Luckily the price for that was free.

Ravendor drew his leg back, the one that was flung carelessly over Magi's shoulder as he attempted to divest him of his pants, and slammed a heel into his face. He didn't use his full strength or the total force he could have exerted from where he was lying, as that would have completely shattered both his friend's nose and cheekbone, but he clearly let his anger and distaste for Magi's plans be known.

The young archer screamed in anger and pain as Ravendor left a vague boot print across his face, temporarily losing hold and control of his prey. Magi was forced back, hitting the cold wooden floor and twisting onto his stomach to protect himself from Ravendor while he raised a hand to check himself for injuries. There was no extra blood, but that had really hurt. He coughed briefly, trying to gather his bearings, when suddenly all the air was knocked out of his lungs as Magi was violently crushed to the floor.

Ravendor had at last come to the final consensus that if he didn't take control of the situation *right now* it was going to come back and fuck him in the ass later on. With Magi distracted he had climbed back up into something of a crouch and tackled him while he had nursed his wounds, jumping on his back so to speak, and at least in this position he was in more familiar territory now.

He managed to get an arm around Magi's neck and forced him into a headlock, but the younger man snapped at him like a wild dog so he had to discontinue that plan in a hurry. Instead, Ravendor forced Magi's head and upper body down against the wooden floor tiles and reached another arm around him at his belly, working blindly but carefully to divulge him of his pajama bottoms.

And then the strangest thing happened, something that Ravendor never would have expected.

Magi stopped struggling and became quiet, still. His chest still heaved with the horny pants of anticipation, but there was obedience there now when there had been none before.

Maybe this was what he had wanted all along. Ravendor stripped him of the rest of his clothes until he was completely naked, every inch of his skin bathed silver by the faint moonlight streaming in from the window close to his bed. Magi felt something light and warm touch his shoulder, and it wasn't until days later did he realize that it hadn't just been a simple touch; it had been a kiss.

Ravendor didn't undress himself any more than he needed to; Magi had already taken care of that for him earlier. He gave himself a few quick strokes to get himself to where he had been previously, and asked himself one last time if he was really intending to do this.

Fuck it, why not? He had already come this far, so why not see it through to the end?

He grabbed his coat lying discarded on the floor beside them and searched his pockets for a small metal canister which he procured in a matter of moments. It was gun oil for his colt .45, he'd cleaned and oiled the weapon earlier that evening but there would still be some left, enough for one more oiling at least. Ravendor smiled as he poured a liberal amount on his hand.

Unable to speak, Magi merely whined like a desperate creature that knew what was coming next and all his body cried out for it to begin. Were he himself he would have felt ashamed at how utterly pathetic he sounded, but in a very real sense he was dying. The tendrils that had grown, that Warren had so cruelly cut and burnt away, that had been a part of it. The mindlessness, the bliss, the *ease* of living… it had all been part in parcel of the alraune's gift. It had been a way to turn around and walk backwards through evolution, past the fall, past guilt and shame and back towards innocence and the opening gates of the Garden of Eden itself.

Losing that, so soon, just a taste…

That, in turn, was death for him. He mourned.

His mourning cry was intermingled with both pain and pleasure as Ravendor lubed himself up and roughly shoved into him. His alraune queen had loosened him up some during the brief stay in her lair so he didn't quite feel like a virgin anymore, but Magi was inexperienced and young. He could have counted all the times he'd done this with the fingers on one hand and still had some left over to spare, but *gods* he had missed this feeling. He'd missed it so very much.

Tight… tight… he'd never fucked anyone this tight before. It was as fresh an experience for him as it was familiar to Magi. Similar, yes, to his experiences with women but different because this was *not* a seduction, this was *not* gentle. It was animalistic, brutal, and simply barbaric in nature. He was pretty certain that he'd be able to feel blood on his lips *and* his cock before long, and that was fine because he didn't care anymore and it felt so damned *good.*

Ye gods, for a second there he had begun to feel like a monster himself.

But when Magi's breathy cries gradually built up in force until they were moans of sheer ecstasy he began to feel like he was starting to get the hang of things properly. Ravendor realized that he quite enjoyed hearing that sound and strove towards dragging it out of Magi's throat as best as he could, even as the younger archer's hot, tight muscles pushed him closer and closer towards the edge.

He was on his hands and knees, head hung low, fingers splayed as he rocked back and forth to accommodate the movement of the other man. He was so *warm*, and, silly as it sounded, he didn't want that wonderful heat to leave his body even for a moment. The sensation of being *filled* after being empty for so long was comforting and maybe, just maybe… it was worth losing the alraune's gift for a chance to experience something like this with his friend.

They found a natural rhythm best suited to them and when Magi could take it no longer he propped himself up on one elbow and reached for his aching, neglected cock; giving it hard, rough pulls in time to the thrusts even though it meant he was going to be as sore as hell tomorrow morning. Time no longer mattered to him just so long as he could live in this single moment, this single encounter for as long as he could.

Ravendor was almost embarrassed by how incredibly turned on he was, with or without the aphrodisiac, but of course he had no knowledge of the true nature of the poison except for what had been discussed in the town meeting prior to going back into the dungeon to save his friend.

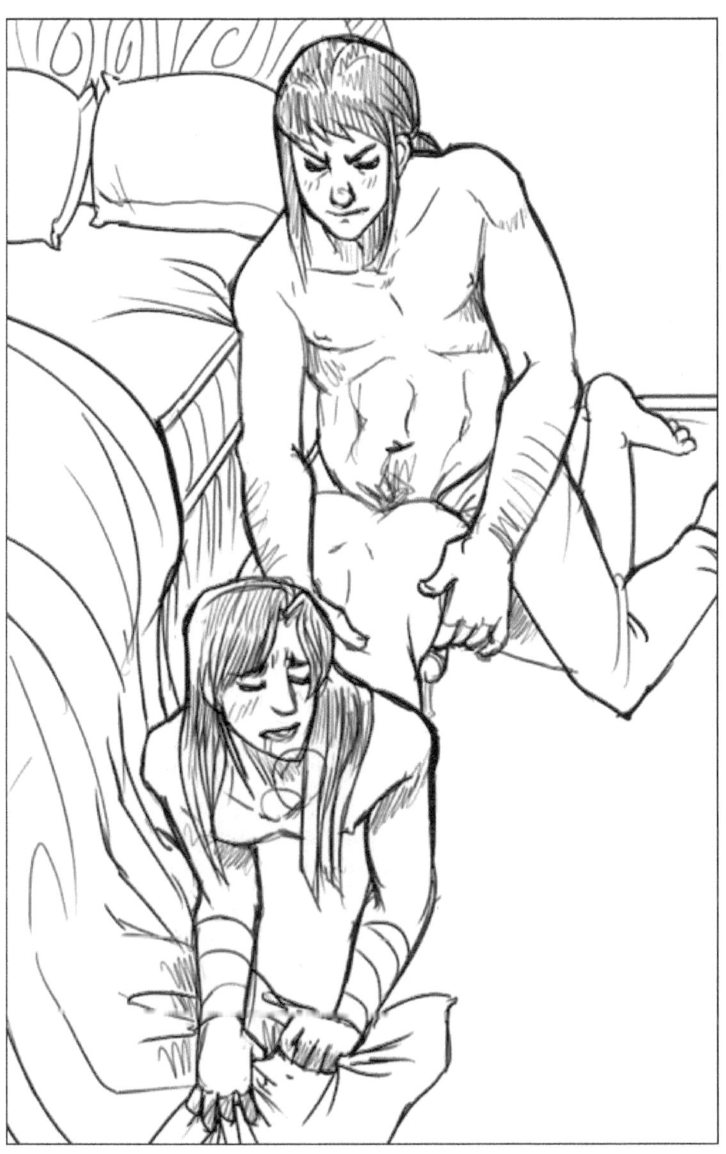

*"He was on his hands and knees, head hung low, fingers splayed as he rocked back and forth to accommodate the movement of the other man."*

When this was over, and that would only be in a few short minutes because this was just too *good* to last, would he ever be able to look Magi in the face again, knowing what they'd done?

Magi came first, letting out a low, slutty moan. His whole body shuddered as the orgasm hit him with full-force, just as strong and as savage as it had been in the caverns of the dungeon. He ground backwards against Ravendor as he buried his friend's cock deep inside him to the root, trying to savor, trying to memorize while his mind reeled in a flash of blissful delirium.

The other man finished moments later, unable to bear Magi flexing so hard against him as he climaxed. He thrust a few more times and then leant against him, holding him steady as his finely manicured nails bit into Magi's chest and side. He was usually a silent lover, and had been up until this point, but when he heard his friend moan underneath him and all the desire and love and lust was condensed into that one lovely sound he couldn't help a little moan of his own slip between his lips, almost like some kind of answer.

They both slumped against one another; Ravendor against Magi and Magi against the floor, panting like they had both tried to run a marathon together. The young archer felt something warm and slick run down against his inner thigh when Ravendor pulled out of him, hot spunk or remainders of the gun oil lube, heated up by the constant friction of their bodies. It could even be blood; that hadn't been gentle sex by any means. For a while they just tried to get their breath back and steady their heartbeats into something slightly more normal, the cursed archer taking grateful, mute comfort in his friend lying on top of him, his head against Magi's shoulder.

Ravendor's arm went around him again much like he had tried to headlock him before, but this time it was different. It was like a loose hybrid of a hug, and Magi didn't resist it. "Is… is that to your satisfaction?" He heard Ravendor ask him, still coming down from that high they had achieved together.

Even sated, with the maddening need to fuck temporarily quelled he was still unable to answer. Instead he disentangled himself from Ravendor and rolled over, not really caring that he had rolled into the smattering of his own spilt essence. The dark-haired man in turn got up and sat back on his haunches, fixing his pants. Magi smiled at him from where he laid, a pure smile, like one the old Magi would have given a friend. It gave Ravendor faint hope that maybe the old Magi could come back after all.

And, with him lying there with his long hair mussed and messy but beautiful and his eyes clear in the first time that felt like forever, Ravendor realized with vague surprise that if given the choice he would have slept with Magi all over again.

The next day Ravendor awoke with a largely unavoidable sense of guilt and a terrible headache. It was bright outside the inn already and light came in through the open curtains, illuminating miniscule motes of dust in the air. He could hear birdsong coming in from the trees outside; though with his headache the tune wasn't quite as sweet as it could have been.

He couldn't remember the last time he had fallen asleep on somebody else's floor before. When he sat up he felt a stab of pain down his back from where the alraune had struck him yesterday. The night before was an indistinguishable, bitter-tasting blur. What had happened to him? Had he gotten drunk and wound up passing out on the floor of someone's room? Or…

When he realized that somebody was lying on the floor next to him the whole sordid late-night meeting came back to haunt him. Magi was sprawled out on the carpet, naked, sleeping the deep sleep of the recovering fevered. His colour seemed to be a bit better today, and his hair was losing that faint tint of green and returning to its normal, blond hue. That could only be a good thing.

For a brief while Ravendor held his aching head in his hands and was silent. There is a unique kind of despair reserved only for those who try to take care of a sick friend and then wake up right next to them the very next morning, and not in the platonic bedside manner way. Magi's kiss… it had made him go temporarily crazy; had transferred a tiny sliver of Magi's madness directly into his blood. He was at least relieved to discover that the only remnants left behind today were his pounding headache.

He stood up cautiously, mindful of his shaken balance, and carefully thought about how he was going to get Magi back into his bed without waking him up and therefore possibly initiating a second assault. The dark bruise at the edge of Magi's mouth looked painful enough as it was, though with the memories of last night Ravendor wasn't sure he'd resist as much as before.

That thought scared him a little. What the hell was he thinking? Ravendor sighed and knelt, putting an arm around Magi's shoulders and pulling him up onto the bed. It was a clumsy effort; he lacked the strength at the moment to do it with much finesse.

The rough handling caused Magi to stir into hazy consciousness. While uttering a soft groan his eyelids fluttered open and they were clear blue, like a cloudless sky on a warm summer day, much like this day.

"Hngh..." He said without much clarity, but then after an extended pause added; "... uh?"

Ravendor spread the blanket over him and then turned to gather up some of his clothes scattered over the floor. His face felt unnecessarily hot, even though he was certain he hadn't blushed in *years*. It was probably just shame. He pulled his shirt back on and neatly folded his coat under one arm. "You will not be leaving this room today. Not until I can be certain you will not attack anybody else." He announced firmly.

Silence filled the room, broken only by Mara's faint singing as she hung up her washing down the street. When he realized Magi still wasn't really able to respond or even comprehend his statement Ravendor moved to the door, gripping the handle.

Before he could leave, however, Magi made a very soft noise that was almost a choke and almost a sigh. "... I'm... sorry..." He managed to breathe at a barely audible level.

It was loud enough for Ravendor to hear. He made a noncommittal grunt that was far from forgiveness and left the room immediately, unlocking it with the master key and feeling much better the very moment he stepped back out into the hallway; free from the smell of sex, sunlight, and the faint scent of his friend. Ravendor uttered a sigh of relief.

As an afterthought he used his inn master key to lock the young archer into his own room. Better to let the youth feel a prisoner rather than let him get free and molest some of the townsfolk. They probably wouldn't take it quite as well as he had. Ravendor felt in his pocket for the familiar touch of cold metal, pulling out his cigarette case and a lighter. He lit one with the practiced ease of a man who had done it so many times it barely required conscious thought.

He breathed out a faint cloud of smoke. Okay, so it wasn't *all* bad. It was better than Magi dying in the night or turning into a gardenia or whatever. All he had to do was pretend that last night had never happened and maybe Magi would follow suit. He had been, after all, out of his goddamned mind. After a bath, some coffee and aspirin he'd feel like a new man again, and *that* was much more practical than standing around like a dazed idiot; staring at the door.

Speaking of that, the door to the far left of him creaked open slowly and Reiyu slipped out into the lobby. He had his sword slung behind one shoulder which could only mean one thing; he was planning a trip within the dungeon today. He smiled meekly at Ravendor who looked at him in silence from behind a stream of smoke.

"So, how is he today? Magi, I mean." He asked in a congenial, yet slightly concerned tone.

Ravendor turned away from Magi's door and became acutely aware of how disheveled he must look to Reiyu or anyone else who decided to pass them by. It was quite embarrassing, but if that happened to be the worst thing to happen to him from this point on then he'd consider himself lucky. "Magi is perfectly fine, he merely requires time on his own so that he may recover." He said coldly.

Reiyu didn't seem to be perturbed by the icy reception. He shoved his hands in the pockets of his jeans and leant against the doorframe. "Is he still poisonous? I only ask because we're neighbors."

"It's unlikely."

"But you're not certain?" The brown-haired swordsman replied in a slightly more worried fashion.

"I am planning to visit Warren later on to find that out." Ravendor said to Reiyu, as if this were common knowledge. He took another drag on his cigarette and blew the smoke away from them. "If you are so concerned then just stay away from him and leave everything to me."

"That sounds reasonable." Reiyu agreed, and then smirked. "I was worried. I heard a lot of strange noises last night, but I thought I must have been dreaming."

Ravendor shot him a dirty look, but said nothing. Reiyu must have taken it as a signal that the conversation was over and locked up his own room, heading downstairs. The older man waited for a little bit and finished the rest of his cigarette in peace, then slunk away at his own pace back towards his room.

He'd feel much better once he got Magi's smell off of him; he was sure of it.

A few hours later after a bath, some breakfast and a fresh change of clothes Ravendor finally stopped procrastinating and headed off to the clinic on foot, located on the other side of town. The summer heat had yet to hit the town full-blast but it was evident in many other little ways, like the curl of dry grass beneath his boots or the constant droning of cicadas creating a white noise in the trees. The heat didn't bother him much; his own home country had also been hot and dry and summer in Adratea was no difference. It was almost nostalgic.

Talking with Mara had been unavoidable; she was a neighbor to his inn and Ravendor sort of suspected that she had been out hanging up washing and gardening simply for an excuse to catch him when he passed by. Doubtless she was a little desperate for news over Magi's condition too. Well, it was better to warn her off now than return to tragedy later. He tried not to imagine Magi attacking her in the same way he had attacked *him*, all hunger and frenzy and hot, hot tongue…

"Uh, Ravendor? Hello? Are you still there?" Mara asked with a tiny smile of amusement playing at the corner of her lips.

He suddenly remembered that he was in the middle of a conversation. "Pardon?" He asked the woman, a little lost.

Mara seemed intrigued by this. "We were talking and you just kind of got this very strange look on your face. Are you alright?" It had almost been similar to the way Darren looked when he talked about Mina, but not quite. If anything, it wasn't the type of expression she expected to see from her neighbor.

And now he couldn't quite remember what he had been talking about in the first place. "I am sorry; I have not been sleeping well lately. I believe it is starting to show." He apologized lamely.

"It must be all the dungeon crawling," Mara agreed, "and everything that happened with your team and Magi in the dungeon. You boys at the inn need to take better care of yourselves. I worry too much about everyone." A group of men living in shared lodgings with no women to take care of them was a sad and disheartening thing indeed.

"I can assure you that both Magi and I are perfectly fine. He just needs to be properly quarantined until the doctor can be certain he will not spread his affliction to-"

*-or simply attack-*

"-others. Until then don't try to visit him. It's for the best."

Mara appeared to consider the warning with a small frown that eventually disappeared. "Well, I don't want to get anybody in trouble. I had the measles once as a child and I remember how that spread." She pulled off her gardening gloves one at a time and brushed dirt off her peach-colored dress, then pointed at him to keep his attention, like a parent reminding a forgetful child. "But promise that as soon as the doctor gives permission for him to have visitors you come here and tell me. Is that okay?"

Ravendor smiled despite his terrible headache. "Would that stop you from ignoring everything I have said and visit him regardless?"

The woman laughed. "You know me too well. I can wait to see him again just as long as I know he's okay, so yes. I'll be good."

Mara's crush on Magi seemed to be painfully obvious to everybody except for Magi himself. Sometimes Ravendor had to resist the urge to say; 'to hell with it' and staple the truth to the front of Magi's tunic and be done with it, but he doubted Mara would appreciate such indiscretion. "Then I promise. You can trust me." He said.

She seemed satisfied with a promise like that and they parted ways, Mara citing that she still had much more work to do and reminding Ravendor that he still had his own personal errands that were not being done. Still, the inn wouldn't *collapse* if he left them until the afternoon or the day after. Magi, as his tenant was also an errand. A responsibility.

Adratea was a small town, easily possible to walk from one end to the other in under half an hour. That was still enough time for Ravendor's mind to wander as he walked. He had been afraid of something like that.

If Magi had been a little quicker, or a little stronger, would he have raped him? Well, he supposed he had been raped regardless of the ins and outs of it simply because he had said no, shouted it in fact, but it hadn't been enough. That almost felt unreal, and it was slightly worrisome that the only thing he could feel about it was dull confusion and a little bit of shame. After all, it hadn't taken him much to get him to stop saying no…

Warren's clinic was a cavern cut out of the rock in Eastern Adratea, near the Guildhouse. Ravendor had heard once that the grant Warren had received to fund the opening of his practice in Adratea was almost entirely spent on equipment and other necessities, leaving him with nearly nothing left to build his clinic. He wasn't very good with numbers and management in general, and it showed. Ravendor went inside, the temperature dropping immediately once he was out of the sun. It was always slightly cool in the clinic, frigid in the winter, but during the summer it was nice and pleasant.

The place was almost empty. Odd. Usually Warren was busy during the day. Ravendor looked around a bit in the silence until he spotted the good doctor slumped over a table, unmoving and still. This set off alarm bells in the gunman's head for a second before he realized that Warren had his elbows on the table, his hands folded over his head. It was hardly the position of someone who had suddenly collapsed.

"Warren." He said as he approached.

Warren groaned in response.

"Are you dead?"

He lifted his head from the table and Ravendor was greeted with a visage he was fairly certain he had seen at least part of in his own mirror at home. He looked absolutely exhausted, as if he hadn't even slept the night before. Regardless of this he tried to smile warmly. "No, I'm fine. How can I help you?" He asked.

Ravendor sighed and pulled out a chair across from him at the table. He sat down. "It's about Magi."

"Oh yes? Is he getting better?" Warren inquired, but then looked sheepish. "I'm sorry about running off so suddenly last night. I shouldn't have done that."

"He seems to be returning to his former self, and that is a relief." The older man explained.

"How about the burns on his arms?"

"I haven't checked them. I was hoping you could come over to the inn and look at them later this evening." Magi hadn't had a proper checkup since he had left the dungeon, and maybe if he was lucky

Warren might finally decide to move him into the clinic and house him there until he was healthy again.

Warren hesitated after Ravendor finished speaking. If he didn't know any better he would say that the dark-haired man looked visibly nervous. It was something about the way he was carrying himself that seemed different. If he didn't feel like he had run halfway across the country and back the night before he would probably ask.

Ravendor moved to light another cigarette and then paused, remembering that he was a guest in somebody else's home. "Do you mind?" He asked.

Warren couldn't help but smile. "Go ahead. We're all going to die of something anyway."

"That does not sound very professional." The gunman said as he lit up, but felt better for it immediately.

"Let me bum one off you." Warren said and managed to catch Ravendor's cigarette case as he tossed it to him despite his tired reflexes. He hadn't smoked since he was a teenager, so it burned uncomfortably for a bit, but he endured it. The conversation died in the quiet and the smoke, the doctor leaning back against his chair until it was only on two legs, bracing a boot against the table and staring at the rocky ceiling. If he was lucky maybe he would spend the entire day doing nothing and he could relax.

"I shagged Magi, just so you know." Ravendor admitted, from out of the blue.

Warren lost his footing and toppled backward onto the floor. He let out a short cry as his back hit the cobbled stones of the clinic, but his seat absorbed most of the shock. He was up again in a matter of moments. "You did *what*?" He coughed, surprised.

Ravendor looked at him as if Warren hadn't just made an ass of himself. He shrugged apologetically. "Just as I say. I thought you might want to know; in case you examine him and wonder who on earth has been boffing him." He thought that that should have been harder to say, but figured that because Warren was a doctor he'd be assured confidentiality.

The doctor shook his head as he climbed back into his chair, but then got up again a moment later to look for something to use as an ashtray.

"You let him kiss you, didn't you?" He accused, producing an empty saucer and setting it down on the table.

"I did not *'let'* him do anything." Ravendor said in a significantly hotter tone, raising an eyebrow. "He forced himself onto me. I am fortunate he didn't shag *me* instead, but as luck would have it I kicked him in the face in time."

He really shouldn't have tried to picture that while he turned away to his little alcove which served as a kitchen. A tiny snerk crept out and immediately Warren felt like a terrible, awful person for it. Rape was *never* funny, no matter the people and no matter the situation. Ever. He turned to regard his friend still at the table, staring off into space. He looked bored. Bored or tired; he couldn't tell which.

"Would you like some coffee?" Warren asked, trying to be the good host.

"Some tea would be nice, thank you."

Warren got to work on said tea right away, reaching for the canister that he always kept on the highest shelf for some reason. "So are you alright, then? About everything?"

"About last night? I suppose so. I have been tortured in worse ways." Though he had his back to him Warren could hear the irony in Ravendor's words.

"You know, I studied psychiatry in med school. If you want somebody to talk to about anything, I'm technically qualified."

His tone did not quaver even the slightest bit. "Ah, you are offering your ear to me? That's very kind of you. We can talk about my father. Did you know he's an utter bastard? He never writes me, not even on the Solstice."

"Ravendor, please. I'm being serious here." Warren sighed. "Magi is your friend. I'd hate to see a friendship go sour if there was something I could have done about it. How do you take your tea?"

"One sugar, no milk please."

Frankly Warren was surprised that nobody in town had run into the clinic with a problem yet. Usually Siro would come in at around this time, but he didn't think that would happen today, mostly because he knew that Siro was still sleeping soundly upstairs. On second thought, it might be even *more* embarrassing for him to come downstairs wearing only his pants and tiredly ask what was going on. Augh, knock on wood, knock on wood…

He brought two cups of tea to the table and sat down again. Ravendor accepted the tea with silent gratitude and for a long time nobody said anything. This was good enough for Warren for now; the silence helped his headache and he knew that when his friend was ready he would speak. Pestering him into talking would only clam him up more.

After about fifteen minutes, when the tea was entering its lukewarm stage and their cigarettes had long since been smoked, Ravendor finally said; "So what should be done about this? What happened to me? After he kissed me… it felt like I had lost my damned mind."

"Alraune poison does that to humans. My guess is that Magi's body started to change on a chemical level long before it began to show physical symptoms, and it affected everybody who came in contact with his saliva. You kiss him once, it compels you to kiss him more, and before you know it you may have double or triple dosed yourself. None of it was your fault." Warren reasoned. "Mina's book said that you and I should be safe though. Magi wasn't a matured alraune when he kissed us, so the nectar wasn't infectious."

Ravendor noticed that Mina's big leather bound book was indeed lying open on Warren's work desk, surrounded by several hand-written notes, some crinkled, as if the author had screwed them up and then smoothed them out again later on. Suddenly he remembered that he hadn't been the only one kissed by Magi the night before, and then a whole lot of things made much more sense to him. He blinked. "Oh, you had to run home to give yourself the vinegar stroke before you exploded? That was why you left us there."

Warren went an interesting shade of red. He wasn't entirely certain what that term meant but he could make an educated guess, and it was embarrassing. "T-To make a long story short… yes. I thought I was going to die, but Siro-"

The doctor realized that he had put his foot in his mouth and grimaced, but it was too late. He thought that Ravendor might have had something smartassed to say about all that, but he merely waited patiently for Warren to continue. Warren sighed heavily. "But Siro is very good to me. I don't know what I'd do without him. We're… dating, you know." He admitted. There, he had said it. Somebody else knew now.

Ravendor thought about this for a bit, and then nodded to himself as if it made sense. "Far be it for me to criticize who you choose to bunk with, Warren. It would be a tad hypocritical, don't you think?"

"It's not really the same thing..." Warren tried to tell him, in consolation. "Listen, something terrible happened to you and something needs to be done about it. Do you want to press charges over this?"

The innkeeper's brow furrowed. "What do you mean?"

"You were the victim of a crime. If you want, once Magi recovers, Siro can order him exiled from town. It's a messy business and I'd hate to think of it happening to one of my friends, but the law exists for a reason. Anybody who rapes or murders should be prepared to face the consequences of their actions."

After Warren had spoken the older man gave him a strange look that he just couldn't decipher. "That is ridiculous." He stated flatly. "Magi had no more free will than I did after he kissed me, and it was a *far* cry from a cretin who makes the conscious decision to attack and molest a helpless victim. I believe that Magi is also a victim in all of this, even more so than I am, and the fact that you want to judge his behavior via such a black-and-white code of conduct when it is clearly a grey area is simply ridiculous."

"Do you really think so?"

"Yes, I do."

Warren nodded in understanding and smiled. "I'm relieved you think that way. Do you think that you'll be able to forgive him for what he did to you?"

"Not yet... but perhaps eventually. After some time has passed." Ravendor took a sip of his tea, realized that it had gotten a little too cool for his liking, and put it back down again. "Anyway, I would just like to forget about this for now, if I can. I feel absolutely exhausted. Do you have anything that might fix that?"

He seemed to have almost expected that question and Warren hopped up a little too quickly for his headache to bear. "I have just the thing." He said brightly and moved to the cupboard behind his work desk, stuffed with various kinds of medicines and pharmaceuticals. He selected a palm-sized glass bottle at shoulder height and returned to the table. “The withdrawal symptoms of the alraune’s aphrodisiac usually leave the sufferer with a huge vitamin B deficiency. I’ve started taking this multivitamin, so both you and Magi should as well. It’ll make a big difference.” He tossed the bottle to Ravendor who caught it easily.

He read the label quickly and asked; “How much?”

“It’s on the house. I think I can spare it.” The doctor grinned broadly at him.

The innkeeper knew that he probably couldn’t in the long run, but he accepted it anyway. He was tired of talking and just wanted to go home. Ravendor rose to leave, stuffing the bottle into his coat pocket. “I trust that this meeting will remain confidential?” He asked calmly.

Warren was surprised that he even had to ask such a thing. “Of course. I have my reputation as a professional to keep.” He laughed. “I’m not like Mieus next door.”

“I will be expecting you this evening, then.”

The younger man flapped a hand at him. It was covered in no less than three different band-aids. Idly Ravendor wondered if they were the result of their dungeon crawl, or merely Warren’s own carelessness. “Sure, sure. I’ll come knocking just before dark.” He assured him, and then became a little more serious. “I hope I’ve been of some help.”

By that point Ravendor was already at the threshold of the clinic, the afternoon sun flowing in softly. “You usually are.” He mused out loud, then added; “Warren?”

“Yeah?”

“… Thanks.”

It was mid-afternoon by the time Ravendor returned home and the inn seemed mostly empty; both Darren and Reiyu had left their door tags in the ‘out’ position to indicate that they weren’t in their rooms. He flipped his own tag over to ‘in’ for the benefit of Warren when he came calling later on, then he went upstairs to check on Magi and make sure he was still alive.

He didn’t knock on the door this time, he doubted that he’d get a real response and just decided to let himself in. Ravendor went inside but continued to hold the door open a moment longer with his boot, thinking that if he let it close again it might lock shut like last time. He released the door and it closed, but there was no click. Reassuring.

Magi had been standing in front of the windowsill, quietly looking outside. He was dressed now, not in his pajamas or his hunting clothes but in simple slacks and a shirt. His feet were bare but his hair was neatly brushed, and it looked like he had bathed. He appeared almost normal again, except for the minute differences one could only see if they knew where to look and the tired, haunted quality in his eyes.

"H-hello…" He said to Ravendor as his friend closed the door behind him.

Ravendor had been ready to assuage Magi's fears and insecurities over what had happened if he had any, but as he was about to speak the old anger and indignation from last night returned, like a repressed memory rising back to the surface. He sighed as he approached the other man. "So what are you today, Magi? The human or the monster? I'd like to know before I get within grabbing distance of you."

Magi's gaze shifted to the floor and it looked like that comment had hurt him. He turned away from the window but laid a hand on its frame, as if using it as some kind of anchor or grounding. "I don't really know." Magi admitted honestly, in a soft voice. "I'm afraid to find out."

So Ravendor got within grabbing distance of him and Magi didn't pounce or go for his throat like he might have done the night before. Instead, the blond hunter looked panicked and stepped back against the windowsill, trying to maintain his distance. "Wait! I don't think that's a good idea. I might flip out again." He pleaded, alarm present in his bright blue eyes.

"But you do seem to have your wits about you, at least." Ravendor commented, not backing down. Magi regarded him with an awkward, guarded expression, one that spoke worlds of what was running through his head. Fear, guilt, shame, and… resignation. Ravendor dropped the dry, businesslike attitude and smiled at him. "I had feared you would remain that mindless creature forever. It does my heart good to hear you speaking again." He said.

The younger man smiled wanly, even a little bashfully over such concern, but he slunk away from Ravendor and the warm light streaming in from the window and walked towards the table, taking a seat. He limped when he walked and moved with the weak, wobbling gait of the long-bedridden. Ravendor felt a stab of guilt over that limp, but he said nothing. Magi sighed in discomfort and he sat down. "Well that's the problem with that, I *wasn't* mindless. Not really, anyway." He paused and thought for a bit. "It was like being in a deep, long dream."

*A wet dream...* He added to himself, but would have gladly died before he said it out loud.

Had he been a more affectionate man, or more open with his feelings Ravendor would have done a lot more than just comment on his relief at seeing Magi sane again. He wanted to embrace him, maybe not like they had last night, but more than simply saying; *'I'm glad you're not insane anymore.'* He didn't have many friends in this town. Sure, many were civil to him but that was just mutual politeness. If he had lost Magi... well, he would have been lonely.

Okay, so maybe he *did* want to embrace his friend like he had the night before, but only a little.

Just a tad.

Not enough to warrant action.

Instead, Ravendor voiced what had been weighing on his mind. "Do you remember what happened to you after we freed you from the alraune?"

Magi merely nodded in reply, folding his arms on the table and leaning forward a bit to take a little weight off his backside. It hurt just as much as he expected. After a few moments he realized that just nodding wasn't enough and he spoke. "I can remember in the same way I can remember what I had for breakfast two weeks ago. If I focus the memories are there, just faint and indistinct... sort of disconnected."

He glanced towards the other man and decided to just blurt out the one, hardest question that had tried to stick in his throat and mind all day. "Ravendor... did I really rape you last night? Please tell me it was only a dream."

To be honest Ravendor didn't really have to say anything at all for Magi to realize the truth. The way the older man paused for several seconds before replying, like he was working on sugarcoating or paraphrasing the answer was affirmation enough for him. If it had only been a dream maybe Ravendor would have laughed, or looked surprised instead. Possibly even indignant. "I suppose it depends on how you interpret it." He said at last. "But no. No. No, Magi. You did not do anything I didn't willingly agree to."

Except that was a load of bullshit and he could see that even Ravendor knew it. He wanted to be kind so much that he was trying to believe his own lies. One of the universal truths about humans that it was all too often they succeeded. But Magi could remember. If one part of the dream was true then the rest of it was as well, and he could remember Ravendor shouting '*no!*' at him even as he continued to divest him of his clothing. He could remember how hearing the protests had aroused him even more.

A wave of sickness, of a wretchedness so thick and foul it was even worse than the alraune's blood filled him up inside. It felt like he was choking on it, and likewise Magi Magemere's eyes threatened to fill with tears. "Oh gods," he ground out in a constricted voice, "you must hate me now. I did something so terrible to you and I'll *never* be able to take it back. I'm a horrible person! I'm a rapist! I'm… I…" He seemed to be unable to get the last sentence out.

Ravendor closed the distance between them in a few quick strides and grabbed him roughly by the upper arms, hard enough to kill the remainder of Magi's words stuck somewhere on his tongue. He was suddenly afraid. If Ravendor whipped a knife out of his pocket and slit his throat with it he'd be completely justified in doing so. It might even be better to die now than live with the consequences of what he had done.

All the older man did though was shake him once to calm him down and shut him up. "Magi!" He said once, loudly and firmly, then softened somewhat. "Weren't you listening? I said that you did *not* molest me. I think it is rather difficult to molest the willing." He explained.

Magi laughed once, a short, clipped, humorless sound. "If that's so true then why did you feel the need to give me this bruise?" He asked, and turned his face to the right to emphasize the dark purplish-blue smear running down along his chin.

Ravendor looked at it and him evenly. "I wish you would not be so melodramatic. It is an ugly mark and I regret striking you. I would take it back from you if I could." Unexpectedly he knelt, his hands on Magi's arms trailing down, past the horrible bandaged wounds until they grasped Magi's own hands. "Perhaps if last night had ended differently and you had shagged me instead of the other way around I might have hated you, and everything you have said would be true. But that is not the case. It is I who took advantage of you, so if there is anybody here who should be feeling like a horse's arse it should be me."

He couldn't help but crack a small smile at that. "And you're not angry that you had to fuck another man? I know that if I were straight I would be pretty upset." Magi suddenly realized that he had no idea if Ravendor was straight or bisexual or what. Sure, he had talked about old girlfriends before but that was a guy thing. Everybody did that.

His friend made a dismissive gesture with one hand. "If it had been anybody else maybe, but there were extenuating circumstances involved. No harm was done. It might have gotten a little messy, but that is what soap is for."

Maybe it was the thought that Ravendor, who was such a stickler for neatness and order and propriety being able to brush this easily aside that caused Magi to finally let go. At first he thought that he was going to burst out laughing, but then the tears started to roll down his cheeks and he quickly turned away, trying to hide such weakness.

For his own part Ravendor just let Magi vent whatever he needed to vent in his own way, rising from the crouch and heading to the dresser beside Magi's bed. His gun holster and colt were lying there beside a half-burned candlestick and he picked it up carefully, weighing the familiar object in his hands. It might have been an idiocy to leave a loaded weapon out where somebody like Magi had easy access to it, but he was just glad to have it back now. Both of them.

Magi wiped at his eyes with the heel of his hand as he watched Ravendor take off his coat, slip and buckle the holster carrying the six-gun with practiced ease, and then put his coat back on again. The young archer felt a fondness for him then that he had never felt for anybody else before, not even Mara. "So apart from 'shagging' you," he began, the idiom feeling foreign and strange in his mouth, "what else did I do to the people of Adratea? Did I attack anybody else?"

"You did nothing they would not easily recover from. You scared Darren nearly half to death and gave Siro a few nasty scratches and bruises." Ravendor glanced at him momentarily, "You also gave Warren quite a thorough snogging if what I have been told is true."

Magi blushed fiercely and inspected his folded arms laid against the table. "This is *so* embarrassing," he moaned, "I am never going to be able to live this down. I'll be the laughing stock of the entire village." Yet even so he felt deep relief in knowing that his own madness had been self-contained, and the casualties had been few. He could not have asked for anything more than that, but in safety and sanity men were selfish.

Ravendor realized that the one reason he had been unable to stay still and pace about the room was that, despite of his outwardly calm exterior, he was filled to the brim with nervous energy. He walked back over to Magi and sat down beside him at the table. Magi felt the urge to lean against him for some reason, but he squashed it silently.

"I would not worry yourself over such thoughts. Like I said before; there were extenuating circumstances and the people of this town are very forgiving. Warren remains the only one who has full knowledge of what really happened to you, and he will not talk. If anything you probably did him a favor." Ravendor advised, remembering the way Warren had stammered upon mention of Siro.

Even with the other man sitting right there beside him Magi suddenly felt very lonely. After long minutes of silence he passed a hand gently over the bandages of his forearm, bandages covering burns which had disconnected him from that other, simpler life; a life where all that mattered was light and water and love from his queen. "Alraune..." Magi uttered in a voice that was only a shade above a whisper, like wind rustling in the grass at night.

"She is not dead. She escaped." Ravendor said gravely. "I suppose if we had had more time we would have hunted her down and burnt her, but getting you out of the dungeon while you were still breathing was our top priority."

Magi said something that was not entirely unexpected. "Good. I think... I think I am in love with her." He admitted as he narrowed his eyes, as if trying to peer inward into himself. "I can't possibly describe what it was like to be connected with her. It was like... it was..."

"Profound?" Ravendor offered helpfully from where he was sitting.

The young archer nodded gratefully, but his smile was sad. "You could say that. It was a lot like..." He struggled to find the right words. He'd been as mute as a dumb animal the day before, but as he worked on it more the language flowed easier again. "It was like feeling the way you used to feel… before you were born."

Before Ravendor had a chance to reply Magi's expression became pained. He was running his fingers lightly across the bandages, stroking it again and again like some kind of cat, feeling the rough coarseness of the fabric with the pads of his fingertips. His vines had been *far* more sensitive to touch, and when Warren had sliced into them in the same manner that Mara had when she pruned the delicate rosebushes in her garden…

Tears prickled in Magi's eyes again as he remembered that sharp surgical pain, eclipsed only by the rolling, roaring agony of the fire. "I don't think I'll be able to come with everybody else if you plan on hunting the alraune. I don't know what I'd do. Maybe I'd be fine. Maybe I'd fall apart emotionally and become a vegetable if you, uh, pardon the pun. I might even turn on everybody. I just don't know. I don't know, and I'm afraid to find out."

For a moment Magi felt horribly alone in the world, but that feeling was soon quelled as Ravendor leant over and took him by the shoulders again, not to calm him down this time but simply as a gesture of comfort, of sympathy. He wasn't especially a very touchy-feely kind of man, and Magi appreciated it for what it was worth. This time he didn't ignore his desire to lean against him, and Ravendor didn't protest so it must have been okay.

"I do not think you will be leaving the inn much anyway. We have the safety of the townsfolk to consider, after all." Ravendor said reassuringly. Something told him that they wouldn't be seeing the alraune again for a very long time.

"What? But how will I earn a living? What about food? What about the rent?" Magi asked, worried. Just the thought of not being able to go outside panicked him a little. It was no less than house arrest, but he guessed that after all he had done he now deserved it.

"Magi, are you capable of going outside and interacting with people safely? Do you believe that you can go next door and chat with Mara without feeling like she will be in any danger? If you can wholeheartedly believe that, without reservation, then fine. Go ahead. What I am concerned about most of all is what happened to me happening to someone else; particularly a woman." Ravendor demanded, his tone suddenly stern.

He supposed that it was probably right of him to be so concerned. He was getting better now, slowly, at least out of that phase when the alraune's curse had sent him half mad with desire, but he was not free just yet. It was that persistent longing feeling, like a smoker's impulse, to do it again and again. If for some reason Ravendor kissed him again that addictive bitterness would still be there, fainter of course, but still there. Still dangerous.

He was wearing those loose-fitting slacks for that very reason; so that if he unexpectedly popped a boner again as the itch got worse he'd be able to hide it. Shame colored Magi's cheeks a light pink. "No… no. I guess not. It's taking a lot of self-control right now to make myself not to want to grab and kiss you again. I'm sorry. I'm really sorry…"

"It's alright, I understand." Ravendor sighed, not wanting to think about it. "Do not concern yourself with worrying about your living arrangement for the moment. I am certain we can work something out." He was fairly adept at money management and postponing or writing off a couple weeks of rent payment wouldn't harm him. He had a thought. "And I do believe Mara would gladly prepare dinners for you if she thought it might help you to recover."

Magi relaxed. That really *did* sound like something Mara would do. He had such wonderful friends, though how he had come by them with his luck he did not know. "Ravendor?" He asked.

"Yes?"

"Are you sure I won't have to pack up and leave under cover of darkness? I've done it before. It wouldn't be anything new to me."

"Not without breaking a binding legal contract. You signed a lease. Six months, remember?"

Magi's lips quirked up into a smile despite wanting to cry again. His chest felt tight. "Is that all?"

"Well…"

"Well what?"

"I would miss you."

Magi hesitated and let the words hang in the air for a moment longer. He was almost sure that Ravendor was just trying to be kind and nothing more, but saying that after sleeping with him the night before was weird.

Good weird. "Does that mean you forgive me?" He ventured, stepping tentatively into new territory and afraid of the results.

Ravendor seemed to look uncomfortable as he considered this, and then abruptly dismissed the idea. His voice sounded a little fainter than it should have been. "Ask me again sometime in the future, Magi. It is too soon right now." He cleared his throat and itched for another cigarette, but ignored it. He'd gone from a pack a day to maybe five or six on average, and he preferred it that way. He was easily addicted to things himself. What he feared most of all right now was becoming addicted to the person leaning next to him. It would be all too easy…

But Magi was patient, and Magi was penitent. So long as their friendship didn't suffer, that was good enough for him.

He hadn't really expected a yes anyway.

www.ingramcontent.com/pod-product-compliance
Lightning Source LLC
Chambersburg PA
CBHW021621030826
48979CB00035B/1476/J

* 9 7 8 0 9 9 2 4 4 5 5 0 8 *